Richard Trewen Taylor

SACRIFICE

"   "

Hedgehog

"All great truths begin as blasphemies."

George Bernard Shaw
Annajanska (1917)

ISBN 1-900094-05-3

This first edition first published in the United Kingdom in 1998 by:

Hedgehog Books
Maunditts Park Farm
Little Somerford
Chippenham,
Wilts
SN15 5BH

Printed an Bound by

Intype
London Ltd
Elm Grove
Wimbledon
SW19 4HE

Dedication

To all, wherever they may live,
who care about Britain
her past and more importantly, her
future.

R.T-T

Also by Richard-Trewen Taylor - in Hedgehog Books

No Post on Sundays
to
be published by
Hedgehog Books
in
Autumn 1999

Future Hedgehog titles:

One of our ships has been hit!
(Absolutely the last word on the Falklands!)
by
Lt Alan D Rapkins RN(Ret'd)
(To be published June 98)

Eve's last chance
by
Bridie Willis
(To be published Winter 98)

*

Bignell
by
Anna Masters
(To be published July 99)

*

ACKNOWLEDGEMENTS

Flt Lt. Stephen Noujaim RAF (Pilot)

The author and publishers wish to thank the following who have
kindly given permission for use of copyright materials:

The Times (Extracts from 1995/96 news items)
Rachel Trickett, Former Principal of St Hugh's College, Oxford.
(Extracts from *Gentility Recalled*).
Dr Caroline Moore, Fellow, Peterhouse, Cambridge.
(Extracts from research paper concerning changing UK social habits).
William Horwood (Quotation from *Duncton Wood*).

© *1989 Big Pig Music Ltd*
Intersong Music Ltd, London W1Y 3FA
Extract from "Sacrifice" performed by Elton John.
(John/Taupin)
Reproduced by permission of International Music Publications Ltd.

*Every effort has been made to trace all possible copyright holders,
but if any have been overlooked,
the author and publisher will be pleased to make the necessary
arrangements at the first opportunity.*

'The President Awoke
momentarily unable to distinguish between
his awful dream and reality.
Reality struck soon enough
with consciousness.
Britain was destroyed and as yet
unavenged and what was
left of the free world looked to him
and his administration to respond effectively
but without destroying
civilisation!'

"This is a story which makes previously heralded
block busters by the so-called household names,
seem like child's play!"
Publisher

*"With its international setting,
it's all here, intrigue,
love, jealousy, suspense
and staggering dilemmas!"*

"Strong Characters, good and evil.
A massive read with something for everyone
and a surprising and satisfying climax!"
A Bookseller

Part One

*Sic Transit
Gloria Britannica*

* * *

'Who did it, Major? It's a simple question and it's the one they are all going to ask me tomorrow, including the President of the United States?'

'We're not sure, General.' The Major adjusted his rimless spectacles and looked nervous, as well he might. McIver was not known for his patience.

'Dammit, we're supposed to have the most sophisticated intelligence gathering network since the beginning of time and you're telling me that you don't know who took out England!'

'Britain, General,' the Major corrected him.

'Britain, England, what's the difference...?'

Johnson suppressed a reply extolling his Scottish ancestry and remained silent.

McIver had smacked his hand on a section of the large wall map covering the greater part of the Ukraine.

'It was from here, wasn't it?'

'There was certainly some missile activity in that area at the time,' volunteered Johnson cautiously.

'God-damn it Johnson,' McIver had said impatiently, 'don't bandy words with me...'

'The strange thing is General,' drawled Johnson, 'there was a small launch ...'

'Yes?' McIver had thundered

'It was going the other way, General'

McIver remembered how he had been stunned, and at the same time confused and annoyed, at this revelation. 'What did you say Major?'

'East, towards China, General, not North West'

'Why didn't you tell me this before?'

'It's only just been confirmed, sir'

'The hell it has!' McIver had yelled.

'Sir?'

'Son, If you're holding out on me your West Point ass won't save you!'

3

'I assure you sir, ...'

'Then explain to me why the Russians would bomb China in order to take out England?'

'Britain, sir.' The Major inserted the correction, his college lecturer background getting the better of his caution. McIver glowered and the Major wiped away the beads of sweat that broke out on his brow. 'Well-er, we don't know – yet, sir...

'Does anybody know? NATO HQ must know, after all they were supposed to be protecting Europe.'

'Europe's OK sir,' replied Johnson, blinking.

The General gave the Major a warning glance which made the recipient flush visibly.

Clearing his throat, the Major announced, croakily, 'The NATO opinion is that they were either decoys – diversions to fool our monitoring satellites, or...'

'Well?'

'It's unconfirmed, sir'

'Dammit, will you get on with it?'

'It is claimed by the Russians that they were fired by unauthorised personnel who had set the wrong tracking codes. They were aimed at Moscow.'

'Moscow!' McIver exclaimed and sat down heavily. 'This gets crazier by the minute.'

'NATO HQ have a team working on it, General, and the Russians are co-operating fully.'

'I'll just bet they are.'

McIver had lit up a cheroot and wondered how he was going to explain all this to the Chiefs of Staff, the President and most of all the President's staff.

'No smoking in this area General,' said the major timidly.

'Are you giving me an order, major?'

The Major stuttered, 'N-N-No sir, just pointing out...'

'Oh balls!' McIver stubbed out the cheroot in his coffee cup. 'Get the hell out of here Major and on your way out, ask Admiral Kearn's aide if the Admiral can join me.'

'Yes sir!' The Major had saluted smartly and quickly left the room.

McIver sighed and tried to disentangle his brain from his emotions. He kept getting visions of his trips to England. The pubs, the red buses, the black taxis, Tower Bridge... His reverie was interrupted by a knock.

'Come!'

Admiral Kearns strode into the room, a stocky man with a permanent fierce, and often intimidating expression, but McIver was unmoved by his presence. 'Well Kearns,' McIver began, 'this is a really fine mess. I...'

'An Air Force mess.' Kearns rejoined sharply.

McIver took a deep breath. This was one occasion when he needed his old rival on his side. 'Perhaps, but what to do? Any ideas? I understand that the President is going all out for a political solution.'

McIver motioned the Admiral to a chair in which he planted himself, making himself comfortable before responding.

'If that's so, he's right. After all, any other response is pure revenge.'

'You've just topped thirty years of defence policy in one sentence, Admiral.'

Kearns flushed, 'Well, there will be no decision without our input. Dammit, a military response is just out of court, we don't even know who did it!'

McIver had put a large hand to his chin thoughtfully, 'You're sure of that, Admiral?'

He was mildly taken aback, as among other things, he had brought Kearns in specifically to impart this news.

'We are not without our own sources, General. Everything we have in the North Atlantic was unable to determine a single source of attack from any quarter, but all contact with the British was lost instantly. We're up against something here which may be unprecedented. One thing's for sure...'

'What's that?'

Kearns continued, 'The longer it's left, the ...'

'Less likely we are to make a military response,' McIver finished the sentence for him. 'Maybe it was planned that way.'

Kearns remained impassive but wished he had thought of this angle himself.

'I'm very concerned about our whole position on this thing. We're wallowing in indecision... whoever did this, we surely know enough to deduce that it was deliberate, and we...'

'We don't even know that yet – for sure. But if it was deliberate it was planned to wrong foot us, and in that they have surely succeeded.'

'Our defence strategy was based on the simplistic principle of a known strike against the United States, a front line NATO state or NATO as a whole. Not an unknown strike against Britain.'

'In war, always expect the unexpected.' Kearns mouthed the platitude smugly.

'But we don't even know if this is war!'

'What kind of crazy talk is that?'

There was what seemed a long silence between the two commanders as both men digested the import of McIver's last remark.

At length, Kearns said, 'Well in the absence of further data, I still think it was deliberate. But hell, you're right about one thing... By moving unexpectedly and covertly, they think they can wrong foot us and frustrate a military response!'

'Yes,' McIver agreed, 'but who's *they*?'

*   *   *

After the President's Emergency Council had adjourned for a sombre dinner, McIver mounted a small dais erected in front of a large white board in the White House library for a post-prandial presentation of the latest information, real and postulated, as to the means, extent and nature of Britain's sudden departure from the international scene.

A laptop computer from the Department of Defense had

been loaded with the latest intelligence and hooked up to a projector which displayed the first slide. It read:

The Attack/Happening/Cataclysmic Event,

culminating in the Destruction of the British
Population/Infrastructure/Culture

Possible Means

a/ Mass Neutron Bomb detonation

NB Need to find out about Red Mercury which kills but may leave the following intact:

i/ Buildings

ii/ Nature? i.e., all other living things (high survival rate expected)

b/ Biological (Deadly virus)

all other living things (lower survival rate expected) dependent on distribution and ambience

c/ Hormone/Chemical contamination

e.g SARIN nerve gas. all other living things (lower survival rate expected) dependent on distribution and ambience

Perceived & Estimated Damage

Widespread fatalities, but few injuries apart from collateral resulting from crashing automobiles, and other vehicles, trains and some aircraft.

Evidence of Governmental, Official/Military surviving presence.

In spite of all possible effort by US, European and other Agencies, none detected or contacted at this time.

There were mutterings from the august audience: 'I can't believe this stuff,' and 'Yes, but WHO did it?' McIver did not respond but pressed the hand control and brought up the next slide, which scrolled slowly down the screen.

This was at first greeted with a stunned silence, then groans of despair.

Contact with US Political, Ambassadorial & Military sources known to be resident at the time.

None, at this time.

US & other national surveillance & intervention.

Proceeding via aircraft, satellite, electronic and surface military (special) forces.

At this second item the President spoke in a voice tinged with relief.

'Ah! at last we have some people on the ground there?'

'Yes sir,'replied McIver, 'But we only have a limited number of personnel suitably equipped.'

'How's that?' It was Admiral Kearns again. 'Are you saying, General that the Army...'

McIver cut him short, 'The highest specification of personal body equipment is necessary. We have to take every precaution.'

'I see,' replied Kearns, 'and just how many personnel do we have so equipped?'

'At this time around fifty.'

'Fifty!' Kearns expostulated. There were also accompanying murmurings from the rest of the meeting.

'Dammit, General. This is the United States, not some banana republic! Is that the best you can do?'

There was an awkward silence. McIver wondered, at this point, if Kearns was overdoing it.

At length, and without a word, he pulled down another screen and nodded to the presentation operator.

The screen was instantly filled with image of a single soldier. But this was no ordinary soldier.

'Mr President, gentlemen, let me introduce you to Supertrooper 2020. A fighting machine, so advanced that it borders on science fiction. The helmet contains a computerised nerve centre. At night the visor is a data screen, with infra red and other systems, giving night vision, map and all the latest data needed to be effective in a particular area at any time.'

McIver paused for audience reaction, (silence) and moved the pointer to the body of the projected image.

'Body armour: super light version of Kevlar vests with ceramic plates to protect vital organs. Under it, a cooling system to control personal climate.' Once again McIver paused in his delivery, but there were no questions or interruptions so he went on. 'The rifle is a combat weapon with two barrels, one firing normal size 5.56mm rounds, the other a 20mm barrel for high explosive rounds. The weapon is constructed of corrosive-resistant plastics. There is a built in laser range finder, accurate over very long ranges in all conditions.'

'Before you get to the boots, General, I'm having a little trouble with the relevance of all this. I mean, is this level of technology really necessary for this task at this time?' This came from Defence Secretary, Richard Scottdale, McIver's political superior.

McIver moved the pointer back to the helmet. 'This contains not only the systems already described but chemical warfare indicators, very important in this context... There is also a shortwave radio...'

'But General, we don't even know if there actually is a chemical warfare situation...' Major General Phillip T. Arnold, Chief of Strategic Air Command stood up, blinked in the light from the projector and sat down again.

'No, we don't. This is why we are assembling this specially equipped force.'

The ensuing silence allowed him to continue, 'I'll skip the boots. Needless to say, they are more than adequate for all known conditions, including radioactive material, as is the whole suit.'

'Yes but only fifty,General? How soon can you assemble and deploy this force?' McIver shaded his eyes and identified the southern drawl of the Deputy Defence Secretary, David Douglas.

'We are dependent, to a large extent, on how quickly the suppliers can deliver.'

The President quickly intervened, 'Have we got any more data on the overall state of the country at this time, General? Infrastructure, communications, that kind of thing?'

'Well sir, the data we have so far is scant. We are presently trying to collate eye witness reports and satellite film, some of which you have already seen.'

'I got more information from CNN!' Kearns again.

'Gentlemen!' The President adopted an almost avuncular tone. 'In-fighting will lead us nowhere. Please continue General.'

'Thank you sir!' McIver gave Kearns a winning glance. 'Anyway I'm glad Admiral Kearns mentioned the media. Sometimes they do get ahead of us.'

'Sometimes...? Humph.' At this interjection it was clear from the acid glances of the political contingent that Kearns was doing himself no good.

He got the message that McIver had the floor and from then on he remained silent.

'There have been some vicarious eyewitness reports and we are collating them to get some consistency. Many of them are bizarre and contradictory...'

'What do you mean by "vicarious eye witnesses", General?' The President spoke quietly and with great concern. Some present, if they had asked such a question, would have made it sound like a criticism. However, the President was not that kind of a man.

'Radar operators, satellite monitors, intelligence traffic... That kind of thing, sir.'

The President was not sure he believed this answer, but did not interrupt his Chief of Staff.

McIver continued, aware that all eyes were upon him, and that his powerful audience was hanging on every syllable of his reply. Yet if they were expecting further real enlightenment, they were to be disappointed.

'I have an intelligence team collating and verifying these reports to elicit any consistent patterns.'

'Is that a difficult process, General?' Defence Secretary, Richard Scottdale studied him suspiciously.

The bastard is just trying to ingratiate himself with the President, thought McIver. But he replied briskly enough.

'Some of the reports are from foreign agencies, Mr Secretary. Accurate translation is involved.'

'Any Russian translation necessary?' asked Scottdale coldly.

'I'm not sure at this time, sir.'

'Can you see me afterwards, General?' rasped Scottdale.

'Damn you!' McIver thought to himself, Scottdale made him feel like some errant high school pupil.

His anger and attention was deflected by another question from the floor.

'It seems that there is no coherent government presence or representation. Is that true, General?' This from the President's Counsel, James Stockman.

'That does appear so, sir.'

The President spoke, 'But how can that be? Surely some organ of government has survived?'

To President Thomas it was this latest aspect which somehow made it all the more distressing. He was so used to the British being there, politically, that somehow now he felt all alone in the world.

'We are investigating it, sir, of course. It may be just communications. We are gradually building up a picture of the state of the country as reports come in. I've got a team compiling a structure map detailing damage, survivors, communications and infrastructure state, but, of course, surveillance can only do so much. The weather has been particularly bad ever since the event, with heavy cloud cover...'

'Or smoke...,' interrupted Kearns mischievously,

'Yes, how about that?' The White House Chief of Staff leaned forward, 'Could it be smoke?'

11

'Some of it is smoke, certainly.' The Air Force Chief, Major General Phillip T. Arnold, announced, 'One of our missions was able to take a sample, and initial analysis does indicate the presence of dust and smoke but until we have more samples and a full analysis...'

'And men on the ground,' interrupted McIver, 'We won't have enough on which to base meaningful decisions about rescue operations, supplies, and even possible hostile engagement...'

'Now hold on there, General...' The President's Counsel, James Stockman, adjusted his rimless glasses and made a crucial contribution. 'We can't go barging into a foreign country, especially with arms, without Congress approval under the War Powers Act!'

'He's right, dammit,' said the President.

'But surely, sir, under the circumstances they'll agree,' said McIver putting down his pointer and hitching up his slacks. Urgency had somehow engendered informality on the meeting.

'I'm not so sure,' Defence Secretary, Richard Scottdale got up to stretch his legs and began to pace the library looking up at the leather-bound volumes. 'You know the Democrats. 'They'll likely insist you have to go through UN channels.'

There were general nods and grunts of agreement to this.

The President's Deputy Chief of Staff asked, 'So what do we have at this stage? We have to give the press something. Otherwise they'll just start making things up.'

'So, what's new?' quipped the President. Nervous laughter greeted this remark. Franks continued, smiling grimly. 'Well General?'

'There is something... we don't quite know what to make of it at this stage...'

'Go on...' urged Franks.

'Nothing really helpful, just some radar traffic from a place called Fylingdales...'

'I know the old BMEWS!' It was the Chief of Strategic Air Command, Major General Phillip T. Arnold. He had been seconded there for a period early in his career and recalled vividly that row of large lonely golf ball shapes on the edge of the North Yorkshire moors. 'But surely, it was decommissioned some years back?'

'We thought so too Phil, but apparently there was some test exercise going on there just before the event. I guess the Brits thought it was secret...'

'But you picked it up...?'

'Yes sir, we...'

'BMEWS, what's that?' interrupted the President.

'Ballistic Missile Early Warning System, sir,' replied Arnold.

'Oh, and were there any missiles, General?' enquired the President leaning forward.

Then the library telephone rang, it was the the British Ambassador.

2

"D'esarmer les forts et armer les faibles ce serait changer l'ordre social que j'ai mission de conserver."

(To disarm the strong and arm the weak would be to change the social order which it's my job to preserve)

(Anatole France 1844-1924)

The Secretary General's car pulled up in front of the impersonal slab of the United Nations Building. Perhaps significantly, one flag was missing from the flag-bedecked concourse: the new Russian Federation tricolour. And one flag was at half mast: the Union Jack.

Serge Lammas, a gaunt swarthy South American, stepped from the black Cadillac stretch limousine. His normally cheerful, sensitive face and purposeful manner, now projected dejection through haunted eyes.

Although he sprang from the car and moved sharply up the steps to the main building with something of his old dynamism, he could not hide the fact that essentially he was, in his own mind, a failure and an organ of a failed organisation. His and its highest ideals had been lain waste in the presumed radioactive dust and death that was now Britain.

He had been there many times and had a great affection for its people, its avuncular influence in the world and its imagery and tradition. Delicate entities in an increasingly selfish and materialistic world. He had gone to school there. He knew that America had few of these qualities. The wealth yes, the material and military power certainly, but little of the subtlety and aging gentility that had still been

14

effective in the most unexpected arenas. Had he not personally witnessed the skill, patience and deftness with which British diplomats had conducted and influenced international affairs, using some ploys, methods and approaches that would have been disastrous in other hands. Many Americans summed all this up as quaint. He knew it was much more than such a banal term could describe. He knew also that everything which made up the positive side of the British national character had died, or had been extinguished as a flame, and possibly would never be completely rekindled.

*   *   *

When he approached the main entrance doors he was saluted by the commissionaire; then made for the express elevators across the marble hall with its wall plaques and figurines of former incumbents of his exalted office. The elevator quickly delivered him to the Secretary General's suite on the top floor of the lofty building.

When he emerged from the elevator two secretaries were awaiting him, each quickly adopting his mask of concern. They escorted him to his office right up to his enormous desk with its imposing chair and onyx ornaments. A great decorative inkstand, a magnificent ivory chess set, a present from a former President of Malawi, with each piece a functional item: the black king which became a cigar lighter when the crown was pressed aside, revealing the flame; the white queen an ingenious pencil sharpener, an impish design with sexual overtones.

In the corner hung the great blue and white UN flag, the carpet also carrying the international motif of the continents entwined in olive leaves.

The huge picture window behind the desk presented the New York skyline with breath-taking clarity. As he stood and looked silently at the view for a few moments it was as if every building awaited his decisions – decisions which must influence the healing of the greatest wound ever inflicted on the international community. The weight of his great responsibility could be felt in this impressive room even more during this brief moment of silence.

The two secretaries, one male, one female, began to speak at once. Lammas held up his hand: 'Please, one at a time.' The secretaries exchanged very brief but meaningful glances. The man bowed in deference to his female colleague, simultaneously encouraging her to continue with a faint but elegant movement of the hand. Dolores Grey delivered her message.

'General McIver would like to see you tomorrow. His office or yours?'

'I wouldn't be seen dead in the Pentagon,' snapped Lammas. 'Call his office and ask them to have him come here. Is there an hour free tomorrow morning?'

'I've already taken the liberty of pencilling him in at 10am.'

Lammas could not help smiling. 'Alright Dolores, phone the General's Aide and confirm.' Dolores nodded and walked briskly back to her office.

Lammas turned to his male senior aide, Brad Chalmers, who was hovering. Devoted to his boss, his demeanour bordered on the obsequious.

'Well, Brad?'

'The President 'phoned, sir. He was very brief. He said he would take it as a personal favour if you would see McIver and devise an agenda of mutual advice.'

'I see. Is that all?'

'Yes sir. A bit cryptic I thought?' volunteered Brad Chalmers.

'Yes, thank you, Brad.' the aide nodded in deference and trotted back to his office.

Lammas had only met McIver on two previous occasions, both of them formal social affairs at the White House. Consequently he did not have his professional measure, although he knew he had a solid reputation as Chairman of the Chiefs of Staff. Lammas had found him a trifle bombastic, but then he did not really like military men.

He scanned the press release of the last words of the President's telecast of yesterday evening, broadcast to the world via CNN:

> "Britain, leading light of Western culture, has been largely destroyed - she cannot go unavenged, but as yet the culprits are unidentified.
> We, the United States, through NATO, must be diligent, and purposeful, but above all we must be prudent and seek with the help of United Nations, to find fitting resolution of this terrible event which affects us all.
> Those proud Britishers who perished, and indeed those who remain, both in their stricken homes and abroad, would not thank us if we were to destroy the remainder of the globe in avenging them."

Lammas put down the paper and sighed deeply. President James D. Thomas was a good man, but he was not a strong one. As such he relied heavily on his advisers. Now, he was a man with a historic and world class dilemma. Put bluntly, it was this: whether or not to avenge the destruction of Britain, because realistically he, and his administration, were the only ones with the means to do so, however the resposibility might be shared. Moreover, Lammas was painfully aware that his organization, the UN, had the reponsibility of legalising any action taken.

In such a situation he knew that Thomas would by-pass the normal chains of command, committees and consultations – although he would undoubtedly pay lip-service to them and rely heavily on the direct advice of his strong Chairman of the Joint Chiefs of the Defence Staff, General George Marshall Lee-McIver.

So, on balance, he was glad of the President's invocation to meet with McIver, to get to know him and to influence him against any precipitous action he might advise. It might be his only real chance to influence events directly at a crucial time, perhaps the only chance for the world itself! A chilling prospect, but he checked himself, stood up and walked to the enormous window, presenting the panorama of New York's East Side.

'But of course,' he muttered grimly, 'to avenge, one must first know the culprit.'

* * *

The pleasantries completed, the two men eyed one another appraisingly. Lammas, dapper, swarthy with penetrating eyes but with a pleasant upward curve to the lips, suggesting kindness. McIver burly, powerful in personality as well as frame.

'Well, General,' opened Lammas, 'an unhappy situation is before us. What is your latest information?'

This was an appropriate opening gambit; Lammas knew that McIver held all the cards where military intelligence was concerned.

McIver gazed for a moment at the enormous desk with its imposing chair and onyx ornaments, the great decorative inkstand, and the magnificent ivory chess set.

'As you know, Mr Secretary...' McIver began in a faint Southern drawl, 'The President is anxious that we should confer, the urgency of the situation precludes usual channels...'

Uncharacteristically, Lammas interrupted him, 'I know that it's unusual for incumbents who hold our widely differing offices, to meet directly like this; after all we view situations from an entirely different perspective.'

Lammas, not normally an impatient man, was mildly annoyed that he had not had his opening question answered; particularly as this was a uniquely urgent matter, there was no time for stating the obvious.

'Just what have you found out, General?'

'You mean do we know who's responsible?'

'Quite so, General, if you please.'

McIver hesitated, and Lammas found himself becoming agitated. It was most unlike him. Things had not got off to a good start between them.

'Well, Mr Secretary, it's like this..' began McIver cautiously...'

Lammas interupted him.'You can speak freely here, General, the place is not bugged!'

'Well, no of course not...'

'Well?'

McIver looked uncomfortable. 'You must understand, it's most irregular to give out classified information on demand.'

Lammas almost lost his temper.

'Good God, General, I'm not a foreign spy and are you not here on the orders of your President?'

'Well, that's just it,' McIver announced flatly.

'Why, whatever do you mean General?' Lammas unclasped his hands from the praying position and leaned forward from the high backed chair, dark eyes blazing.

'Why, the President is not *your* President is he?'

'Oh, I see, you mean I'm a foreigner and I'm not to be trusted.'

'I wouldn't put it quite like that, Mr Secretary.'

This was getting nowhere. Lammas decided to take a positive tack.

'General,' he said confidentially after a pause, and not unkindly, 'First of all, we may as well both get used to the idea that we have got to work closely on this. This situation is the most extraordinary tragedy in history. You have been sent here on the highest authority to which you answer directly, and I.....,' Lammas hesitated,' I represent, for the moment, the international community - the rest of the world, if you will. So let's skip the formalities, stop prevaricating and get down to this most urgent business in hand. You can begin by calling me Serge. May I call you...?'

Lammas suddenly realised that he did not know McIver's first name.

'George,' McIver revealed directly and without hesitation. Lammas was almost sure this paragon actually showed relief. Things were beginning to turn his way, perhaps.

'Very well, George', said Lammas leaning back, 'Shall we

begin again?'

'Well – er Serge,' McIver began, as if he was revealing the whereabouts of his last penny, 'it's like this...'

'Yes, General?' prompted Lammas.

'After probing the most likely sources and several conferences with our remaining allies, we have eliminated a number of scenarios and sent up some Dragonflies..'

'Excuse me?' queried Lammas, leaning forward.

'Dragonfly is an advanced drone..'

'You mean an unmanned spy plane?' interjected Lammas.

'Well, yes - Dragonfly can hover over targets of military interest for up to twenty four hours.'

'Twenty four hours?'

'Yes,' McIver went on, 'they're called Dragonflies because they can flit and dodge like insects.'

'How big are these things?' enquired Lammas, genuinely fascinated.

'Twenty seven feet with a forty nine feet wingspan.' McIver went on, forgetting his former reticence in his temporary enthusiasm for his topic. 'We had a Pentagon briefing a few weeks back, about these babies and I was interested enough to put them to the test in the current situation.'

'I see,' replied Lammas thoughtfully, 'please go on General, er – have they reported anything yet?'

'They have sophisticated cameras which transmit live images via satellites. You could see a window in a building and get its latitude and longitude. Then in a normal operation – which this isn't...' He paused looking at Lammas almost quizzically, 'you could pass the data on to bombers. We targeted all the most likely areas..' McIver was in full spate now,

'Excuse me, General.' Lammas interrupted again.

'Yes, Mr Secretary.... er, Serge?'

'Did anybody track incoming missiles?'

There was an awkward pause. The question hit McIver like a slap in the face. He was concerned. How much did Lammas know to ask such a question?

'No sir,' he said at length, almost apologetically, 'that's

the strange thing.'

'Oh, you missed them then?' prompted Lammas.

'No, and by all accounts we've been mighty diligent about this.'

'I'm sure you have.' replied Lammas.

'There weren't any.' McIver stated flatly. The lie was almost a reflex action.

There was a brief silence while Lammas digested this piece of misinformation.

'But how...?' he began.

3

"Sic Transit Gloria Britannica."

On the twenty eighth of October 1998, two days after the event, the following leader appeared in the *New York Times* and was syndicated across several leading newspapers throughout the United States and Canada, with the notable exception of Quebec.

> *"When a loved one has died, it is difficult to accept that they are not going to come walking through the door once more. One lays a place for them and they are greatly missed for their character and their special ways, their humour and their resolve; the time we spent with them and how they affected our lives, our hopes and our dreams. History too, is affected by such characters. How much more so then when a nation is lost, particularly when it is a nation which helped shape the modern world, a nation which was instrumental in saving it from tyranny not once but twice, a nation which contributed great culture to the world: Shakespeare, Milton, Keats, Macaulay, Dickens, Trollope, to name but a few, an innately innovative culture which had pioneered the most significant of inventions, fundamental now to most developed nations' way of life: the steam engine, the railway, the steam ship, the first calculating machine, forerunner of the computer, and in more modern times, the military and commercial jet engine and its later development, the fan jet, the hovercraft, the first electronic wrist watch and pocket calculator, great military inventions such as the first battleship and the battle tank, the aircraft carrier angled deck and steam catapult and so much more.*
>
> *Britain past: prominent in world class civil engineering, contributing great bridges, power stations, tunnels, marine telephone cables and the commercial use of*

nuclear power, leader in medical discovery, bestowing penicillin, immunization & vaccination.

In entertainment, music of all kinds developed from medieval composers to modern day leaders, internationally acclaimed orchestras and conductors, once home of some of the world's greatest performers and proponents of both native and exotic art, notably of dance – what now of the Royal Opera House Covent Garden?

What now of the admired British theatre, not only exponent of the great indigenous bard, but home of world class actors and performances of all kinds, from tragedy through popular musical and all genres to the most sophisticated comedy.

The British cinema: though earlier glories had faded, had still provided the very finest screen performances, and latterly, unsurpassed special effects techniques, on which Hollywood increasingly relied for its world wide box office hits.

But truly the most momentous legacy of all is the English language, widely spoken and used, indispensable in its clarity, succinctness and variety of expression, envied and never to die, disseminated world-wide by the great British educational establishments and publications; distinguished British authors, classic and contemporary, living and dead, promulgated in 'Nation shall speak peace unto nation' by a contemporary, and some might say, increasingly controversial, BBC and by its many satellite-toting competitors.

And what of the, presumed, political vacuum left behind? Britain the compromiser, the contributor, the persuader, the negotiator, past conqueror and administrator on the world stage. Who would the United States, the European Community, the old Commonwealth of Nations, turn to now for considered advice and the centuries of experience of its institutions?

Most immediately, what of its surviving people? Many, of course have survived abroad, some surely in the homeland itself, (we do not yet know) but if so, they must surely be shocked, bewildered, disoriented, stunned in disbelief. They must be contacted, rescued, supported and reassured that the United Nations, the United States, and all other friends of Britain, will come to their aid.

Words are inadequate but our hearts go out to them – and to their families, friends and colleagues. Be assured, lasting help is on the way."

Later, the piece was criticised in some media circles for being over long, over sentimental and even mawkish. There were also murmurings in some official circles, that it made promises that might be difficult to keep. International reaction ranged from hysterical concurrence – from most English speaking nations – through to ominous silence from some of the Eastern regimes. One or two (somewhat self consciously) even engaged in open celebration. But, in truth, the world's media and political institutions were still stunned, and reaction was therefore, for the most part, still in its infancy.

Yet, before the event, all was normal, striving, hopeful and chaotic as the infinite variety of characters went about their daily lives, blissfully unaware of what the near future held for them. Britain, a socially stratified society even unto its end was an integrated middle ranking industrial power, ostensibly in genteel decline.

*   *   *

Inbound from Brussels to Birmingham, Robin Goodchild, had, as was his habit, switched off the autopilot and began the second stage of the descent into Birmingham International Airport. Approaching from the East, the lights of the East Midlands conurbations appeared as fine amber necklaces, strung out and sparkling on endless black velvet.

Thin cloud scudded under the nose of the elderly 737, intermittently obscuring the panoply below. Then, a continual, thread of just perceptible diamonds and ruby, with occasional amber settings, appeared, the beginning of the M42 motorway. He turned his head slightly to his right and nodded to his co-pilot, who applied the first flap setting slowing the little airliner perceptibly. Such was the rapport between the two men that words were unnecessary. Goodchild yawned as the plane bucked gently in the low level turbulence.

Later, at 20.50 Greenwich Mean Time on a damp, early September evening, the little Boeing lowered its wheels and lined up with the fast approaching runway. The twin track of white lights beckoned and rapidly widened as Goodchild, gently raised the nose, then moments later came the slight screech and thump as the main wheels contacted the black shining tarmac. As he pushed the control column forward the nose wheel also came home and the white lights rushed past on either side at well over a hundred miles an hour. Once again the nod to his companion and practised hands moved the thrust levers to reverse. The plane's twin under-wing engines responded with a sudden great roar while rapid loss of speed accompanied a slight shimmy of the nose wheel. Goodchild gently toed the big brake pedals above the rudder controls causing the 737 to lose even more speed as it calmly approached the runway end.

Back in the terminal, he had difficulty applying his mind to the tedious matters of turn-round and debriefing as visions of Julia invaded his thoughts.

'Hey Robin! Are you with us?' It was his relief captain 'Bob' Marley and yes, he was also a talented coloured man just like his musically historic, namesake! However, the notion flashed through Goodchild's brain that Marley's demeanour and speech was in many ways more British than his own.

'Sorry Bob. My mind was elsewhere.'

'And I bet I know where.' Marley accompanied the retort with a perceptive wink.

In that same middle England, only two months earlier, a small but most significant part of the national culture, amid the beauty and variety of the English late summer countryside, some typical and not so typical citizens, had been about their daily tasks and social pursuits.

The fuming, whizzing, stinging cocktail of sweat, sound and pain bound up the personal, present environment of Jacqui Strakes as she hurled herself once more at the accursed little black ball. She hated squash, so why did she play it? She hardly knew. It was perhaps a mixture of attempting to please and keep up with her fast friends, together with a forlorn chase toward the physical fitness that had always just eluded her. Then there was the even greater and more elusive goal; parity with the svelte swankiness of her superior friend, Julia McMahon.

She paused at the sad end of yet another conceded game, the sweat perversely ignored her sodden head band and ran unhindered down her florid forehead. Panting and gasping for breath, she looked at Julia, looking amazingly cool in both appearance and demeanour. Her long legs emphasized by her still crisp, (even after six games) short white dress. Julia smiled serenely – irritatingly confident.

'Don't give up on me yet, Jacq,' Julia said, wide eyed, hands on hips, holding her racquet like a riding crop.

'I'm sorry,' panted Jacqui, 'I'm knackered!'

'Nonsense, we've hardly started.' Julia's small, but shapely breasts, rose and fell rhythmically as she spoke. The only outward sign of her recent past exertions. 'Only one set to love.'

'Only!' muttered the defeated Jacqui to herself. Then she watched in amazement as Julia began swinging her racquet aggressively toward the court floor, then bounding up and back on her expensive, trainer clad, toes.

'My God, where does she get her energy from?' thought Jacqui. Then something hit her and everything went black.

A voice from afar, which sounded much like her own, said faintly and wistfully with an echo, 'Why can't I be like her? Why?'

*   *   *

Jack Prince downed his third pint and glanced at his watch. 'Bloody Hell,' he muttered, 'she'll kill me!'

'Who?' said the crony at his elbow.

'Who'd yer think?'

'Ah.' said the other.

Jack pushed past him in mild exasperation and made for the Gents.

Five minutes later and several ounces lighter, he made his way through a throng of rather ageing Fords, Vauxhalls and Peugeots in the *Black Horse* car park. His was one of them, the most battered and faded, but it started at first turn of the key.

Amy Prince was a short stocky woman in her late forties, fadingly attractive but still bright eyed and occasionally vivacious. Now with the Sunday joint in the oven, approaching *bien cuit,* she was annoyed.

She wiped the condensation from the kitchen window and peered out. Where was Jack? Where was he? Then suddenly she began to feel rather unwell.

*   *   *

A sound like a clash of symbols and a chorus of steel knitting needles emanating from the engine of a battered Morris Minor announced Jacqui Strakes' imminent departure from the Byeford Country Club. Julia McMahon, her friend, would follow as usual in her smart white BMW saloon. Jacqui peered through the grease smeared windshield and eased the little car into gear with her aching left wrist. Once again, Julia had beaten her at squash.

'Perhaps being a left-hander is my real handicap,' she consoled herself. The car jumped, then gained momentum under protest from a worn first gear pinion joined by a shrieking clutch thrust bearing.

'I'll have to get myself a new set of wheels soon,' she groaned to herself.

As always, the smart white back end of Julia's trim 316 appeared before her after an effortless passing manoeuvre with a cheery toot on the way to the *Shoulder of Mutton*, their favourite local inn, beloved of the gin and tonic set.

'Smart cat!' growled Jacqui. 'Trim bum, trim boot that's Julia. Never mind, she's first, so perhaps she'll get the first round of drinks in!' but on second thoughts, her long acquaintance with her friend told her this was unlikely.

Then something unexpected happened. Some way ahead on the damp, early autumnal lane, Julia's car seemed to do a slow waltz on some wet leaves in the hollow, and gently, and seemingly ever so slowly, kiss a large American convertible gently on its ample cheek, as it made its way ponderously up the hill that they were travelling down.

'Oh my gosh I know that car!' was Jacqui's first thought. However, an instantaneous pang of remorse brought her mind sharply back to the matter of Julia's safety.

'Marcus, what can I say?' Julia was apologising, a fairly rare event for her, 'I don't know what happened.., I...'

'Never mind the car, are you alright?' enquired Marcus with genuine concern. Julia McMahon and Marcus Payne, failed barrister, now computer consultant, of South African origin, age uncertain, but somewhere between thirty five and forty two, was now an established member of the County set. His more regular mode of transport was a green sports car with pop up headlamps.

Jacqui arrived noisily; the couple, which in Jacqui's view they had instantly become, completely ignored her.

'You are sweet', cooed Julia gazing into Marcus's eyes.

Jacqui groaned, experiencing minor nausea together with her annoyance. Also her wrist hurt, and heaven knows what Julia's squash ball had done to her skull. Julia had said that she had always fainted easily, while the Country Club coach, who was also a paramedic, had examined her and said he thought she was OK but that she should see her doctor to make sure.

*　　*　　*

Later, in the *Shoulder of Mutton* Jacqui was at the bar getting the drinks. She was spending her rent money now.

'What were you doing in that American barge anyway?' Julia enquired, sipping the lager Jacqui had placed before her. She leaned on one elbow and gazed steadfastly at Marcus.

'It belongs to a friend of mine. An American actually...'

'No, really?' enquired Jacqui, almost managing to mix innocence with sarcasm and slopping the drinks.

Julia shot her a steely glance at this out of character interjection, which then withered into mere disdain, as she picked up her glass.

'Yes, he does some work for me occasionally so he was returning a favour by lending me his car,' Marcus continued.

'Oh, he works for you does he?' interrupted Jacqui again, determined not to be left out of the conversation.

Another snake-like glance from Julia. 'Oh, Jacqui stop interrupting and go and get some more drinks.'

'I've just got the last two rounds!' retorted Jacqui indignantly.

'Oh, well here you are, here's the fiver you owe me.'

'What?' Jacqui was flabbergasted.

'You know,' Julia went on, 'for losing at squash! You can give it me back next week'.

'No, no, you sit down I'll get them,' volunteered Marcus, gathering up their glasses.

'Cheers Marcus, you're such a dear,' chirped Jacqui, copying Julia's style.

'I don't know what's come over you, you're behaving very oddly,' rasped Julia accusingly, when Marcus had passed out of earshot.

'Oh really,' said Jacqui coldly, gazing intently out of the window.

4

"Facilus Descensus Averni."

(It is easy to go down into Hell)

Five miles above Southern England, Captain Lex Noonan, United States Air Force, banked his Lockheed ER2 spy plane, one of only two built for NASA, a much modified successor to the U2, in which Gary Powers was shot down by the Russians during the height of the Cold War. Capable of atmospheric and geological analysis, it carried sensors able to directly analyse minute particles suspended in the air.

For the aircraft itself, it had been a long flight from Moffet Field, Dakota, USA, but Noonan had only taken it from its intermediate positioning stop at McGuire USAF base in upper New York State. With its long range cruising capability the ER2 had easily made the UK in nine hours, cruising at over over sixty thousand feet – a height at which the curvature of the earth's surface is clearly visible.

Noonan eased his position, sweating slightly in the full pressure suit, and reflected on the three hour pre-take off oxygenation session, which all pilots flying this type have to undergo. His busy brain still had time to muse on why (unlike him) Concorde passengers, who flew at similar altitudes, could travel in casual clothes, converse with one another, eat *cordon bleu* food and drink champagne! Following this train of thought he wondered what had happened to Concorde now. Air France still operated them of course, and maybe some British Airways Concordes were still flying or positioned in one or two airfields abroad. Perhaps there was even one in the States at the time this thing happened. As a boy, twenty two years earlier, he had marvelled at the slim white bird as it came into Washington and could not understand the protests at this elegant visitor, although he could still recall the ear splitting crackle and roar of its powerful engines on take off.

Below, the cloud tops were beginning to thin and occasional glimpses of the ground were just visible. He programmed the auto-pilot, reduced power and the aircraft began to descend.

A few minutes later a dull bleeping and a flashing orange light on the lower instrument panel attracted his attention and his first reaction, which he suppressed, was to climb, increase power and get the hell out of there! It was the radiation warning monitor.

He reached for his radio transmitter switch, thought better of it and switched on the voice recorder instead:

"November 3rd, 09.50 hours. Position, eight miles South of Birmingham, descending to flight level six-zero. Strong indication of ambient radiation, actual dose to be obtained from flight data recorder, ...intensity level is intermittent but suggests recent neutron detonation..Am continuing descent. Noonan. Out."

Some ten minutes later as he passed below six thousand feet he began to feel the slight buffeting of upcurrents as the November sun warmed the lower air levels and the ground surface itself, still nearly a mile below.

The familiar patchwork landscape of middle England came into view – familiar from his F111 days at Upper Heyford. He had been the last to fly out when the base closed. As a senior captain with two tours in England, he was a natural choice for what was becoming an increasingly unenviable task.

Continuing his descent through five thousand feet, noting the scudding stratus and the flexing of the thin white wings, he was suddenly aware of another warning light, red this time, flashing ominously on the special surveillance panel. Under the light were the stark words 'Nerve Agent.' Nerve gas! As a reflex action momentarily bordering on panic, he reached for the air conditioning panel and fell back in his seat straps relieved – the control was set to "recirculate". The cockpit was hermetically sealed from the outside atmosphere – and anyway, his suit would protect him. It was just that, well... quite naturally, he didn't like the thought of any of that stuff near him!

Steadying the slightly bucking aircraft with one hand, he reached again for the record switch:

"Noonan. 10.13 hours, over Daventry, England, Nerve agent warning. Will attempt to capture atmospheric sample."

Then, as an afterthought, glancing at the silent VOR indicator, and with a touch of pathos in his voice, he said, *"Daventry Beacon silent."*

Reaching down to the surveillance panel, he moved the small lever to operate the sampler pod in the aircraft belly. 'Time to get the hell out of here !' he exclaimed, leaning back and glancing at his fuel gauge. Enough for the hour plus trip to Ramstein Air Force Base, in Western Germany and a little left over for a possible diversion, although this would be a problem as few other runways were long enough to take him.

*   *   *

Amor vincit omnia.

(Love conquers all)

Goodchild carefully parked his car, a small and unpretentious blue Volvo, and walked gingerly up the gravel path to the white painted front door of Julia McMahon's cottage. The brass knocker gleamed in the late summer sun undeterred by the water droplets that shone on it from a recent shower. He was relieved that no other car stood in the driveway or anywhere else about except for Julia's white BMW.

He hesitated before using the brass knocker, not from any concern about marring its pristine condition but more from the butterflies in his stomach. He was not very good at what his parents used to call courting. He had no idea what he was going to say, neither could he think of a suitable excuse for calling. He would much rather be landing a plane in fog at an unknown airport than be where he was standing now... and yet...

'Robin! How nice...' He started back as the door was flung open and Julia filled his vision with a kaleidoscope of colour, vitality and more than a suggestion of Chanel. 'Julia...,I...'

'Oh come in, come in.. you can put the flowers on the hall table!'

'Sorry? I haven't brought...'

'Just a joke Robin,' Julia chuckled. 'You'll know better next time, won't you? You forgetful flyer you!'

'You seem in a good mood...,I...'

'Of course, we're alive aren't we? It's a lovely day!'

'Well, it was...'

'What?'

He cursed himself for his gaucherie. 'I mean the weather,' he added quickly.

'Oh, don't be so gloomy Robin. Have a drink.'

They had passed through Julia's brief hallway and into a chintzy lounge. The sun suddenly shone defiantly through the diamond leaded window, illuminating Julia in mid-room like some celestial super trooper.

'You've just missed Marcus,' she announced giving him a blazing smile, 'Oh and...er Jacqui,' she added as an after-thought.

'Oh, really,' replied Goodchild sitting where Julia indicated. He didn't really care for Marcus Payne, a somewhat pretentious, as far as he could determine from Julia's past verbal gales, kind of failed South African lawyer.

'How's Jacqui keeping?' he enquired.

Julia frowned 'Jacqui? Oh, same as always. Jacqui's Jacqui... you know.'

Goodchild processed this snippet of disinformation, then decided to change the subject, but Julia got there before him.

'Well Marc...er Robin, and what have you been up to?'
As can be imagined, this verbal slip did not go unnoticed.

'Oh, you know the Brussels milk run.'

'Robin! You make it sound so mundane. You're an airline captain for God's sake!' Julia chortled.

'What about you?' replied Goodchild, ignoring the polite protestation.

'But you haven't got a drink,' Julia sidestepped, 'what am I thinking of?'

'Nothing for me, Julia, but don't let me stop you.'

'Oh, Robin you're so... sensible,' or even boring, she thought to herself, then loudly with a smile, 'OK, perhaps a small sherry for me. How about a nice cup of coffee for you?'

'Later, that would be nice,'

'Oh, you're stopping then?'

Goodchild almost blushed.

'Only teasing.' Julia winked wickedly, then added genuinely Goodchild hoped, 'You know you're always welcome.'

It occurred to Goodchild that Julia had still not asked him why he had called, a fact for which he was grateful. Then the phone rang.

*   *   *

In the Maryport Estate, in a Northern England city, Martha Brennan dreaded nightfall. She looked up nervously toward the boarded up window in her spartan kitchen but there was only the sound of the electricity meter whirring her pension away. Then faint shouts came from outside. She quelled the tremor in her breast with a thin hand. They were back – her tormentors. To a woman of her age and background it was incomprehensible – this persecution, this hate, never mind the lack of respect. Some, she had been told, were as young as five and so beyond the law! What were they doing out at this hour? What must their parents be like? She sighed deeply, then to console herself, automatically switched on the electric kettle. It seemed to her that the comfort of a warming drink was now one of the few comforts that remained in her life.

As Martha gazed blankly at the black and white photo portrait of her dead husband, on the dark heavy wooden side board, she bit her lip and a small tear began, but quickly she brushed it away. She looked at the telephone which seldom rang and thought briefly about ringing her son in Australia but railed at the imagined cost.

Sitting down before a low fire sulking in the grate and a blank television screen, she experienced one of her occasional, quite vivid recollections of her childhood, when she, her siblings and contemporaries used to wear their best flowery dresses on sunny Sundays, and after Church, skip and laugh along the dark forbidding streets. The vision seemed like another lifetime, another planet, another country - which in many ways it was. She hated England in the nineties, she felt betrayed and alone. The noises outside were getting louder now and a stone rattled against her boarded window.

*   *   *

'What you have to remember about ex-pats is...,' chattered Julia pouring out the fresh coffee, filling her small pine furnished kitchen with its rich aroma, 'that they have to justify their exile to others by running down the old country - justified or not!'

Goodchild said nothing, his mind had wandered elsewhere.

'Er, sorry Julia...I was...'

'Honestly Robin,' she chided him good naturedly, 'my best truisms are wasted on you! I was talking about Marcus Payne.'

Goodchild felt something approaching relief. He had recalled something of what she had said after all, and to him at least, it sounded like just the faintest criticism of a rival.

'Oh, you mean the chap on the phone?'

35

'No, I mean the milkman. Look out..' She leaned over him to get down the cups that hung on the pine dresser, giving him a waft of Chanel which made his head spin and his loins stir.

'I thought he was South African?' Goodchild said, sipping his coffee. It was hot.

'He was.'

'How do you mean?'

'He had to leave.'

'Oh why?'

'I'm not absolutely sure, something about the government of the day and his practice...'

'You mean the government before Mandela?'

'Oh yes, I mean old Nelson's a sweety....isn't he?' Julia raised her perfect eyebrows quizzically.

'I don't know I've never met him,' Goodchild replied flatly.

'Did you know they used to shoot elephants with machine guns?'

'You mean the South African army? Yes.. I did read something about it.. from helicopters I believe, working with UNITA in Angola, then selling the ivory - tons of it.'

'Beasts,' spat Julia, an animal lover.

'Quite,' said Goodchild, once again deep in thought.

'Honestly, Robin you're always...'

'Always what,' replied Goodchild, unnerved by her tone.

'I dunno.. thinking, I suppose. I can hear the wheels of your brain whirring from here!'

'You're right, I was thinking about Payne.'

'Oh, where does it hurt?' giggled Julia, knowing full well what he meant.

Goodchild ignored the witticism. 'I mean, what's he doing here – exactly?'

'Marcus? Oh I don't know... having a good time, I imagine.'

'Yes, but where does he get his money from?'

5

The British Ambassador in Washington, Sir Iain Taylour, was in the uncomfortable position, of being the senior surviving representative (overseas) of Her Majesty's Government. As such he was interlocutor to the rest of the world, most immediately with the USA, NATO, the British Commonwealth of Nations, and the UN, although strictly speaking the Ambassador to that august body was still Sir Percival Praed.

Taylour's 'office' was an historic 'first' and certainly unique. Unfortunately, it was not only unprecedented but also unpaid, and diminished by the depressing circumstances that gave rise to it. However, this did not stop others coveting it.

His latest telephone conversation with the US President had not been particularly helpful or conclusive. Personally, he doubted President Thomas's ultimate resolve in effectively handling the whole situation. Yet, he had to admit that he too found arriving at a policy of response extremely difficult at this stage of events – not least of all because no one seemed able to judge precisely who, or what, was responsible for the destruction of his country and probably most that had been dear to him.

Yet, like the President, he felt extremely alone. The grief he felt for his home, extended family and friends, was only mitigated by the myriad of responsibilities threatening to engulf him. Naturally, his first solace was communication with what remained of his fellow countrymen and women. In his case this meant not just his immediate family and staff, but his fellow Ambassadors, thinly spread about the world, following the latest and pre-catastrophic diplomatic economies, almost the last act of the final Her Majesty's Government. He wistfully enjoyed using the video conferencing suite, placed at his disposal by the Americans, as it gave him a unique opportunity to see some familiar – and hopefully, friendly faces.

Accordingly, when the equipment was available, and time differences allowed, he would communicate with his diplomatic colleagues, exchanging information and sympathies and generally doing his best to console them (and himself).

His first task was to arrange a series of British Ambassadors' meetings at the UN in New York. He had cleared this with Secretary General, Lammas, who had promised to chair one of the gatherings. However, when he was told that the Chairman of the National Security Council and the US Chiefs of Staff, General George Lee McIver, was also to preside over several of the meetings, he felt uneasy.

Admittedly, there was no precedent for what had happened, and so to a large extent policy and procedure had to be formulated 'on the hoof '. Nevertheless McIver represented the military establishment, and, being an inherent pacifist, Taylour was anxious about the military taking the lead – especially the military represented by McIver, heading the now unfettered, and as he saw it, unrestrained combined forces of the USA and NATO. He decided to speak directly, and if need be, obtain the advice of the only surviving UK Ambassador with recent military experience.

*　　*　　*

Rear-Admiral Lloyd Hope-Watson RN retired, Her (presumed late) Majesty's Ambassador to Hong Kong, took Taylour's call in his cool, ivory decorated office overlooking the Straits.

His had been an unusual appointment by an incumbent

Conservative government, who recognized that, although it was no longer appropriate, possible or affordable to retain a British military presence East of Suez, they might well combine diplomatic representation with the next best thing. While the succeeding socialist government elected in 1997, decided that he was safely out of the way in Singapore, where his right wing views might be satiated.

For his part, Taylour had considered carefully before making this call; he knew that Hope-Watson had tried to reach him several times since the event. Indeed, Taylour had received, but not responded to, a number of his faxes, offering advice and requesting information.

'Hello Iain, nice to hear from you at last!' This form of address was not quite a rebuke – after all Taylour was still his superior in diplomatic rank – but near enough to put the sensitive Taylour on notice that his 'performance' was being monitored.

Taylour decided to seize the high ground before Hope-Watson.

'Lloyd, I'm sorry I haven't got back to you. But as you can imagine, I have been rather busy.'

'Of course, I understand.'

'I should have liked to have included you on video conference but the time difference was against us, I'm afraid.'

'Iain, I'm just here to help,' Hope-Watson responded in an avuncular manner, 'Just tell me what you would like me to do?'

Taylour softened.

'Well, first of all, I have to tell you not to worry about funding – we're getting access to all overseas, government related accounts and a special fund has been set up by the IMF and the UN to continue paying all British overseas missions; that of course includes Ambassadors and their staffs....'

'That's very gratifying, Iain, but I must tell you that was the furthest from my thoughts at this moment.'

Another inherent, if not quite stinging, rebuke.

Hope-Watson took advantage of the short, ensuing silence

to press home another point. 'Have you any reliable information about what's happened, on the ground I mean?'

'Lloyd, I must tell you straight away that kind of information is classified – and I'm surprised you asked it.'

'A natural enough question surely – after all, one is enquiring about the survival or otherwise, of one's country.'

'Not on an open line, Lloyd – surely, you of all people, should know that!'

Round Two to Taylour.

'I did in fact call you specifically in the hope that you might give me some benefit of your military experience,' Taylour continued, somewhat testily.

Hope-Watson made no reply.

'Are you still there, Lloyd?'

'Yes, Iain? I'm still here.'

Taylour relented somewhat, 'I'm sorry Lloyd, did you have anybody special back home?'

Again Hope-Watson made no reply.

'The fact is,' Taylour went on, 'information is very scarce at present, until...'

'Until?'

'Well, please don't repeat this to anyone, not even your aides. Please use the scrambler now – ready?'

'I *hope* I can be trusted, 'replied Hope-Watson stiffly. He pressed the green button on his receiver.

'Of course,' Taylour was almost apologetic,'the fact is the Americans..'

'The Americans?'

'You disapprove?'

'Better than the French I suppose, please go on.'

'They're doing a series of surveys.'

'On the ground, you mean they've landed?'

'No, no, by air and satellite, that sort of thing.'

'Why can't they land?'

'Lloyd, I must impress on you that this is in the strictest confidence. The press haven't been informed yet.'

There was again silence at the other end of the line.

'It seems there may be nerve gas.'

'My God. Poor devils. What about er... radiation?'

'That too. Small amounts though.'

'Ugh! Makes one feel, well almost like an, an orphan!'

'Quite. It's a sickening business. One can't quite take it all in. Look Lloyd, I can't honestly tell you any more. What I mainly called to ask you is, I'm calling a conference of our main Ambassadors at the UN in New York. It's rather short notice I'm afraid.'

'When?'

'November the fifth, funnily enough.'

'How appropriate.'

Taylour sighed, 'Yes. Can you make it?'

'I should think so, after all, UK Singapore trade isn't what it was!'

'Quite. Look here, I'm going to send you an advance agenda via the diplomatic bag, and all the other details you'll need. Oh, and a short questionnaire. You might fill it in on the plane.'

'Oh?'

'Yes, as I said at the beginning I need your advice about, well, military matters.'

'May I ask why?' enquired Hope-Watson.

There was a short silence from Taylour this time. At length, he replied, 'I'm having to deal quite a bit with the American military. Well, to be quite frank, Lloyd, one doesn't want to be outflanked. No pun intended!'

At the end of the conversation Hope-Watson slowly replaced the receiver, leaned back in his bamboo chair, and smiled faintly. He rose and walked to the window. He had learned quite a lot after all, but most of all perhaps, he actually felt needed again. He lit a cigar – it tasted good.

*   *   *

Back in his office, McIver reflected on his meeting with Secretary General Lammas. It was true they had agreed a draft agenda for a coordinating meeting between the US Defense Dept, the UN, NATO and the senior British

Ambassadors. However, he – or more specifically, his military persona – felt somewhat outmanoeuvred by what he judged to be a diplomatic fudge. As he saw it, the priority was information gathering. Find out what physical state Britain was in, provide all possible assistance, then determine who did it! But even he had to concede that this order of events was almost the diametric opposite to conventional military thinking.

After Major Johnson, McIver was normally the first to see the intelligence photographs, which were now coming from three main sources – the Dragonflies (launched from the carrier Lexington, patrolling the Western Approaches); a handful of U2s and their updated successors from Mannheim; and the orbiting 'spy' satellites, hitherto primarily used for arms control.

The ER2s were also carrying out atmospheric sampling missions to detect the presence of harmful substances, or agents. Early analysis had confirmed significant amounts of SARIN and short to medium range Alpha and Beta radiation. In order of flexibility of operation, the Dragonflies came first, followed by the U2s and finally the satellites.

McIver was only too well aware that the Dragonflies were tactically under the control of Admiral Kearns.

Thermal imaging data was also available on the U2s and the satellites. This enabled Major Johnson to build up a 'heat' map which, when computerized, made it possible to overlay any radiation hot spots and nerve gas contamination data gathered from the U2s, onto the thermal heat areas obtained. The computer system display was colour coded, red for heat (including living mortal and mammal presence), orange for nerve gas and green for clear areas.

Naturally, Johnson was very proud of this system. Nevertheless, the situation changed hourly - mainly in accord with the weather, particularly the prevailing winds, monitored as well as could be achieved, near the surface and at two thousand feet above it. Accordingly, McIver ordered that an hourly refreshed Emergency Structure Presentation (or ESP) be delivered to the emergency operations room he had set up at the Pentagon, together with hourly weather reports. This process formed the vanguard of his *priority one* (agreed militarily – even with Kearns) which was, information about the theatre of operations.

Conversely, the feedback he received from diplomatic and political circles, was that precedence should be given to *priority two*: namely, to determine and assist all signs of life. At this stage, McIver considered this to be impracticable.

Later however, some interesting facts began to emerge which went some way toward fulfilment (in part at least) of priority two.

Large areas of the British mainland seemed relatively unscathed – at least by all available visual and physical determinations. This fact had been alluded to at the first Presidential briefing at the White House and was now confirmed by the latest reports. McIver had passed these on to the United Tactical Rescue Force (or UTFOR). But UTFOR was still being formed under a British Wing Commander ('Some kind of British Air Force Colonel,' as Kearns had reported somewhat grudgingly).

'Why, Ted? What's your problem?' McIver had enquired at the last joint briefing.

'I would have liked to have put my own man in charge of that Rescue mission.

'Well now, Admiral...'

'Don't you think we might use first names since we are going to be working closely together on this?' Kearns interrupted him.

'Of course Ted, but we're not going to be that close from now on.'

'You mean you want me to lead the sea landings?'

'Something like that. But first, I was going to say two things: one, we must allow the British to lead any rescue of their own countrymen and women. Secondly, there will be no rescue mission proper until my special monitoring and clearance forces have determined exactly what we're up against here.'

'Oh yes, Super Trooper,' rejoined Kearns somewhat sarcastically, recalling the White House briefing, 'by which time, any survivors will be dead!'

There was a brief silence between the two commanders, shortly broken by McIver.

'I have taken advice on this Ted,' said McIver quietly.

'Which is?'

'That there's little sense in the rescuers suffering the same fate as those they are attempting to rescue.'

'You're the boss,' said Kearns grudgingly. 'I just hope the Brits agree with you.'

'It was them, I asked,' smiled McIver, a little sadly.

*   *   *

This then was the Survey & Rescue side of Operation *Broken Arrow*, as it was officially named. Thereafter, the world's press had a motif for its almost continuous headlines, in papers, journals, TV and radio.

Later, after some sustained pressure from McIver, backed up by the Supreme Commander of NATO, the President had authorized McIver to form an *Offensive Response Subcommittee* at the Pentagon. The UN was not informed of this.

6

The ominous grey black outlines that formerly slid in and out of the large scenic dock that was Faslane, and even before that, the Holy Loch, were no more, and silence was all about, except for the crying of the gulls and guillemots.

Admiral Edward J. Kearns, Chief of United States Naval Staff, and task force commander designate, approached, but the throbbing engine of his less than ornate US Navy barge could not yet be heard. For it was still many nautical miles to the West.

There was a heavy green grey swell and the Admiral, ironically, not the best of sailors, was uneasy. Yet, who knows, perhaps excitement caused his incipient nausea. The tremor behind the high ranking waistband of the heavy blue reefer coat, (shielded from the chill wind by a six foot standing marine) stemmed from a disobedience of a superior he considered his inferior. A dangerous juxtaposition.

The barge approached the Firth of Clyde, far from its snug berth high in the ramparts of the far off USS Lexington, whose great bulk Kearns could not risk on such a journey.

At the limit of its normal range, the small, but capable vessel, with extra fuel aboard and the best helicopter crew briefed to seek them out if they did not report at the pre-arranged times, bucked its way over the, now white capped, swell, past Garroch Head to port and Little Cumbrae Island to starboard - at 10.30 hours GMT. Visibility was still good, but falling slightly.

'Coxswain, what time do you estimate Dunoon?'

45

'If the wind doesn't change, 11.50 hours, sir.'

'Very good. Report our position to Lexington.'

'Aye Aye, sir'

'He's Loco,' thought the Coxswain, bent to his task at the mildly ornate wheel.

Behind him, his Commander in Chief surveyed the purple, misty coastline through powerful binoculars.

* * *

> *"The Grass will grow in the streets of
> a hundred cities, a thousand towns."*
>
> (Herbert Hoover
> American Republican
> 31st President
> 1874-1964)

Back in the calm warmth of the USS Lexington bridge, Captain Wade Brannigan, USN, checked his watch with the bridge clock, scowled and wished he had some one to share his disapproval with. He walked slowly into the office through the open white painted steel door signed in red: *Captain.* Once inside, he closed the door, opened the small safe and took out a folder marked *NATO Secret.*   He opened the folder and read halfway down the first page:

OPERATION 'COUNTER STRIKE'
Primary Delivery method
<u>ROYAL NAVY</u>

Nuclear Submarine Armament
Sea (via upper atmosphere)
to Surface, Re-Entry Missiles.
TYPE:Trident D5

Warheads 1 to 14 (Max) per missile.

ONE MISSILE PER TARGET

(5 Warheads per missile)

Warhead Charge
(1) Non Nuclear HE 500 Kg (Torpex or Amatol)
(2) Dilute Nerve Agent SA22

There was more, much more, but he could not take it all in at that moment.

Brannigan, visibly shaken and pale, sat heavily behind his small desk, clutching the file. Then suddenly, he rose, crossed quickly to the door, closed it as silently as possible and applied the lock. Returning to his desk, he picked up the next sheet and began to read, beads of sweat breaking out on his brow.

'My God!' Brannigan exclaimed when he had finished reading, closing the file with a reflex action. 'Where did Kearns get this from?' His pre-occupation was interrupted by the telephone.

His hand trembled slightly as he raised the receiver.

'Yes?'

'The C in C's barge has reported entering the Firth of Clyde, Sir.'

'Very good, Yeoman, keep me informed of further reports.'

'Aye Aye, sir.'

After the call, Brannigan sat heavily on his day bunk and looked at the liquor cabinet door, white and innocuous.

*   *   *

Kearns sat shielded from the wind and the eyes of his subordinates, in the covered section aft, and began to feel better. He reached into his reefer and took out a small leather covered flask. He had kept it with him since the occasion of his first command. It had been a present from his mother. He looked at it briefly, unscrewed the cap and bringing it to his chilled lips, took a generous swallow. The Bourbon tasted good.

He could rely on Brannigan - he felt sure of it. Not only

was he a protégé, the Captain also had a problem, about which only he knew, and Brannigan knew that he knew. His power over him went beyond the chain of command.

Kearns plan was to visit the British Navy nuclear submarine base at Faslane and then go on to the former United States Navy base at Holy Loch. McIver would never have allowed it, of that he was certain and by the time he found out, Kearns would have done what he had to do and be armed with knowledge which would give him the advantage in the President's Council. Knowledge was power – but only in the right hands at the right time. The high school boy from Milwaukee was beating those Ivy League bastards at their own game. He knew it was a gamble, perhaps the biggest of his life – certainly of his career.

Suddenly, to starboard, through a sullenly lifting mist, a flashing light – Cloch Point. Kearns heart leapt, until reason won and told him the lighthouse was automatic and probably had its own power source. 'Dunoon, 11.50 hours, sir,' called the Coxswain.

'Very good,' replied Kearns flatly, failing to congratulate the sailor on the accuracy of his estimate.

*   *   *

Back in his office, in the Pentagon, McIver reviewed progress following the morning meeting of the Commanders and Commanders in Chief, assigned to Operation *Broken Arrow*. There was one notable absence – Admiral Kearns.

Apparently, Defence Secretary Richard Scottdale, had acceded to a quite extraordinary request by Kearns, that he should join the Lexington, currently patrolling in the Western Approaches to the English Channel, and sail her under his flag, to Scotland on a personal, high level surveillance of the Faslane and Holy Loch region, (but had given assurances – according to, and on the orders of, Scottdale - not to land) the object being to find out what had happened to the British nuclear submarine fleet.

As an ex sub-mariner, Kearns had specialist knowledge

as he had served aboard a US nuclear submarine at Holy Loch.

Needless to say, McIver was not pleased. Indeed, on learning about the mission (by coded fax) he was so angry that he had to confine himself to his quarters for thirty minutes before taking any action, or making any form of contact with others. It was a device which had stood him in good stead in the past, without which his explosive temper would surely have sunk his career, without trace, on several occasions.

It was true that he had assigned Kearns command of the Lexington and a small task force to carry out close surveillance and provide communications and tactical support. She was one of the sources of the intelligence photographs, via her Dragonflies.

He had also detailed Kearns to lead the sea landings. But recalled impressing upon him two principles. One, allowing the British to lead any rescue of their own countrymen and women. Two, that there should be no rescue mission proper until the special monitoring and clearance forces had determined exactly what they were up against. He remembered that Kearns' response had been less than satisfactory.

This had been the last straw, and he had re-drafted the *Broken Arrow* operation order to ensure that Kearns returned to Washington, to take up the crucial naval planning role, which was not unreasonable considering that he was, after all, Chief of Naval Operations.

Now this!

'Dammit!' McIver thumped his desk, 'Ted Kearns is too old to play boy scout!'

He walked to the oak cabinet in the corner of his austere office, and took out a bottle of Johnny Walker. He seldom drank, but this was an exception. It was plain that Scottdale was trying to undermine him and that Kearns was taking advantage of the fact.

He stopped, held up the bottle and looked at it, appreciating its golden colour against the harsh white lights.

'Now, I get it.' He drawled.

In the mirror he caught his reflection, and very nearly smiled.

* * *

Approaching Holy Loch, Kearns' barge made passage with Strone Point to starboard and Ardnadam to port, oblivious of the splendid foreign owned estates just visible through the thin mists – some Dutch, some Belgian, some American.

The Survey & Rescue side of Operation *Broken Arrow* was progressing – albeit somewhat unofficially, toward a possible first landfall.

7

"Every End is a Beginning."

(Anon)

Taylour sat listening to the Elgar Violin Sonata in his Washington Embassy apartment. Outside in the small atrium that formed the entrance to the Embassy compound, was a small flowering cherry tree. Its frailty in the pale November sun combined with the music, invoked thoughts of Malvern, which was not only birthplace of the composer, but also where Taylour went to school. What of Malvern now? he wondered.

Rising from his green leather chair, he walked to the window. Gazing out rather mournfully, he reflected on his initial contact with Hope-Watson. This had culminated in the conference of senior British Ambassadors, held somewhat ironically on the fifth of November, at the UN in New York.

The advance agenda he had sent Hope-Watson via the diplomatic bag, had suffered heavy revision by the US Military. Their priorities were clearly not his own. As to the short questionnaire, regarding military matters, he had asked Hope-Watson to complete on the plane – he had to admit to himself, that he had been been naive in using such a device, for although he had made no secret of its purpose, he should have known that a man like Hope-Watson would not impart information and hard won knowledge, gratuitously. Information which Hope-Watson might use to increase his own stature at an appropriate time.

Indeed, some might say that Taylour had been a fool, but he could never admit that, even to himself.

Yes, he had certainly needed advice about military matters. Unfortunately, his military attaché in Washington had been on leave in England at the time of that most terrible of events, the details of which, even now, were unclear and conflicting.

At the time, there had been no reason why the attache's leave should not have been granted – after all, things had been quiet militarily, ever since the abortive Chinese annexation of Taiwan. He remembered it well. At the last moment, when the world had braced itself for a super power, military exchange, the Chinese had suddenly deferred to the presence of a mighty US naval force in the Taiwan Straits, successfully led by a certain Admiral Kearns.

At all events, he now kicked himself for confiding in Hope-Watson.

* * *

Lammas was speaking slowly and deliberately into the telephone handset, held lightly but firmly in long slender fingers, a shaft of sunlight catching a single gold ring.

'Mr President, far be it for me to criticise General McIver. It's just that he has the ball and we are all waiting on the sidelines. Without information we can do precious little.'

There was a pause while he listened to the President's reply.

'Yes, I understand that.'

Another pause.

'Of course, by all means…'

A long pause this time.

'Thank you, Mr President. I'm most grateful.'

On replacing the receiver, Lammas afforded himself a faint smile. At last, he had the go ahead to start assembling what might prove to be the biggest aid operation in the history of the UN. Thomas had even promised the lion's share of the funding. 'We must ensure that the legal instruments are in place to hold him to that promise,' Lammas muttered darkly. 'Anyway, thank God. I just hope we may be in time after all this delay.'

He leant forward and pressed a button on the intercom.

'Ah, Brad, is that you? Good. Would you please arrange a meeting of heads of departments for tomorrow…, yes. I should be free to address the meeting at 11.30am, Yes. It is UTFOR at last! Thank you Brad.'

Lammas had been particularly grateful that the President had given him the news for the go-ahead personally. He didn't really care for McIver.

*   *   *

"Nature alone cannot dry our tears."

(A.E. Housman
English Poet
1859-1936)

As Kearns had expected, except for the birds, there was no observable sign of life at the old US Polaris submarine base. "The Bombers", as the former occupants had been known.

As he looked about him, from the undulating barge, the misty horizons rose and fell and the whole vast area had a forbidding air. Perhaps it had always been so. But now it seemed, not only chill but withholding of some dark secret, penetrable only by a sixth sense. Its menace was only a suggestion.

He had ordered the Coxswain to cruise slowly round the edge of the vast dock, their wash slapping the concrete sides and wooden piles of the loading piers. Dark, rusting crane derricks, towered above them, silhouetted against the grey November sky.

Kearns scanned the shore with his powerful binoculars. He called on Marine PFC Wales to take the yellow water-proof video camera from its locker and video the whole scene.

The Coxswain looked at his chronometer.

'12.50 hours sir. We need to move on to Faslane if we are to be out of here by dark, and we can't rely on the weather.'

'I assume you know how to use that radar set, Chief?' rasped Kearns, temporarily lowering his binoculars.

'Yessir.' acknowledged the Coxswain.

'Daylight is a luxury on this mission, Chief, to be used only for observation of our objectives, not returning from them.'

53

'Aye aye, sir.'

'Movement on shore, sir!' called out PFC Wales.

'Where, man?'

'Between those sheds!'

'It's a dog!'

The black labrador began to bark. It was a mournful bark, that echoed from the empty buildings and reached toward them, across the grey water.

The echo seemed to dominate the whole area.

For the first time in an eventful career, Kearns didn't immediately know what to do. It soon passed.

'Marine, I want you to shoot that dog!'

PFC Wales, an animal lover, gulped. 'I – I can't sir!'

The Coxswain, ahead of them, turned from his wheel and stared aghast at both his subordinate and his Commander-in-Chief, appalled at both of them for diverse reasons, one for giving such an order, and the other for such fearful disobedience.

'OK, Private, hand me your sidearm.'

The marine obeyed his awesome superior, as if in a trance, taking the heavy Browning automatic from its holster and offering it, butt first, with a trembling gloved hand.

'Now, stow that camera and go aft,' Kearns spoke slowly and menacingly. If he hadn't needed every hand he would have placed him under close arrest.

'Chief, I want you to get in close. As close inshore as you can.'

The Coxswain turned back to his wheel and felt sick, a rare experience for him.

The Labrador ran, still barking, to meet its fate, toward them right up to the steep concrete ramparts of the dockside, the dark water slapping below. The Coxswain aimed the barge's bow using one of the large iron mooring rings, set in the rust streaked, green stained concrete.

As they approached, the Coxswain reversed the twin screws and the motors roared. The dog barked in a frenzy now, prancing on the very lip of the dockside, its black form in relief against the Scottish sky. A perfect target.

Kearns aimed the Browning and fired as the boat dipped in their reflected wash as it rebounded back from the concrete ramparts.

The Coxswain closed his eyes momentarily, not wanting to see the dog fall dead, into the deep, cold water of the dock. Then, from behind him, came a crash. Swinging round he saw Kearns, collapse, a look of astonishment on his rugged features, onto the damp, but polished deck. A large round hole was between his still open eyes and blood oozed thickly and darkly, starting slowly down the bridge of his slightly curved nose.

The Coxswain, for the boat's safety, turned quickly back to his wheel and toward the bow. Looking up in fear, he saw that the dog was still there, its head cocked to one side now. It had stopped barking and began slowly to wag its tail.

8

> *"The nation*
> *(Britain) has given all*
> *to the common man.*
> *A nation which owes its success to*
> *the uncommon man."*
>
> (Noel Coward
> English Playwright)

British Embassy, Washington
November 19th, 1998

The large bound desk diary for 1998 lay open on Taylour's desk, exceptional in that it allocated two A4 pages to each day. They were needed. The entry on the first page for November the eighteenth started with a list of headings which needed to be addressed, and for the most part delegated.

<u>Items annotated on Agenda of First Meeting of
Ambassadors Nov 5th 1998 but unresolved</u>

1/ FRANCO – GERMAN EUROCORE (military
   involvement/resource)?

2/ IRELAND. Why are the Americans keeping quiet about this?

3/ UK FORCES, Germany (military involvement/
   resource)?

4/ NATO (political/ military involvement/resource)?

5/ UK FORCES CYPRUS?

6/ Convene/ Co-ordinate/ a UK Military
   Committee with real powers Comprising(at least) :-

   (a)   ARMY: 1 General or Brigadier

   (b)   RAF : 1 Air Commodore and/or Group Captain

           1 W/Cmdr (– Nerve Gas specialist)!

ROYAL NAVY:
1 Admiral, 2 Captains, 1 Commander (one at least
with nuclear submarine experience).

The list – one of many – was, as always, incomplete, so with great reluctance Taylour had to resort to a laptop computer – for which a classical education had not adequately prepared him – in order to carry forward his increasingly complex plans. Occasionally, especially when he was tired late at night, he feared they might overwhelm him. It was then that the whole situation seemed unreal, and also when he thought of his estranged wife – who had been living in London. Unrealistically, he had even tried ringing her once; the unobtainable tone was sickening. And so, work was his therapy and his antidote for the emptiness he felt inside.

At all events, he was beginning to realise just how massive his task was. For although some might say he was merely a temporary political, rallying point, his workload was real enough and growing daily; to the extent that he had called on the British Ambassador to the UN, Sir Percival Praed, to help him form a 'Co-ordinating Committee.'

He hoped that such a committee – yet to be adequately named to reflect the auspicious tasks it would be called upon to perform – would become the *de facto* British government in exile.

Taylour was determined that such an important role should not be consigned to some UN, US or EEC sub-committee (which the agendas and moods of several meetings, he had attended recently, had seemed to suggest). Indeed, he feared that without a firm stand on his part, it was an imminent possibility.

The Lion might be singed, but it was not going to lie down, defeated in some foreign back water! He also planned to form some kind of broadcasting facility to become the new voice of Britain. He hoped that this might include both radio and television In addition, one of his principal secretaries in charge of Information Technology, had suggested pages on the Internet. This had made Taylour feel his age!

However, before announcing his plans to the world press, or consulting the US State Department, EEC or the UN – Taylour felt it politic to gather together as many specialists (preferably British) as he could find, and to form them into advisory bodies, making informed recommendations on all likely courses of action. In this way, the overall position would be stronger when liaising, or negotiating with, the many concerned countries, organizations and agencies. They particularly needed someone good with languages to work with the EEC. How he missed the often cursed, and taken for granted, resources of the Foreign Office.

He had been disappointed with the response from the senior European Ambassadors, namely those representing Brussels, Paris and Berlin. Their attitude seemed strangely defeatist. In fact it had crossed Taylour's mind (angrily) that they had been away from Britain and its sense of history for far too long, and had therefore become too European in their thinking. Britain, and everything it had stood for, was very important to him.

He sensed that this was also the case with Hope-Watson, except that the ex-admiral's views appeared somewhat extreme for Taylour's taste – it was an uneasy alliance.

Hope-Watson had volunteered to represent, not only Far Eastern British interests, but also the ex-patriot community world-wide. Taylour had pointed out that *they* no doubt had their own associations. But Hope-Watson had insisted that they would now have to be co-ordinated, and probably persuaded, to return to the homeland, as soon as possible, to rebuild Britain as a nation. He had seemed particularly keen on social reconstruction for, as he pointed out, much of the infrastructure, according to latest reports, appeared intact.

At all events, they would soon know at first hand, because at last UTFOR had the go ahead and the race to organize the operation was in hand. Indeed, it was continuing apace, twentyfour hours a day.

McIver's Super Troopers had given the go ahead for a

number of decontaminated landing points. The US Navy would provide the ships and the token British contingent would lead American and NATO troops, followed by the UN aid workers.

The first task would be to re-establish communications: telephones, radio & TV. For it would appear that all means of communications had been disabled – possibly by neutron radiation, or by more precise and deliberate means.

Meanwhile, on the political level, the whole situation was becoming more highly charged by the day, and vested interests were beginning to emerge and, in some cases, to actually "set out their stalls" – as one of Taylour's staff had put it – some quite openly, others more covertly. For example, Taylour was aware of a developing rift between European and American power sources.

After a slow start, he was getting increasing reports and communications of all kinds, that indicated a belated European Community (EEC) involvement, indicating an attempted European take over of the whole situation. This was clearly overt.

However, Taylour put Hope-Watson in the other category. He felt that, although he was open about the ex-patriot question (which had consensus), he sensed that the ex-admiral had a hidden agenda.

*   *   *

*"I used to be indecisive,
but now I'm not so sure."*

(Boscoe Pertwee)

In the light of the imminent UTFOR landings and with the diminishing likelihood of news of, or from, UK nerve centres, such as Northwood (the Joint British Services Command Centre), Whitehall, Westminster (or Fylingdales), Taylour was relieved to receive news of the arrival next day, of the British Military contingent, and apart from the obvious need for their contribution to UTFOR, Taylour hoped for news not yet released by the Americans, or of which they were unaware. For, in spite of his enforced self discipline, the possibility of his wife's survival began to occupy him increasingly.

Taylour's appointments' secretary, an effete but efficient man called Charles Braithwaite, had thankfully (from Taylour's viewpoint) taken charge of the computer and had assigned acronyms to all visiting and participating parties for its database. This military contingent was henceforth to be called the BOSC (The British Overseas Services Contingent).

BOSC comprised senior officers from the old British Army of the Rhine, Northern Ireland, the Falklands and Cyprus, including some from his old Regiment! He especially welcomed the opportunity to speak with the Royal Navy and Royal Air Force officers among them, the latter having been 'marooned' in RAF Germany, several years before the scheduled final withdrawal of that force, after a continuous presence of some fifty years.

A Wing Commander was able to tell Taylour informally, (without a little embarrassment) that RAF Germany had managed to get off several sorties, after the Event, but had had no prior warning – there having been nothing on the radar and a complete communications blackout. Therefore, these flights had been no more than reconnaissance, a role which they reluctantly handed over to the Americans because they had more suitable aircraft. Moreover, they had been quite unable to make contact with any RAF station or any of the other numerous Ministry of Defence Establishments.

Afterwards, Taylour contemplated glumly the irony of a once proud service, being in the event, literally impotent in the defence of their homeland – in the face of the unknown and the utterly unexpected.

Together with the contingent recently dispersed from Hong Kong, as far as was known, BOSC represented the only senior British military presence, of any significance, left in the world, apart from several small units scattered across the globe, serving with the UN, and of course, the military attaches at the larger Embassies.

Anticipation of their arrival caused Taylour to feel buttressed against the increasing US political, military and other enervating pressures, which had assailed him these past lonely weeks.

When he finally returned to his apartment, late that evening, exhausted but elated, the telephone rang. Taylour answered it with a reflex action. It was the British Ambassador to Ireland, speaking from Dublin!

* * *

Singapore

June 1998

Before the Event

Hope-Watson was relaxing. He leaned back in his wicker chair, drew on his Havana cigar and caressed the crystal tumbler. He was doing some of his favourite things, almost simultaneously. But above all, he was doing what he enjoyed most – talking. His companion was not an equal partner in the conversation.

'Britain? In the sixties we were going to join the space race, remember, Blue Streak, Black Night, Woomera and Concorde? Now, what is it, eh? The latest social trend, as far as I can make out, is something called, 'Ladism.' And the pinnacle of technological and commercial, achievement? The mobile 'phone – made elsewhere, of course – pathetic! While here in the Far East, they're leading the world...'

'What's Ladism, exactly?' asked his companion with mild interest, interrupting Hope-Watson's flow.

'Heard it on the World Service yesterday. As far as I can make out, it means the popular classes indulging in a vicarious obsession with football – we used to call it soccer...'

'How vicarious?'

'I mean they never actually play it, they just watch it on TV and talk about it endlessly, punctuated with expletives.'

'And..?'

'Drink fizzy beer, roar round in cheap motor cars, fight one another, frighten and occasionally rape old ladies. That sort of thing.'

'You don't miss it then?' observed his companion, mischievously.

'I miss what it *was*, should and *could* be again,' Hope-Watson replied bitterly.

'Aren't you just being a terrible old snob? Anyway, things will surely soon be different – very different.'

'It may not be as simple as that.' The shoulder muscles tensed slightly behind the white dinner jacket, and the wicker chair creaked under Hope-Watson's bulk as he leaned forward. He rose and walked to the veranda.

The evening air was heavily scented with a range of aromas, some exotic, others less so and exclusive to the Singapore Straits. A breeze sprang up and rattled the veranda awning.

'I think the last straw was when they got consultants in to examine the workings of Oxford.'

'Oh, and what did they examine, exactly? Town or Gown?'

Hope-Watson swung round, scattering cigar ash to the wind, and gave him a withering look, 'Why the System! The very heart of the place – the tutorial system.'

'Oh, that.' His companion, ten years Hope-Watson's junior, held his glass up to the moon and examined it.

'And look at state education,' Hope-Watson went on, 'a shambles.'

'Always was,' replied his companion flatly.

'Then, selling off Greenwich – bloody scandalous!'

'And that was the Tories!'

'Hmmph!'

'Of course, you were there too, weren't you?'

'It's alright for you,' barked Hope-Watson, helping himself to another gin and proffering the bottle toward his companion's glass, who declined, 'you're a bloody multi – national!'

'That's companies, Lloyd. I think you mean an international. Anyway, you've had too much gin!'

There was a long pause while Hope-Watson leaned over the balcony and glowered at the distant lights.

'By the way,' his companion resumed, 'any news from our friends?'

'Yes,' said Hope-Watson turning round and fixing him with a fierce stare, 'that's why you're here!'

'That's my Lloyd – always so welcoming!'

'But first,' Hope-Watson continued with great emphasis, 'we need to make sure that our people assimilate into the local communities. I hope you can arrange that?'

'You mean like the Irish?' The other man gave an almost shrill laugh and leaned back in his chair.

Hope-Watson stubbed out his cigar angrily, in a large crystal ashtray.

'Something like that, but I hope they might be a *little* more subtle.'

'With a smile and an expensive accent, eh?'

'No, not necessarily. Look here, this is important. It's not a game, we need *all* stratas of society. Is that clear?'

'Sorry, I'll remember, "Old Uncle Tom Cobleigh and all", eh?'

Hope-Watson did not answer, but slumped back in his chair.

When his companion excused himself to go to the toilet, he hardly heard him.

He began thinking of Oxford again, the High, the rotund Sheldonian Theatre, Christchurch with its elegant Tom Tower and Meadows. The Mitre Hotel, where he had got drunk as a first year student, Wytham Woods, among whose bluebell glades he had lost his virginity, all those years ago. Then the wonderful stroll back to Wytham village for a refreshing drink in The White Lion, the pleasant drive back to College in the open MG. He could still smell the hot oil and the tar from the melting road – it had been so hot that day in 1958. Forty years ago!

He had been back recently. Things had changed, but not for the better, in his estimation. The first impression was the traffic. "My god, wall to wall traffic," as a lady American tourist had observed.

The way people dressed – even the girls – especially the girls! Few wore a dress, or if they did, they wore brown boots with them – grotesque! During the day, at least, many girls dressed either in shapeless black and looked more like men, or obscenely tight leggings, some admittedly brightly coloured, but hardly in good taste. Whereas some male students resembled women, sporting not just shoulder length hair, but pony tails and earrings!

Then there were those young men, he presumed to be of the Town. Lager drinking skin heads people called them, on account of their shaven heads – in contrast with the students! Those with rings in their nostrils! – came as a special shock to him.

Apart from the occasional business suit and academic black gown, the rest of the population seemed to be in some form of transatlantic uniform, comprising blue jeans and gaudy tee-shirts, advertising some foreign beer or sports equipment. On their feet they wore "white" training shoes, of conspicuous size and design, with huge tongues sticking out from the laces. On enquiry, he heard that these "trainers" cost up to eighty pounds a pair, or the equivalent in Euros. Ironically, he discovered that many brands were made in cheap sweat shops in the Far East, especially Korea and Thailand, some by children, and might be had in such places for around ten US dollars. That was the multi-nationals for you, he thought. And presently, here he was entertaining one of their lackeys!

He strove to convince himself that it was for a higher purpose.

'Yes, Britain was at the end of an American culture garbage chute,' he mused sadly.

At that point his companion for the evening returned from his ablutions.

'I'm sorry to interrupt your reverie, Lloyd. Are you still with us?'

'Yes,' said Hope-Watson briskly, 'Here's what I want you to do.'

9

*"A nation is in terminal decline when
its citizens are unwilling, or unable,
to speak the whole truth -
about themselves."*

'Hello, Iain? Are you still there? It's Brian Pace. You're obviously surprised to hear from me!'

Taylour was indeed surprised. In fact he was literally speechless

'Brian! My God, you're alive !'

'Obviously, old man.'

'It's wonderful to hear your voice!'

'And you too, dear boy, but listen, what's concerning me is that you haven't been *told* that most things are OK in the dear old Emerald Isle. Weren't you told?'

'Well, no. At least, not verbally, Brian,

'I don't quite understand, old man?'

Taylour struggled for an adequate reply. The simple truth was, incredibly – in the maelstrom of the past weeks – that he had quite forgotten, and had therefore never actually asked about, Eire!

'We've been inundated with information in every conceivable form, Brian. Mountains of paper, faxes, reports and E-Mail too, as you can imagine...'

'Yes, but even so, are we that unimportant?' Pace sounded hurt. 'Seems a bit rum, if you don't mind me saying so?'

Taylour, his fatigue temporarily assuaged by joy and adrenalin, felt a cold shudder of concern. He masked it with the first question that came into his tired mind.

'But Brian, why didn't *you* call *us* before now?'

'Tried to, old man, couldn't get through.'

'I – I see,' replied Taylour, lamely.

There was an awkward pause. At length, Taylour went on, 'I'm sure we've tried to call you – and a good many others besides.' He was about to say, 'I was *told* we could not get through, either,' when realisation struck him, and he stopped himself – just in time. 'Look here, Brian,' he continued, regaining some of his old authority, 'you must get over here as quickly as you can. Can you get a plane?'

'Well, I *think* Aer Lingus are still operating. The trouble is...'

'What is it?' prompted Taylour, anxiously.

'Well, its just that all the flights seem to be fully booked.'

'Fully booked,' rasped Taylour, with mounting apprehension,'who by?'

'The Americans, old man.'

'You mean, the American Military?'

'Exactly so, old chap.'

Some time later, when he had finished the call, Taylour remained in his chair staring fixedly at the wall. On it, there was the usual portrait of Her Majesty the Queen. Below it, he read and re-read the second motto of the British Crown, *Honi soit qui mal y pense.* Evil be to he, who Evil thinks of it.

*　　*　　*

McIver strode into the meeting, at the Pentagon, waving to the *Broken Arrow, Military Response Committee* members, to regain their seats. He sat slowly at the head of the table and, having settled himself, removed his insignia adorned service cap. Suddenly, he realised he didn't like any of the faces turned toward him, and he trusted them even less.

'First of all,' he drawled,' I want us *all* to pay our respects to the late Admiral Ted Kearns, who died in the performance of his duties.., I......'

'Yeah, how about that?' said a Marine Colonel incredulously, turning to his companion.

'What happened there, sir – we heard such wild rumours?' said another.

'That's right, ...something about a dog?'

'And shooting himself with a marine's side arm!' It was the Marine Colonel, again.

'Forget the dog' McIver thundered. Then quietly. 'The rest is true, I believe.'

'You mean suicide?' an Air Force Colonel almost shrieked.

'No, and I'm disappointed you could think such a thing about a man like Admiral Kearns. Sounds to me more than a might disrespectful.'

'I'm sorry sir, I...'

'Never mind. If you must know – it's unconfirmed of course – but it seems there was a ricochet.' There was a hushed silence as they stared at their Commander. 'From the dock wall, if you must know,' McIver went on.

'You mean he was killed by his own shot? Je-sus, I hope he wasn't a Texas man!'

McIver gave the exponent of this remark a warning glance.

'But what was he doing there, anyways?' said a two star General seated next to McIver.

'That needn't concern you all at present. Now, do you mind if we get on, because I'm just a might busy, right now! Now Tom, if you'll lead off? What have we got so far?'

Major-General Tom Stone, McIver's senior aide, stood up and approached the large wall map, extending the telescopic pointer he held, as he went.

He pulled down a list next to the map. It read as follows:

Suspect Agencies responsible for Attack
on the United Kingdom

(Including the whole of England and strategic areas of Scotland and Wales but excluding the Republic of Ireland Northern Ireland, The Scottish Isles and Channel Islands).

Provisional List

Dissident Russian Military Factions

Irish Republican Para Militaries.

International Terrorist Cell

(Libya or Iranian backed cell – London based)

Power cell within the EEC.

North Korean Special Forces

Chinese Special Forces (Including Long range missiles)

There was silence, then muttering.

Stone was apologetic, 'I know this is a pretty crude list...'

He glanced back at McIver.

An Air Force General said, 'If I didn't know you better, sir, I'd say you were playing a little joke on us!'

'We have to consider every possibility at this stage, no matter how crazy,' Stone replied defensively.

'Hell, yes, but shouldn't it be a *considered* list, based on real evidence, and surveillance? What we know to be so'

'Never mind that,' said a Marine General, 'this is the first time I knew that only England, Scotland and Wales had been attacked and Ireland, and those islands excluded!'

'Yeah, how about that?' queried the Air Force Colonel, looking round at his colleagues to gauge their reaction.

They all turned and looked at McIver once more.

McIver did not speak immediately but crossed to the map and stood next to Stone.

'First, I want to tell you that this not a political Committee. Our job is to review *all* intelligence we have on this – no matter how wild – and then make a series of decisions, leading to detailed recommendations for our political masters.'

The Marine General, stood up, and resting both muscular arms on the table, looked intently at McIver. Then he spoke, slowly and deliberately.

'If you don't mind me saying so George, this sounds more like you're leading us through the mushroom syndrome.'

There was an almost tangible frisson which rippled round the long room. The silence, though actually brief, was memorable.

'Excuse me?' queried McIver, peering at the speaker.

'Fed on shit and kept in the dark!' thundered the Marine General, fearlessly.

An electric wall clock, whose face displayed the military twenty-four hour notation, acquired a loud tick, almost certainly not noticed by any of the officers present, before this moment. Now its alternating metallic voice held the floor.

Otherwise, the silence was longer this time, during which McIver looked briefly at the floor and then at the Marine General, whose former impenitence, began to wane very slightly into sheepishness.

'Well now,' McIver said at length, 'I don't know about mushrooms but I do know a little about responsibility and duty.' Here he looked directly at the Marine General, who stood his ground, but nevertheless, replied in more measured tones.

'Look George, I'm not trying to be disrespectful, or even to score points. I'm just trying to get to the *whole* truth here. We need that if we are going to make any really *responsible* recommendations.' He sat down.

'OK,' McIver conceded, holding up his hands in a conciliatory gesture. And after a despairing sidelong glance at Stone, he said, 'I'll lay it on the line for you.'

* * *

Dominating a part of the North Yorkshire Moors skyline, there are a row of very large, white golf ball shapes. These are the covers for the radar heads of the old BMEWS, or Ballistic Missile Early Warning System. Although, ostensibly redundant by October 1998, the Nuclear Attack Warning Centre, Fylingdales, as it was then known, was nevertheless, re-equipped and active on 26th October, a date more important than any in Britain's long history.

* * *

As Julia prepared herself to go out that evening, she suddenly felt an involuntary tinge of guilt. She stopped gazing at herself in the mirror and put down the blusher. It was as if Robin was staring back at her from the mirror with a hurt and disapproving look.

'Damn you, Robin,' she whispered to herself, 'you don't own me!' She got up to remove herself from this imaginary censure and stood looking out of the window. 'In fact,' she went on, 'I hardly know you.'

A chaffinch swooped and perched on the window sill, head on one side, regarding her inquisitively. She froze, then slowly reached for the crust from her impromptu supper, but the bird flew off, calling, it seemed to her, in an accusatory tone.

Outside, she shivered in the chill October air, before stepping into her car and driving off to meet Marcus Payne.

*   *   *

Marcus had chosen well. Not only was the restaurant comfortable and discreet, the menu was comprehensive and fairly priced. Not that he minded that at all. At least, not on this occasion. The subdued stereo system was playing his favourite Brian Ferry tape as Julia walked in, turning a number of heads, including the women's – always a sure sign of a very attractive woman. He got up and smiled what he hoped was a tantalising smile.

Julia's response was dazzling. Her eyes lit up, sensuous full lips parted and perfect white teeth flashed in a unison of recognition – and all for him. For a split second he felt like a king.

10

Li Chan Hope-Watson, the Admiral's Chinese wife, was arranging flowers on the big Steinway when her husband came down for breakfast. It was nine o'clock and the sun was struggling through the usual Singapore warm vapid mist.

'Darling, you're late!' she said brightly, turning.

Their relationship had long passed the stage where they slept together.

'Yes, I had a bit of a heavy night.'

'Oh, yes. That man, who was he?' his wife enquired, deftly clipping the wet stems.

'Nobody you need concern yourself with,' replied Hope-Watson, sitting at the immaculately white silk clothed table and picking up a neatly folded *Straits Times.*

Li Chan, knew better after twenty years of marriage, not to enquire further, but moved into a well practised routine and brought a silver coffee pot to her husband from the heavy oak sideboard and served the dark brown fragrant liquid without another word.

*   *   *

The RAF Group Captain sat down and looked gravely across Taylour's desk, so intense was his gaze that Taylour began to feel uncomfortable – almost as if he was under suspicion and about to be interrogated, which was absurd. He told himself his vulnerability arose from too many late nights and overwork.

Taylour had asked him about possible survival rates

71

following the disaster. The Group Captain, who was an expert on Aviation Medicine, answered directly and controversially, 'What I can't accept sir, is that there has been little or no communication at all from Britain since the calamity.'

'I have been wondering about that myself. It's strange how one accepts it, but there has been so much else to deal with.' He was about to mention the telephone conversation he had only the night before with the Ambassador to Ireland, but decided to wait and see what the Group Captain knew.

The Group Captain, nodded and went on. 'You see sir, there must have been a large number of people who were on board a number of aircraft at the time, or perhaps in submarines, or other places which have their own quite separate environments.'

'Yes, I see,' replied Taylour non-committally.

I mean, sir, can a communications blackout be that total?'

'You tell me, Group Captain, you're the expert.'

'Well, it's not really my field, sir. Communications, I mean.'

'No, no, of course, I was forgetting,' acknowledged Taylour. 'Do we have a communications expert in your team?'

'Not as such, sir. But I do know of someone.'

'Oh, who is he?'

'It's not a "he" sir, its a "she".'

'I see. An American, I imagine?'

'Why, no sir, she's English. Her name's McMahon. Julia McMahon.'

*   *   *

Lammas had just emerged, emotionally exhausted from yet another emergency session of the Security Council. They had gone over much of the old ground again, but they had made some progress.

The UTFOR landings had started, each group being led by

a small band of specialist British Officers from Ambassador Taylour's BOSC group.

Early reports had ranged from confusing to very disturbing: determining the extent of the damage; the number who were dead or alive; the state of the infrastructure; whether or not it was safe to intervene. And above all, any evidence as to just who – or what – was responsible.

The terms of the latest UN resolution stated that if, and when, it was found that the original population had fallen under 50 per cent of that before the Event, a Commission should be set up under Rear Admiral Sir Lloyd Hope-Watson RN (Retd), to investigate and co-ordinate the re-population of Britain which would then be called 'New Britain'. This Commission would report to The British Co-ordinating Committee chaired by Sir Iain Taylour (the de facto British Government in exile). The election of a new Parliament would be co-ordinated by Sir Percival Praed; who, if it was found that the Royal Family had perished, would be appointed provisional President of New Britain under a new constitution, yet to be determined.

This new constitutional arrangement was dependent upon agreement with the EEC in Brussels and whether or not any members of the British Government or Parliament, had survived. For, if they had, they would need to be consulted and their views fully taken into account. Consultation with members of the British Commonwealth of Nations and various expatriate committees through Hope-Watson would then follow.

Lammas was increasingly concerned about developments, in two areas.

Firstly, there was increasing evidence that casualties were heavy, especially in the urban areas, where there were many bodies, particularly in precincts with predominantly ethnic populations and other districts previously known for drug and crime problems.

In the more 'desirable' districts, there were far fewer bodies and many of these were later found to be alive but comatose!

In spite of immediate advance searches of the centres of former government, and the Royal Palaces, little evidence of human life was ever found, only confirmation of 'official' fears, which had predicted a heavy death toll. As might be expected, many Establishment figures of high rank were among the casualties, but none recovered.

Surprisingly however, animals and wildlife seemed relatively unaffected. For example, Regent's Park Zoo carried its full complement of inmates, most of whom were alive, when found, but very hungry!

Even the pigeons in Trafalgar Square had survived! But as the ornithologist in the UN contingent had reported, they were among the hardiest of the feathered species.

There was still much to learn and discover.

But as the reports came in, they were assimilated and the appropriate action taken. A firmer physical picture concerning the state of *New Britain* began to emerge.

One officer later described the empty, echoing streets and the procession of trucks removing the dead, with the pigeons and other birds, wheeling normally overhead, as most poignant and unreal.

'It was not a dream. It was not a nightmare. It was worse than both of those. It was a microcosm of the end of the civilised world.'

Lammas' second fundamental concern was the gathering political storm. And as it was being conducted on an international scale, he felt it was incumbent upon him to hold things together and try to ensure that matters proceeded on an ethical and balanced course.

The latest UN Security Council assessment had been that: *"Britain had been destroyed by an as yet UNKNOWN agency. The motivation was as yet, unknown. However, there was also a possibility that it had been destroyed by more than a covert force – or even by an unfortunate chain of events!"*

The United States NATIONAL SECURITY COUNCIL's assessment was that: *"Britain had been substantially destroyed by a KNOWN or UNKNOWN ENEMY by means yet to be confirmed, and that an expansionist China may be behind it*

74

(presently vehemently denied by Beijing) following the recent shelling of Taiwan, the delayed Hong Kong Accession, and demands for the handover by Portugal of Macao, to whom Britain recently provided diplomatic and token military support."

The last sentence echoed the United Nations:

"However, there is also a possibility that it has been destroyed by more than a covert force – or even by an unfortunate chain of events!"

Lammas stared at this last pronouncement glumly. Was this the sum total of his influence with the US Military?

*   *   *

In an office in the Avenue Louise, Brussels, an EEC Commissioner read the latest UN communiqué and frowned as he donned his dark blue Crombie, an acquisition from his last visit to London, before making for the elevator to go down to his Mercedes, which would take him to Brussels Zaventem Airport, for the Sabena flight to New York.

In his car, he considered his brief: to persuade Ambassador Taylour to accede to a European Parliament motion requiring that Britain – or *New Britain* – as the Americans would insist on calling it – should re-confirm its commitment to the Treaty of Rome and re-endorse the credentials of the British European Parliament Members at Strasbourg, failing which, he was authorized to threaten economic sanctions.

He paused in his deliberations to reflect. Gazing mournfully out onto the damp motorway that led to the Airport, past the impressive Headquarters of NATO, he could not help feeling that the influences NATO represented were in ascendency, whereas his, the EEC, offered only a socio-economic dogma – perhaps obsolescence – for not only had the rules changed, but the very game itself.

For his part, he meant to impress upon Taylour – and the Americans (by whom Taylour seemed unduly influenced) that although gathering military intelligence concerning the cause of the disaster was important; equally, sounding out European and world opinion; getting international consensus, about the way forward, should *also* be promoted. It was crucial to use the momentous event as a turning point in international relations, otherwise all those people had perished for nothing!

However, as the modernistic ramparts of Zaventem airport loomed, the EEC Commissioner could not help feeling that events (and the UN!) had overtaken him and more particularly, the organization which he represented.

*   *   *

McIver too was travelling by car at that very same time except that whereas the time in Brussels was 16.30, in Washington it was 10.30 in the morning.

With the fall well in progress, russet leaves fell and blew damply into the path of his anonymous green service Chevrolet. He was uneasy. He had been wrong footed by the Marine General's question and it had exposed gaps in his own knowledge.

He was even more uneasy following a meeting with Defense Secretary, Scottdale.

What had particularly disturbed him was when he reported the first findings of the *Broken Arrow* Troops heading the UTFOR Landings. In fact, the conversation still reverberated in his brain:

'It seems Mr Secretary, that some of the marines had an unusual find.'

'Oh, what was that, General?'

'Contaminated diesel fuel, sir.'

'Nothing unusual about that surely. It's bound to be contaminated, isn't it?'

'No sir, you don't understand. We have set up analysis labs on most of the bigger ships. You remember there was one on the Lexington. That's why Admiral Kearns wanted the dog shot, to see if...'

'Yes, yes,' interrupted Scottdale tetchily, 'do get on,

General. I have a meeting with the President in less than an hour.'

'Well, sir,' continued McIver, after holding his breath, 'that diesel was specially laced.'

'What do you mean?' Scottdale fixed him with piercing blue eyes.

'I mean, sir,' McIver went on firmly, squaring up to his political master, 'that two of my guys were hospitalized when the stuff was heated in a test tube.'

'You mean it blew up?' Scottdale replied in a manner mixing caution with derision.

'No sir, it was the vapour it gave off.'

Scottdale did not reply.

'You realize what this means?'

McIver paused for a response but got none.

'It means, that wherever that fuel was used, people were going to become very ill or die!'

'Any medical reports?' Scottdale said at length, stonily.

'I was coming to that, Mr Secretary. A large number of the fatalities in rural areas died from a syndrome, which the medicos are beginning to relate to this oil.'

'How can they do that?' snapped Scottdale, leaning back in his chair and glowering at McIver over his rimless spectacles.

'Because, they now have my boys' condition to compare it with,' replied McIver simply.

'Oh, and just how do they compare the dead with the living – you said your guys were only ill. The Britishers were all dead, weren't they?'

'Not all sir, not all by any means.'

He remembered Scottdale's astonishing reaction to this news: shock, then anger followed by a palpable confusion. McIver had never seen anything like it. Was he ill?

Scottdale had left the room, suddenly.

McIver remembered that on his return, Scottdale had spoken with uncharacteristic softness, but with perceptible menace.

'I have called the President and you are to present

yourself at the White House Library or Map Room. The Marine Guard will tell you which – at 1500 this afternoon.'

He had then turned, as if to leave, paused and added, almost as an afterthought, the real germ of his message.

'Bring with you the latest videos and photographs emanating from the latest UTFOR reports, and any other information about the landings and, in particular, the survivors. The purpose of the meeting will be to devise an 'appropriate' press release.'

To McIver, this was something of a watershed. Hitherto, the press had not only been kept from reporting and filming the scene during the UTFOR landings. There was a virtual press blackout. The world's media were, quite naturally, baying for information and (exasperated by the Military) were canvassing the UN and even some unauthorised sources.

Would a mere press release satisfy them? McIver doubted it.

11

*"Western Culture doesn't
have a secret worth keeping."*

(Joe Orton, British Playwright
1933–1967)

When Jack Prince got home, he was alerted by the smell of burning from the steam – filled kitchen. Annoyance turned to alarm when saw the prostrate body of his wife on the red quarry tiled floor.

The effect of several pints of strong bitter beer at first prevented him from deducing the cause of his wife's condition, until he saw the now empty jam jar on the floor near the Aga cooking range. An iron framed kitchen window, unsecured, banged open and shut in the light breeze; there was an imperceptible odour in the air in spite of the potatoes burning in the pans which had long since boiled dry.

He bent over his wife cradling her and calling her name feverishly, his mind filling with panic. At length, he carried her to the couch in the shabby living room and he tried everything he knew in a frantic attempt to revive her. It was to no avail, and soon a great sorrow vied with his panic. What was he to do? He looked up desperately. He must call an ambulance; then realisation of the likely cause of his wife's death hit him.

An ambulance was out of the question. He must call Marcus Payne.

*   *   *

Payne was just getting into the Buick when the car phone rang.

He was not pleased to receive the call.

'I thought I told you never to...'

At the other end Prince was sobbing.

Payne suppressed his anger and for the first time in his thirty nine years, he knew real fear. His mind raced as he strove to deal with the situation and he cursed himself for relying, even briefly, on Jack Prince. With an iron effort of will, he recovered his composure and his dispassionate mind began to formulate a way out of the unwelcome crisis.

'Pull yourself together, Jack...' For the first time he used Prince's first name, realising that the situation demanded some semblance of sympathy – a rare, and seldom to be repeated, lapse where he was concerned, but if needs must...

'Look, old chap, are you sure she's..?'

He recoiled from the receiver as Prince's grief poured out. Prince was clearly completely unhinged by the situation in which he now found himself.

Payne then spoke clearly and directly into the microphone, and as he spoke, in a detached way he listened; it was like a stranger speaking – and he merely an eavesdropper.

* * *

'Julia? It's Jacqui.'

'I know, Jacqui. I recognise your voice!'

Jacqui was too excited to acknowledge the mild sarcasm, 'I've just seen something you'll be interested in.'

'Oh yes,' replied Julia, balancing the telephone receiver on her hunched shoulder and continuing to paint her nails.

'Yes – it was Marcus's car...'

'Well, aren't you the lucky one?' remarked Julia archly.

'I'm serious, Jules.'

'Well go on then – and don't call me Jules. It's so, so...'

'Working class?' prompted Jacqui, helpfully.

'Well, tasteless anyway,' Julia acknowledged mildly, not wishing to expose any obvious prejudice. 'Which car?'

'What? It's not a very good line,' crackled Jacqui.

'I said which car? He's got two, hasn't he?' Julia raised her voice slightly and changed ears.

'Has he? Oh.'

'Oh, *do* get on with it, Jacqui, I'm busy. I mean is it so

very unusual that you should see Marcus's car, anyway..?'

'It's *where* I saw it, that's unusual...'

'Just a minute,' rasped Julia, bracing herself for something unpleasant. Before you go on, *which*, car was it, that you saw?'

'That big American thing...'

'Oh,' responded Julia, a little crest–fallen, realising that there weren't many Buicks in the Cotswolds. 'O.K.,*where did* you see it?'

'Outside Jack Princes's House.'

'Good God! What could he possibly want with that awful little man?'

'That's what I thought,' agreed Jacqui.

'Really, Jacqui, you are a little trouble–maker, 'Julia cried, blaming the messenger, 'there's probably some perfectly rational explanation.'

'Oh yes, what exactly?'

'Well – I don't know, 'Julia floundered for a reason. 'Perhaps he wanted Prince to do a job for him?' she ended brightly.

'Really? I wonder what job that might be?'

'Why, what ever do you mean?'

'You do *know*, what Jack Prince is?'

'I don't know, some sort of tradesman, I imagine.'

'He's a drug dealer,' replied Jacqui flatly.

Julia's voice changed and aquired a hard edge, 'You'd better come round.' she said, and rang off.

*   *   *

"As to experiences; happiness:
nothing is ever quite perfect,
if it is perfect,
it doesn't last."

(Anon)

Goodchild had tried several times to call Julia but all he could get was her answerphone:

'Julia McMahon is sorry to miss your call. Please try again soon, or leave a message after the tone.'

He put the telephone down for the fifth time that day, a Sunday, and frowned. He was due to fly to Brussels that evening and had hoped to arrange a meeting with Julia for when he returned on Monday evening. He knew it would be very difficult to reach her at work. GCHQ, Cheltenham, did not encourage private calls – not even to their Senior Communications Officers.

A rigourously self-disciplined man, he wondered how it was that he should allow himself to become obsessed with another human being. It was a new experience for him; indeed, there had been times in his career and at school, when he had been alluded to as a homosexual. But he could never bring himself to think, let alone utter, the inapposite alternative word 'gay'. In any case, there was no question of it being true. He knew this, which, to his mind, was all that mattered. The question was, did Julia?

Concentrate on work; that was the answer. Friends were difficult. He seemed never to be around when they were, and vice versa.

On Monday evening Goodchild returned from Brussels and drove from Birmingham International Airport to his modest cottage in the North Cotswolds.

On entering the cramped hallway, which smelled very slightly of mildew, his heart leapt optimistically; the answerphone light was flashing. 'You fool,' he told himself, 'It could be anyone. Probably someone from work.' He pressed the button and Julia's mellifluous tones reverberated around the confining stonewalls.

'Hello Robin, sorry to have missed you. Please call me.'

He stood and listened for some time to the buzzing that followed the message, before walking into the small lounge and pouring himself a scotch. Then he rang Julia.

On the way to Julia's cottage, he stopped in a country lane. He got out of the car and walked slowly to an old five bar wooden farm gate, one of the few that had not been replaced by tubular metal. First he breathed in the fresh air and smelt the earthy smell of early autumn. The sun still shone and a blackbird went through its endless repertoire of beautiful phrases. The view was one of successive undulating vistas, green, brown, blue and distant misty purple and mauve. The breeze sighed in the oaks, ash and birch; their occasionally falling leaves brushed his face. A rabbit rose and bolted across the field before him. He sighed deeply then returned to his car, temporarily refreshed.

12

*"Do not make friends with a hot–tempered man,
do not associate with one easily angered,
or you may learn his ways
and get yourself enslaved."*

(Proverbs 24:25)

Hope-Watson was holding court in his favourite place. Home ground. He had dressed for dinner, as was his custom at weekends. His dutiful wife had left him to entertain his only guest, while she busied herself in the kitchen, or supervised the two servants. Whatever it was, her husband was not thinking of her at this time and that was not at all unusual. He regarded the tall slim young man, lolling in the brocade armchair, quizzically, then politely answered his latest question.

'No, not everyone will be ...er, affected...'

'You mean murdered.'

'Really, Payne, such emotive language will...'

'You mean,' said Marcus Payne leaning forward,'that there will be a privileged list...'

'A list certainly,' agreed Hope-Watson affably, pacing back and forth, puffing on a large Havana, 'and they will get instructions on how to act in good time.'

'What kind of instructions?'

'Well now, do you remember the old "Protect and survive" message, broadcast on TV in the old, cold war days?'

Payne stared at him, trying to absorb the enormity of what he was hearing.

Hope-Watson removed a pale pink card from within his dinner jacket – rather like a wedding invitation, thought Payne, but it had no curly edge, normally associated with that most innocuous of documents.

Hope-Watson read from the card:

'From the specified date, do not drink mains tap water. Use bottled water only, for tea, coffee and for cooking.

Baths and showers should not be taken.

For selected areas (to be notified on the specified date but broadly speaking, cities and conurbations) leave the area for the country. When there, observe the <u>water rules</u> stated above and stay clear of <u>roads, service stations and vehicles of all kinds</u>, including farm tractors). Those who can, should consider travel abroad, for plausible or imperative reasons, which could be questioned at a later date.'

'Well, precious few concessions there, except perhaps for the old boy network.' snapped Payne. 'Who's on this privileged list?'

'Well now, I thought you already knew that,' countered Hope-Watson.

There was an icy pause between the two men, as each tried to assess what the other knew. Never was the maxim "Life consists of making decisions from insufficient data", more fitting.

'This ad hoc delivery system of yours – why, it's archaic and bizarre!" sneered Payne.

'Oh?'

'Yes, and there's something else ...,' Payne blurted out. Then, recovering some of his old composure, 'that even *you* don't know.'

The final part of his statement was enunciated deliberately and crisply, with an edge of menace, from which, by now, Hope-Watson was largely immune.

'Really?'

'Yes, something that will make this, this, prank of yours...'

'Prank!' Hope-Watson was suddenly incandescent. 'Do you realise what went into this? The planning, the resources, the organisation, the people...'

Just as suddenly, Hope-Watson stopped himself, shrugged, and slowly drew on his cigar, watching the aromatic smoke drift upward to the ornate ceiling.

'But then what would you know of such things? You're a loner aren't you, Payne?'

'I'm not interested in your opinion of me,' snapped Payne, 'what concerns me is your motives...' Here there was a just perceptible tremor in his voice, and his tone became husky. He cleared his throat.

'Do you really think you can wipe out a nation with...with tainted water and, and doped fuel...?' He stopped, a patina of perspiration breaking out on his pale forehead, the tiny beads of moisture glinting in the light from the crystal chandelier.

'But there's something else, isn't there? Come on, out with it!'

'Well, you seem to have all the answers,' Hope-Watson remarked nonchalantly, but fixing him with a fierce stare.

'We both know...' Payne paused. He was feeling progressively unwell.

'Yes, Marcus?' Hope-Watson enquired, rising from his chair. He walked slowly toward the Steinway and sat on the stool. 'What is it that we both know?'

He opened the keyboard lid.

Payne stood up abruptly, and in doing so, knocked over his glass, its contents soaking slowly into the deep carpet.

'Tch, tch,' chided Hope–Watson, 'getting jumpy aren't we?'

'You bastard!' croaked Payne, swaying.

'Oh dear, are you ill?' Hope-Watson responded with mock concern. He did not look round as Payne crashed to the floor, but placed his large hands on the ivory keyboard and struck out the first chords of Parry's 'Jerusalem', which very deliberately drowned out Payne's last choking gasps.

*   *   *

McIver was beginning to feel the strain of the past weeks. He realised that he had been working almost non-stop and had slept little, or at most, poorly. His body was beginning to call time. Even his wife, who was neither sympathetic nor caring by nature, had said he should rest. Yet he knew that if he eased up events would quickly overtake him.

He desperately needed to delegate, but when he ran through a shortlist in his mind, the characters he pictured there were either not up to it, (he judged) or not wholly trustworthy.

There was, however, one person he must see before he could think of resting.

*   *   *

Barry Hartog, graduate of Harvard and Massachussetts Institute of Technology, was in shock when he heard the news, on emerging from a "mind cleansing" break in a mountain monastery above San Francisco. The main discipline of the Order was complete ex–communication from the outside world, so he was only belatedly aware of the Event which had recently rocked the civilised world.

When he returned to his Los Angeles apartment, the first message he played on his answerphone had been from McIver. He was acquainted with the General through Phil McIver, the General's son. But over time it transpired that his relationship with the General had eclipsed that with the General's own son. This, as can be imagined, had led to familial problems.

The telephone message had been brief:

'Hog, (Harthog's college nickname), it's George, please get yourself to Washington as soon as you emerge. I need your help on this British thing.'

*   *   *

In his office at the Pentagon, McIver had written the following planning entry in his big desk diary, for November 30th 1998, in preparation for a significant, and perhaps, crucial meeting:

'Two colleagues and I are headed for California for a meeting with the President.

Subject: Ostensibly, "Budget Planning/Defense" The

Meeting was unofficially *billed as a "show-down" between me* & *the other side, (Sec State for Defense) but has good support from the State Department, CIA, National Security Council* & *the Joint Chiefs of Staff.*

Graphics & *Display have become a fetish with me. Multicoloured bar charts, bold lines going up, down* & *sideways, arrow headed pointers, boxed in highlights – anything to simplify the complex issues involved. Jim Stephenson, the Secretary of the Interior, impressed on me the importance of being explicit:*

'The only way you can solve the big, complicated issues,' he joked, 'is to elevate them to the highest possible level of incompetence.'

I note that the new Deputy Director of the CIA is an Admiral. This made me think of Ted Kearns, and how much I miss the old buzzard! Yet, he could still be the key to this whole thing. Perhaps Hog might shed some light?'

*　　*　　*

Meanwhile, on the other side of Washington DC, in the offices of the Central Intelligence Agency, the Deputy Director's desk diary was locked in his personal, high security safe. It contained the following advanced entry for November 30th 1998:

<u>President & Chiefs of Staff Meeting</u>

Subject: Billed as "Budgetary"
but (inter alia) "Broken Arrow"

My Brief:

An ambiguous assignment. On the one hand, I am
expected to direct the real investigative work as to the causes of 'Broken
Arrow', while the military just flounder around. On the other, to 'keep secrets', the full import of which cannot be ascertained either by me, or (I
suspect) by those prevailing upon me, at this time.

My Contributions to the meeting:

Subject: BROKEN ARROW

Item (1) CLASSIFICATION: 'Restricted'
Main Destructive Sources & Methods
SARIN gas posioning. Localized Neutron Blast & Radiation.

Item (2) CLASSIFICATION: 'Restricted'
Theatre communications
(Presentation by General McIver)

Item (3) CLASSIFICATION: 'Most Secret'
Possible Involvement of RN TRIDENT D5
(The above to be divulged to sub–committee only)

Item (4) CLASSIFICATION: 'Secret'

The positioning/delivery methods,
of SARIN gas, Other Toxic agents & Neutron
Devices.
(To include contribution by General McIver)

Item (5) CLASSIFICATION: 'Most Secret'
The likely perpetrators
(The above to be divulged to sub–committee only)

Item (6) CLASSIFICATION: 'Restricted'
Target damage reports
(Presentation by General McIverincluding
British military sources).

13

The Event

Sunday had been a normal day in Aldershot, in Bristol, in Cambridge and Chepstow, in Derby, in Erith, Kent, in Frimley, in Guildford, in Halifax, in Ipswich, in Jarrow, in Kings Norton and Keighley, in London and Manchester, in Norfolk, in Oxford and Pangbourne, in Quedgeley and Quainton, in Ruislip and Rugeley, in Stanmore... But no, it had not been quite normal in Stanmore.

But it had been a normal day on the North Yorkshire moors, even at the bleak, rain swept ridge which anchored those, apparently bloated, now dirt streaked, once brilliant white against the darkening Eastern sky, golf ball shapes, gargantuan in size: Fylingdales BMEWS, Ballistic Missile Early Warning System. The hum of the cooling fans in the radar consoles and the air conditioning, combined into their special lullaby until RAF Corporal Ken James saw something on his radar screen.

But his sighting was fleeting and unconfirmed by any other operator, and therefore was not acted upon. So when he protested, he was called into his commanding officer's office.

'I definitely saw something sir, then it had gone.'

Squadron Leader Lionel Badham looked the NCO straight in the eye, then relaxed, leaning back into his chair until it creaked in protest from his 185 pounds, having satisfied himself that there was nothing on the screen presently, or indeed on any other screen in the room.

'Very well, corporal, I accept you saw something. But there is no trace of it now – probably a flock of birds – or anaprop•Certainly not significant enough to warrant an alert.'

'Better safe than sorry, sir.'

'Don't be impertinent!' snapped Badham. 'I don't need you to teach me the job.'

'I'm sorry sir, I didn't mean to be rude, but we could play back the computer log, that would show...'

'Corporal, you're doing it again!'

'Sorry, sir...I...'

Badham stood up, placing his hands on his desk, with arms straight, the two broad and one narrow blue ring of his badge of rank, displayed on each arm, firmly on view to intimidate his young subordinate. He lowered his tone and spoke slowly and deliberately for maximum effect. Much more effective than shouting, someone had told him at Staff College.

'I have already ordered a computer play back at the end of the shift. If we see anything unusual, you will be called. That's all, James.'

'Yes, sir.' The NCO saluted, none too smartly, turned on his heel and left the Squadron Leader's office.

Badham leaned back in his chair again, when the corporal had left and turned to his adjutant, who was present throughout the interview, sitting quietly in the corner of the room.

'What do you think, Harry, could he have seen something important?'

'Difficult to say, sir. I got to his screen pretty sharpish. I already checked that there was nothing on mine.'

'You saw nothing on his?'

Soames shook his head. 'Nothing.'

'Oh well, we'll soon know when we play back the log. Long playbacks can be very disruptive in mid-shift and we've got a deadline to meet on this exercise. After all, live sightings are not really our responsibility.'

*   *   *

• *a spurious radar reflection.*

Two F3 Tornado interceptors and one GR1A Tornado bomber, scrambled on information from a later Fylingdales alert, and climbed quickly from their Leeming and Conningsby bases to 15,000 feet, their twin RB199 engines in reheat, rending the early morning mist with noise and purple blue fire.

Squadron Leader Barnes, captain of the leading aircraft, a Tornado F3, had confidence in his aircraft, whereas others often criticised it for its lack of agility in a 'dog fight.' However, he knew it was never intended for such an outdated role, and that this approach had been vindicated in the Gulf War. Even in the Falklands, of which Barnes was a veteran, he neither experienced, nor knew of any close-in aerial combat.

Like many modern military aircraft, the Tornado was primarily a 'fire and forget' missile platform. The big built-in radar scanner might compromise agility, but it enabled strikes from a longer range than most, and the multitude of weapons carried, exceeded that of nearly all likely adversaries.

Barnes called the ground based Fighter Controller. 'Mission W3A-47A and B to Firtree, at angels one five zero. Vectors please?'

The reply was immediate.

'47A – B, this is Firtree. Climb to Angels Two Five and head Three Six Zero degrees. Report over Point Alpha.'

But both the alert, and Barnes's confidence were short lived, as five MIRV bomblets were released from their mother missile – re-entering the earth's atmosphere above them, at over 2,000 miles per hour – exploding over their pre-planned target areas. Seconds later, their small neutron detonations rendered all electronic communication void.

Across the country, both in and above urban areas, there followed a series of shattering, thunderlike, explosions from these ERWs - Enhanced Radiation Weapons, or *very small* hydrogen bombs, originally conceived for battlefield use, designed to kill in up to six days, by brief but deadly neutron radiation. The associated blast was localised, and affected only buildings in the immediate area of a detonation.

In rural areas, almost within the same timespan, all vital communications, military and civilian, together with key government installations, were destroyed, not only by the ERWs, but by manifold and covert means, from within and without.

Meanwhile, the Tornadoes' TV displays became instantly blank and all communication was lost. An air-bursting bomblet at three thousand feet over Ipswich and Martlesham, destroyed Squadron Leader Barnes' aircraft and sent the second – control surfaces damaged – into a high parabola, from which it did not recover. The third aircraft; the GR1A, flying at lower level – which was its role – escaped. Unable to establish any contact with a ground station, it ran its infra-red reconnaissance videos, then set course East, for any serviceable RAF base in Western Germany able to receive it.

All then was momentarily silent, apart from a distant rumbling, which marked the ending of one era and another's beginning.

* * *

At just one of a hundred local, national, BBC and commercial radio stations, in the middle of the opening announcement, the control console swelled to twice its size and shattered, sweeping the duty operator and presenter through two wooden screens and a glass paned panel, into the outer foyer.

There, their entrails hung bleakly, dripping from the dusty tree that graced the reception atrium.

* * *

At 5.07 am, just as the manageress arrived to open the Luton branch of McDonalds, all the windows of the shop front blew in, lacerating her back and skull. She died instantly. A bluish light flickered briefly before the building disintegrated.

*   *   *

To the North West, at a Liverpool TV studio, during the shift change between the early morning news and Breakfast TV, a shattering roar – a sound that was more *experienced* rather than heard – left the duty engineer, gasping for breath, before he was cruelly crushed by a heavy camera dolly, at once stripped of all electronics to the bare, base metal.

At the same moment, a startled female presenter, just arriving for the early morning broadcast, was deafened, eardrums burst, and stripped of her designer suit and underwear. She careered at fifty miles per hour, five feet above the disintegrating parquet floor, toward a startled porter. He died instantly as one of the presenter's stiletto heels pierced his windpipe.

In Liverpool's Toxteth district, an early morning milk float careered from its normal course into the path of an oncoming bus, which in turn, reared over the flimsy vehicle and crushed it, as if it were a matchbox. The milkman was already dead, but then so were most of the passengers on the bus. The bus driver was rescued, having been cut from his cab, but died later in hospital foaming lightly at the mouth. Two hours later, the rescue firemen were taken to hospital where they lay for some days, alone and unattended, unable to speak or move.

Shortly afterwards the hospital burnt down, as there were none of their colleagues left to fight the fire, or to rescue the by now, mercifully, unconscious injured.

*   *   *

In the sprawling car assembly plants of Longbridge, Luton, Derby, Swindon, Ellesmere Port and Cowley, Oxford, one minute all was brightly lit bustle and noise – light and life. The next, chaos and semi-darkness descended as all power was cut. Shouts were heard but briefly, and a great confusion reigned while all communication ceased.

Fires started and were uncontrolled, for the emergency services did not respond. They had their own problems, the total loss of radio, telephonic and computer communication, which had instantaneously ceased to exist.

Some units already on call, undeterred, drove blind into their local scenes of confusion and devastation – and then, in turn, suffered their own individual fates. Many died heroically, some painfully, others pathetically.

* * *

At the London School of Economics, off Houghton Street, in the Aldwych, Xavier Troon, cleaner, heard a rumble, then saw dust rise ominously from the Senior Common Room floor. Suddenly, scalding whiteness filled the air as the boilers below erupted, and his poached body was flung upward, before becoming lodged, steaming and screaming, in the collapsing roof beams above – a shocking, but surprisingly isolated incident, in West Central London, on that fateful morning.

Dr Jean Sallis, the School secretary, arriving early at the scene of devastation, had looked about – aghast! Then glancing upward, saw the bloated, cooked, white, body of the cleaner. She retched, then vomited, sobbing into the smoking void, below.

For the Court of Governors of the School, recruiting a new Director for that establishment was to become a secondary priority, for it was not just a janitor that was lost, but the whole central building. Yet mercifully, loss of life was restricted to the one fatality, due to the hour.

* * *

In London's Brixton, Southall and New Cross districts, the foetid streets, damp and sticky from a previous nights', eating, drinking, drug taking; fighting, fornicating and defecating, trembled then vibrated as, above, an ear splitting rending sent the sodium vapour street lamps quivering, then bursting, their posts snapping to become monstrous, angry lances – propelled at violent speed. Then at various crazy angles, they shatteringly, penetrated shop fronts, and fatally impeded the now faltering, early morning traffic.

*   *   *

To the North, in Yorkshire's Bradford, the remaining blackened Victorian, mill chimneys were felled like leafless trees, and whole rows of terraced houses crumbled along with many businesses and corner shops.

*   *   *

To the West, in Bristol's St Pauls and Montpelier, the buildings on one side of the A38 road which leads to the City Centre, exploded, blocking the carriageway with masonry and the occasional blackened body.

A dense dust cloud rose above the clanging alarms, screaming babies and barking dogs. Then a thin white mist mingled with the dust and only mechanical sound remained. All life extinguished, except... high above on a toppling ochre, builder's crane, a pigeon cooed triumphantly, then croaked with annoyance as the structure gave way beneath its gnarled claws and crumpled, crashing downward, adding to the chaos below..

*   *   *

And so, nationwide... that misty, late October, English day...

As one, all chattering radio and garish television transmission ceased as if it had never been. The speakers died and the screens darkened.

The lights went out as the dawn came, and not just through any programmed, time switch.

*　　*　　*

While to the North, on the Maryport Estate, on the periphery of a previously proud, north eastern town...

Martha Brennan saw to her amazement, just as her radio went off and her early morning kettle stopped boiling, and the lights went out, ... the great pylons that carried the floodlights that had illuminated the Saturday Football festivals, sway and topple, hesitate, then crash to earth – sending up a cloud of dust and surprised starlings.

She began to feel ill, and went outside to catch her breath. By her back door step there were two dogs, in spasms, foaming at the mouth. Martha hobbled back inside and picked up the vintage black telephone, for the first time that month.

Sobbing, and trembling, she rang the first of several numbers, but there were no replies. She dialled 999 for the very first time in her life – but once again, no one answered.

Then she stumbled and fell, unable to move or speak, her stiffening muscles aching as she gasped for breath, her despairing soul calling soundlessly for help, her very being rent with unanswered questions. Had she not kept her faith? Had she not raised a family unselfishly? Had she not been honest and hard working? Was this then to be her reward? To die alone and uncomforted?

The great unfairness of it all overwhelmed even her physical plight, and then that good soul challenged her maker, in unspoken, questioning prayer.

She received no response, save to die there quietly in her humble home, surrounded by the mementos of an austere life – her long troubles at an end, at last. With one consolation, the ethos of a mutant age and culture that had spat on her principles and revoked her memories, was slowly dying outside.

14

"Kill all your darlings!"
(Tolstoy).

British Embassy, (Consulate)
28 Rue Joseph II
Brussels

USA (Consulate)
25 Boulevard du Regent
Brussels

Before the Event

In early September, 1998, both the above missions had received the same letter from an anonymous source. At the time neither recipient took its contents seriously.

A British first secretary had later paraphrased its contents in a telephone conversation to the Ambassador, who was shaving when he received the call. It was an electric shaver and was consequently rather noisy, especially since it was, *per force*, so close to the receiver.

Sir Brian Carswell, as British Ambassador to the European Communities, was preparing for a meeting at the Council of Ministers – and was behind in his preparations; consequently he was even less receptive when he learned the main content of the letter. He quickly decided that whoever wrote it was clearly deranged. In any case, what was one to do with such a letter, even in the unlikely event of its being a credible threat?

That evening, something brought it to mind when he was in conversation with the US Consul at a Brussels diplomatic function, ostensibly in the interests of furthering trade.

'Do you mean to say that you got one too,' Carswell expostulated.

'I did, sir, yes.' The American Consul was a serious man, who seldom smiled. Unusual for an American, Carswell thought.

'Well, what did you make of it?'

'I sent it to Washington.'

'You did what?'

'I thought the CIA ought to look at it.'

'Did you now?' mused Carswell, rubbing his chin. This chap is going to make himself a laughing stock, he thought. We shan't be seeing much more of him.

*   *   *

September 1998

British Embassy, Washington

Before the Event

When Sir Ian Taylour took the call from Carswell he was a relatively happy man. He had the posting he had always dreamed of. He liked America and the Americans – or at least most of them. True, his wife spent a lot of time in London, but they did get together once or twice a month, which at their age (mid fifties) was not so uncomfortable, because their relationship had always experienced periods of separation.

He did not care for Carswell; he was a little too European for his taste, which was probably why (Taylour reflected) he held his present appointment.

'Yes Brian? How nice to hear from you,' lied Taylour convincingly – an unfortunate feature of his trade.

'Iain, long time no see. Look here...' Carswell began imperiously, 'Do you have any contacts in the CIA?'

'Well no. At least, not directly. Why?'

There was a short silence, during which Taylour could just hear Carswell having a muffled conversation aside with someone at his end.

'Sorry about that,' Carswell continued, 'Look, it's a bit difficult on the blower. I'll send you something in the Diplomatic Bag. Please look out for it. I'm sure you don't get that much from Brussels – lucky beggar. My regards to your wife,' Then the line went dead.

'Extraordinary!' exclaimed Taylour and he slammed down the receiver.

At that time (Late September 1998) Taylour's workload was not too great. He had taken Carswell's call in the Embassy library, where he had found time to scan through a book his wife had sent him from London.

The book was the result of an academic study on modern British social behaviour by an Oxbridge Social Affairs unit. It determined a current and increasing trend of loutish behaviour, including slovenly or aggressive dress, swearing, cheating and an increasing use of brute force. The author, a former Principal of an Oxford College, commented in a critique of feminism, that,

> *'Political correctness has proved no substitute for bad manners...' and,*

> *'When courtesy disappears men inevitably prevail for the simple biological reason that they are stronger. Women, without some code of deference or respect, become increasingly, victims.'*

As he flicked through the pages, Taylour read further and could not help smiling, if a little sadly.

> *'Being a lady did not demean women, as feminists claim, but provided them with necessary protection.'*

He just had time to read a final passage and ponder its moment before taking yet another call.

> *'The idea of being a gentleman does not repress men's individuality. Politeness isn't a restraint...Manners are a language, rich, flexible and infinitely subtle. Gentlemen were in their element in society.'*

After taking the call, he slammed the book shut, sighed, and returned to his office.

Before the Event

Hope-Watson put down the book he had been reading, lit a cigar and strolled to the window. There on the window seat was an old copy of the London *Times*. A large piece of cigar ash fell on its yellowing pages and as he brushed it away, an article caught his eye and he began to read.

'When Shoko Ashara, leader of the Aum Shinrikyo (Supreme Truth) cult, ordered his disciples to mass produce the deadly SARIN nerve gas and to test its power on theunfortunate commuters of Matsumoto, a town north of Tokyo in 1994, it was said at his trial that it was the start of a doomsday plot to eliminate countless numbers of innocent people.

His followers had apparently driven a truck to the town to release the gas, produced – according to the prosecution – at the commune, by the cult's misguided scientists.

However, the true objective of the attack was to test the power of the gas by killing judges, sleeping in the courthouse dormitory, for these judges were due to rule against the cult in a property matter.

It was said that Ashara had planned the experiment to assess the effect of SARIN as a weapon of mass murder in densely populated urban areas. With an initial death toll of seven dead and one hundred and forty four injured, the Matsomoto courthouse incident was a mere dress rehearsal for what followed in a Tokyo subway, where, eleven died and more than four thousand were injured.

The plant which produced the seventy tons of gas, originally invented by the Nazis, was enough to wipe out entire cities.

Hope-Watson finished reading the article, folded the paper absentmindedly, and said 'Mmm,' out loud to himself. Then he walked to his desk, picked up the telephone and dialled an international number.

15

America has twenty three major airports. Chicago O'Hare, the world's busiest, handles a million passengers a week – a superb airport – but truly massive.

Barry Hartog, having just arrived from Los Angeles, peered round for the United Airlines transfer desk to check in for his onward flight to Washington DC It was a little before 14.00 Eastern Standard Time.

As something of an airline buff, he knew that United Airlines served some ninety domestic destinations from there and American Airlines, seventy four. Most transatlantic flights being timed to arrive at 13.00, giving just enough time to transfer to a bank of domestic departures between 14.00 and 14.30, Hartog's onward flight to Washington was due to take off at 14.37.

At last, settled in his seat, on the taxiing Washington plane, Hartog relaxed for the first time that day. From here on, his journey should be relatively stress free, for he knew McIver would have a car waiting for him at Washington National airport, in spite of the fact that the Pentagon was just across the street from the airport complex.

*   *   *

McIver studied the young computer expert from under bushy eyebrows and tried to put himself in his place. The shock of Britain's sudden demise had clearly affected Hartog deeply and this was the first time he had the opportunity to discuss it, and get the reaction of someone in authority. It was obvious that Hartog could still not take it in and the liberal anglophile in him was looking for someone to blame.

'I can see you're still very upset by this,' said McIver gently.

'You're damn right! I go away for a few days and when I come back the whole of England has disappeared, for Chrissake! What were NATO doing? I'd like to know.' Hartog waved his hands despairingly. Apart from the deep affinity that many Americans felt for the country that gave them their language and much else beside, Hartog had many British friends and connections.

McIver sighed with genuine regret. His memories of England were as fond as Hartog's, or indeed any American's. He was stationed there in the sixties, and it was in the quiet Suffolk lanes that he had courted his wife. He leaned forward and tried to give the distraught young man some reasons.

'To say it was a surprise attack, is an understatement! There were none of the usual political warnings – at least...'

McIver was grateful that Hartog was so engrossed in his own grief that he did not pick up on the hesitation in his last sentence and so he continued, uninterrupted.

'There's increasing evidence that there was some kind of internal coup...'

'That's a load of bull!' was Hartog's explosive reply. 'Where are you getting this from.'

'The usual sources,' said McIver quietly.

'I just can't believe that we, NATO, the world, the UN, could let this happen.'

Hartog buried his head momentarily in his hands.

'Well, of course, it's history that many of the great military attacks were a complete surprise and unwarranted. Take Pearl Harbour...'

Hartog interrupted him, angrily, 'Pearl Harbour was a picnic compared with this!'

'Your reaction is typical, I've heard practically the same words from a hundred others over the past weeks.' It was true. Sometimes he got the impression that he was personally responsible for the outrage.

Hartog was suddenly contrite. 'Sure, look I'm sorry. I just can't...'

'Don't be, you've got to get it out of your system.'

'I have, for now...Listen George...'

'Yes, Hog...?'

'Do *you* know how it happened?'

'No, that's why I called you.'

'Well, I don't see how I can help you.'

'Listen, Hog..., I'm sticking my neck out on this. I need your expertise, but I can't tell you all the details. Security is really tight on this...'

'But you must have plenty of computer guys at the Pentagon...'

'Not as good as you, and I'm not just saying that.'

'Is that the only reason?' Hartog was tired, but his intuition was working.

'Look, you're tired,' McIver countered, 'we'll discuss it all in detail tomorrow.'

*   *   *

Taylour was not looking forward to his meeting with the EEC Commissioner. It was not that he was against the EEC *per se*. It was just that he had enough on his plate already. Moreover, he had the distinct feeling that this visitation was more likely to add to his troubles than to detract from them. Of course, it was entirely possible that the Commissioner was authorised to offer much needed funds for the reconstruction of the country, but Taylour felt sure that, in that case, there would be a *quid pro quo*. Also, he felt a strange feeling of vulnerability in anticipating the meeting. Yet, he could not quite determine why. The nearest he could get to it was the premonition that the Commissioner knew something that he did not – something he should know but not be informed of by an outsider. But then, Taylour was a sensitive man, perhaps too sensitive for the position in which he now found himself.

*　　*　　*

Julia McMahon heard the squeal of Jacqui's Strakes' arrival only too clearly, and as might be expected, temperaments were frayed. Julia had been shocked at the news of her latest beau's choice of associates, then rationalising, told herself that there was probably a simple explanation. Anyway, how did Jacqui know that Prince was a drug dealer? It sounded quite preposterous and she was about to tell her so, when something rather unexpected happened. Coincident with Jacqui's noisy arrival, Julia found she had other visitors – the local police.

Later, when Julia tried to normalise the situation, by making a pot of Earl Grey tea for her disparate, and somewhat unwelcome visitors, to her horror, she found herself in tears. When Jacqui came into the kitchen to find out the cause for the delay, she was rewarded by her haughty friend throwing her arms around her and asking her advice.

'What am I going to do, Jacqui?' Julia blubbed uncharacteristically, 'I'm so – so...'

'Gullible?' suggested Jacqui, somewhat tactlessly.

The truthful thrust of the remark was enough to stop the flow of Julia's tears almost instantly and put her on her accustomed mettle.

'Tact was never your metier, was it Jacqueline?' snapped Julia, pulling away and drying her eyes on a tea towel.

'My what?' asked Jacqui innocently.

'Oh, never mind. But you're right, of course. I have been a silly mooning cow.'

'Golly!' remarked Jacqui, unaccustomed to such self deference in her friend.

'Look,' said Julia, fully recovered, 'take this,' thrusting the tea tray at her companion, 'and stall them for a bit. I'm going to make a phone call...'

'Who to, your lawyer?'

'No, silly. I'm going to telephone Robin. He'll know what to do.'

'Robin Goodchild?'

'Who else?'

'Well, I must say, you're a cool one...'

'What do you mean'

'Well Jules, I've got to tell you this...'

'Tell me what?'

'You're like a child at a fireworks party.'

'Why, what ever do you mean?'

'When one banger has exploded in your face, you reach back into the box for a damp squib.'

'Oh, get out and entertain the fuzz. Tell them I've gone to the loo...'

16

Part Two

*"I am become death,
the destroyer of worlds."*

from the sacred Hindu text, Bhagavad Gita
(Song of God)

California, USA
November 30th 1998

After the Event

McIver had emerged from the President's meeting perplexed. He had a strong impression that he had been outmanoeuvred politically. And although one might argue that, as a senior soldier, politics were none of his business, he knew this was a naive view. Any officer reaching his rank was obliged to embrace the political realities, which ultimately directed his every professional action. Moreover, it was not unknown for previous incumbents of his job to become President!

But, acknowledging that he was out of his depth politically, was one thing; being excluded from sensitive information and vital decision making, was another.

The new CIA Deputy Director's contribution to the meeting had been substantial, and much of it a revelation to McIver – beginning with Item One on the Agenda.

In flat monotones, the CIA man had outlined the origin of upwards of thirty tons of SARIN nerve gas, distributed in – of all things – imported personal computers, probably originating from the Far East, into the UK over the six months preceding the cataclysmic events of Monday, the 26th October 1998.

Then, with as much emotion as an attorney reading a Last Will and Testament, or a disillusioned diner perusing a restaurant menu, he delivered what, to McIver at least, was the *piece de resistance*.

Under the heading of 'Application', the ex-sailor CIA director droned on...

'The detonation of the concealed devices, containing capsules of SARIN was initiated by the code word 'Counter Strike' over the INTERNET world wide computer network. The geographical origin of the detonating command is not known at this time.

Having delivered his bombshell, the retired Admiral had cleared his throat and sat down to a stunned silence.

After this, Item Two, McIver's first contribution to the meeting came as something of an anticlimax. This was somewhat irksome for him as he had envisaged this as his "party piece", but now he had been upstaged by yet another, somewhat disagreeable, Admiral!

McIver's presentation concerned 'Theatre Communications', which as McIver demonstrated, were inhibited by the pulse effect of numerous neutron bomb detonations which appear to have been "placed" over or adjacent to, important centres of communications, such as TV and radio stations, transmitters, repeater antennae, telephone exchanges, etc.

There was nothing new about this phenomena. It had been recognised almost since the advent of nuclear weapons, although it had never been put into effect on such a scale before, or with such deliberation. And this revelation was little more than had already been drafted into the UTFOR Press Release approved by Scottdale.

Nothing very stunning there. No... but McIver's explanation of the paralysis of the SARIN victims...? Here he was able to bring in something of his own which might unseat complacency and reveal any disingenuousness on the part of his political superiors. Here was something that even the CIA man might be unaware of...?

'The communications blackout was consolidated by the

paralysis and death of most communications workers and many users of the systems. However...'

McIver paused for effect but, looking up, registered only blank faces in his powerful audience, some of whom were still in mild shock from the previous speaker's revelations.

'Not all were so affected,' he went on, 'that is, not by the nerve gas, because quite simply there were not enough releases to cover the whole country and I believe this was intended...'

'Why, what ever do you mean by that, General?' asked the President, leaning forward.

'Just this, sir,' replied McIver, gaining confidence, 'this attack was *meant* to be highly selective. Certain areas were targeted and others neglected. The first level targets were, as we know, the communications centres and centres of power. It was necessary to...'

'Now see here, General,' retorted Scottdale, 'I think you're exceeding your brief...'

'Let him finish,' said the President with uncharacteristic sharpness.

McIver went on to mention the effects and tests on the contaminated diesel fuel, and how it seemed to have been deployed in many, but by no means all, rural areas. He outlined how with such an imprecise lethal agent, there were probably many "collateral" deaths. He reported that UN health experts were also testing water sources and found many of them to be contaminated with a variety of substances, some lethal. He described how the many survivors seemed to be in a state of natural shock, but more significantly, from the point of objective analysis of the catastrophe, a large number – perhaps the majority – were suffering from amnesia.

He outlined how work was underway to determine, more accurately, human losses, and perhaps more significantly, those who may have escaped. This was to be achieved by accessing public records, but he had to point out that this had proved far from easy, as many records, paper, electronic and micro-fiche appeared to have been deliberately destroyed – either before, during, or immediately after the event.

'After the Event?' interrupted the President, 'Why, what ever can you mean by that, General.'

'Mr President, we time the initial attack at 5am Greenwich Mean Time on Monday, 26th October, 1998. However, it is clear that there were insurgent forces on the ground, before, during and after the attack, who were suitably equipped and informed to ensure their own safety – largely by being in the right place at the right time.'

'And who do you think these forces were, General?' It was clear to McIver, by his Commander in Chief's form of words, that he had already been briefed by the CIA on this subject, and therefore probably already knew the answer to the question, or at least *thought* he did.

McIver, feeling all eyes upon him, knew that much depended on his answer, even perhaps his career.

'Well, sir, I'll have to take a raincheck on that one. Whoever they were, we haven't found them...'

'Then how do you know they were ever there to begin with?' interrupted Scottdale, sarcastically.

'They left traces of their presence...' McIver was particularly careful not to say "evidence".

'Oh, what traces?' said Scottdale.

'It was a job for the forensic team,' countered McIver, quickly.

'There were no native police experts, either fit or available, and unfortunately all the US forensic expertise appeared to have urgent duties elsewhere.'

'Oh, and where were these urgent duties...?'

'At the time, sir, I didn't know. However, I have since been informed that they were in Eire,' replied McIver, glancing at Scottdale for his reaction. But there was none he could detect. Just the inscrutable hostility toward him, which he could feel, but not fathom.

'I see' said the President, once again (to McIver, at least) almost revealing an exposure to information to which McIver had not been made privy.

From that point, McIver continued without further interruption to the point in his presentation where he summarised the main destructive agents used in the perpetration of the attack. He did this by use of a coloured slide, which he carefully placed on an overhead projector.

1. The ERWs (mini neutron weapon)

(Method of delivery uncertain, but probably incoming missile or satellite release, origin as yet uncertain).

2 SARIN bomblets concealed in imported personal computers

This item had been hastily included in McIver's straggly hand.

3. Contaminated diesel fuel and public water supplies.

4. 'Commando' attack squads

(Presumed responsible for tertiary destruction of vital (and other?) installations, not destroyed by other means).

The President noticed the 'and other' installations, in the last item, and queried its meaning.

Once again, McIver thought it odd that he should query such a comparatively minor point, rather than more pressing matters such as the origin of the incoming missiles, or satellite bombs.

He would have liked to have known the answer to the last question himself – he was uncomfortable being in this position. For, if others knew and he did not, more than his peace of mind would be compromised.

17

*"Nor shall my sword
sleep in my hand"*

From the song "Jerusalem"
by Joseph Parry

**United Nations Building
New York**

After the Event

Lammas was in his office on the thirty-eighth floor of the UN building. He leaned back on the shiny leather sofa, sighed and allowed himself a moment of self-congratulation. His mind went back to the quite extraordinary quick-fire sequence of events which had culminated in a US revelation that a Russian rocket, or rockets, were responsible for the British catastrophe, followed by a covert proposal to retaliate with a precision attack on the command centre and launching site.

This proposal, which had come direct to him from the Secretary's office at the Department of Defense, stipulated that there was no time to go through the usual channels (UN Security Council and NATO). Moreover, there was the question of the obvious Russian veto!

He had immediately telephoned the President, who was unavailable, and then General McIver, with whom he felt he had at least some rapport because of their previous meetings. However, once again he had great difficulty in reaching him.

The monotones of the Pentagon answering system repeated the same frustrating message:

'You have reached the Chiefs of Staff suite at the Department of Defense. Please leave your number and message after the tone, and the party or section named will get back to you.'

Later that day, a Major Wilbur Smith had called to say that General McIver was away from his office, and to ask if the matter was urgent.

Lammas had confirmed that it was of the utmost urgency – indeed, a matter of international security. There was a short silence at the other end of the line. Then the aide said he would be sure to have the Chairman (McIver) call, and asked if he could he have an evening number.

'It will be the same number you're calling now, Major,' replied Lammas, contemplating yet another long working day.

When McIver eventually rang at 9.10 that evening, sounding very weary – and not a little wary, it soon became clear to Lammas, that although he tried to conceal the fact, incredibily, McIver actually knew little, if anything, about the matter!

The following day, Lammas was at length able to persuade the White House, through his contacts at the State Department, to approach the Russian Ambassador and impart to him the serious consequences of the revelation. At first, as might be expected, he hotly denied the whole thing. However, over the next twenty four hours, in a series of telephone calls and two postponed meetings, it was agreed that there might be something in it, and that there might have been "an unfortunate accident".

* * *

The disintegration of the Soviet Empire and its pervasive influence in Eastern Europe was one of this century's most momentous events. Suddenly, long forgotten nations have returned to the world stage and at the same time new ones have been created.

In their struggle for independence and stability, one of the first things these nations do is ...?

The firing of a twenty year old RS18 strategic nuclear

missile from the Baikonur launch site in Kazakstan (although internally reported as 'excellent' in result and pronounced fit for further use by the Russian military) unfortunately co-incided with the devastating attack on the United Kingdom on October 26th,1998. For although the missile's trajectory had been in the opposite direction, the six warheads falling harmlessly on its target near the Kamchatka Peninsular in the Russian Far East, it had been embarrassing, to say the least, for the new Russian Democratic state. The Americans wrongly reported the launching from the Ukraine.

These events had taken a great deal of explanation and caused considerable alarm and confusion on both sides. The fact that it was the twenty sixth launch carried out by the Strategic Missile Forces command, which came into being after the Soviet collapse in 1991, cut no ice with the Americans who, if it had not been for the intervention of Serge Lammas, Secretary General of the UN, would have prevailed on NATO to launch an aerial attack on the Baikonur launch site on the very day that Colonel General Dmitri Ilyich Vokarov, leading Russian soldier, head of the Strategic Missile Forces general staff, was celebrating his fifty seventh birthday.

As it was, he merely received an international telephone call on the secret scrambler line, an unusual event in itself. In fact it would have put the fear of God into him, had he been a believer, but it was the identity of the caller, and what he had to say that gave him sleepless nights thereafter.

When Colonel General Vokarov received the call from the Russian Foreign Minister, speaking from the United Nations in Washington, he was shocked. Firstly, to receive a call from someone so senior, and secondly because of the proposal that had been put to him. If his career, so far, had suffered from his own innate honesty, here indeed was a watershed.

If he understood the Comrade Minister correctly (he could not free himself of the old habit of the communist style of address) he was to technically underwrite an apology by the

Minister to the international community, for a rogue pair of missiles fired in the early hours of Monday the 26th October 1998, which had escaped the earth's gravity (due to a faulty propellent charge), circumvented the globe on latitude 52° North and released their twelve warheads over Britain.

While an increased propellent charge might explain the prolonged trajectory, or even the nearly two degree increase in latitude, how was it to be explained that the RS18s were armed with live neutron warheads of a highly sophisticated type which, as far as he knew, his country did not possess?

When he put this question to the Minister, he replied, 'I think you'll find that one of our neighbours possesses such a weapon, Colonel General. And by the way, you never received this call. Your further instructions and authentication will be sent to you very shortly. Needless to say, I shall deny any knowledge of the matter,' and put the 'phone down.

A few days later Vokarov received a small package by special courier.

When he opened it with an old bone handled Cossack dagger he lovingly used as a paper knife, a computer diskette fell onto the toe of one of his polished brown boots. His dog, Chaika, barked and ran off with it, thinking it was a toy. When he retrieved it, it was damp and bore several teeth marks. It took him some minutes to clean it, every second of which he suffered great anguish. For if the data on it was damaged, how could he possibly ask the Comrade Minister for a replacement? When he nervously inserted the diskette into his personal computer, it took some time to discover what was on it. When at last he found a program which would read it, he felt sure there must be something missing, for all it appeared to contain was a number of disparate newspaper articles, which he read in turn with increasing bewilderment:

"China to build Su-27 fighter in $2bn deal with Moscow. China and Russia have reached agreement on the joint production of Su-27 fighters, far superior to anything currently flown by the Chinese air force. Between 40 and 60 will be assembled by S......

> Hong Kong's Ming Pao newspaper quoted defence sources in Taiwan saying that the deal would not challenge the island's superiority in the air..."

There was a foot note to the damaged article which was just legible, it read...

> 'China has imposed tighter controls on use of the Internet and other international computer networks, the state run Xinhua news agency said yesterday. Networks will be required to use official channels and pledge that they will not harm state security – AP.'

Delving into the envelope once more, Vokarov found a single sheet of paper clinging to the envelope interior. He read it, re-read it and turned pale.

CIA UNLEASHES SPY TEAMS ON FOREIGN FIRMS

The British Foreign office has expressed concern over a strategy by the American CIA to spy on foreign companies, including the UK, to gain US competitive advantage. The CIA Director planned to ask US spies to recruit agents inside foreign business and to use electronic eavesdropping to gather details of company operations. This gave rise to tensions in the area of intelligence cooperation (MI6).

The scheme was discussed with US Congress members and given preliminary approval by the US President, who gave it not only approval, but priority.

The Plan caused divisions within the CIA & the US Administration. However, France, Russia and Japan, are considered the worst offenders in gathering economic intelligence.

It soon became clear to Vokarov, that in spite of the risks, he must confide in someone, mainly because he needed help to make sense of 'his instructions.'

18

'What do you know about hacking?'

'You mean computer hacking?' replied Hartog.

McIver nodded.

'What do you want to know?'

'Well, first of all, a little background. I can tell you this. Hackers attacked the Pentagon computer system as many as 250,000 times last year.'

Hartog whistled. 'As many as that?'

'Yes, and they gained entry on two out of every three attempts.'

'That many?'

'Mmm, but it's not quite as bad as it sounds because ninety per cent of the attacks were on unclassified systems, which make up most of the Defense Department traffic. But once in a while....'

'Yes,' replied Hartog, leaning forward, he was beginning to get interested now.

'Well, there was an incident not long back,' McIver continued, 'when some jerk from London...'

'You mean London, England?' Hartog interrupted, excitedly.

'Yep.'

'What happened?'

'He took control of the computer network at a top Air Force Research Laboratory.'

'That sounds scary. Did he do any damage?'

'He put all of the laboratory's thirty three sub-networks off-line for several days. Files were rummaged and repairing the break-in and adding security 'patches' cost half a million bucks. And that's not all,' McIver went on, 'It seems he may have been working with a foreign agent!'

'Who says?' enquired Hartog.

'The CIA.'

'Oh them, they're paranoid.'

'Maybe, but this was the premier Air Force Command and Control Research Centre, which works on weapons systems, artificial intelligence and radar guidance. During the attacks, they stole information on methods used by the Air Force commanders to relay secret intelligence and target information during wartime.

'Why are you telling me all this?' asked Hartog, not unreasonably, sipping his scotch.

McIver suddenly looked very serious, almost vulnerable. 'Look Hog, I don't want to tell you more than you need to know, but without sounding too melodramatic, I think you have an opportunity here to help your country.'

'George, you seem very worried by this...'

McIver laughed bitterly, 'Let's just say I don't mind admitting to you, that I'm getting a little out of my depth..'

'You mean technically?'

'No, I don't just mean technically.'

'You mean – politically?'

McIver nodded.

'That's very worrying, George,' replied Hartog seriously, shaking his head.

'I know, Hog. I know.'

*   *   *

*"If your relationships are good
you don't need a contract.
If they're bad it won't help you."*

(Anon)

Colonel General Vokarov had confided in someone whom he felt sure as he could trust, regarding his "instructions" recently received so vicariously from the "Comrade" Foreign Minister.

And so it was that he revealed the nature and cryptic content of these instructions to a trusted colleague – of the necessarily similar rank. After some hours, spent working together on Vokarov's personal computer, and in learning the translation program supplied, they discovered that the first and last line of each article, when sorted, gave what his confidante was able to identify as an Internet code. But that was merely the first revelation. Further study revealed a series of access codes which they laboriously tried in turn, working through the night, consuming many cigarettes and not a little vodka.

At 03.00 hrs Central Russian Time, having transferred their work to a more powerful but discreet computer within the complex, they discovered to their amazement, that they were accessing what appeared to be a Chinese Defence computer system. And when the remainder of the coded portion of the sort program - supplied to Vokorov, was applied to the rest of the text of newspaper articles he had received, it de-coded the instructions needed to fire the latest Long March missiles from China to North Korea and beyond.

They ransacked the available Chinese translation programs and swore at one another until they were at last able to uncover the notation they sought, and finally to translate it. There, in an obscure directory, were the words: "Enhanced Radiation Weapon, Warhead." The Chinese did have ERWs, the kind that had crippled Britain.

* * *

McIver had resisted telling Hartog more than a little of what he believed about matters leading up to the Event, and even less about the political skulduggery since. His forbearance had been difficult, as every nerve, sinew and inclination had induced him to trust another human being. However, his military discipline and regard for the younger man's well-being had been enough.

It was now becoming increasingly clear that not only was he being kept at arms' length from the political decision-making process, but possibly even when that process involved actions for which he might later be held responsible.

McIver's conversation with Lammas had been embarrassing to say the least! He had tried to disguise his ignorance but knew from previous meetings that Lammas was not a man from whom one could easily hide facts.

The next day McIver tried to contact Scottdale without immediate success and once again he had to employ his time-tested tactic of confining himself, incommunicado, to his quarters, to wait until his fury had subsided. On emerging, he was told by an aide that Scottdale would see him that afternoon.

However, on arriving at Scottdale's office he found Deputy Defence Secretary, David Douglas, waiting for him and when he naturally enquired as to the whereabouts of Richard Scottdale he was told, by Douglas, that Secretary Scottdale was with the President at this time. He was then offered a drink which he declined.

McIver knew from former meetings that he was able to intimidate Douglas with his mere presence, something he could not do with Scottdale. Here was the opportunity to get more out of the Deputy Secretary than the weaker man intended.

'Well, General,' Douglas opened, as McIver sat regarding him impassively, 'I think we both know why you're here.'

'Yes, Mr Secretary, I guess we do.'

'Would you like to lead off, General?'

'OK, I'd like to know why I was not consulted, or indeed informed, of this... proposal. No dammit, threat, made to the Russians...'

'Yes, yes. I can expl...' laughed Douglas nervously, but McIver was in full flow now and not amenable to being interrupted.

'And not only that,' McIver went on, leaning forward, 'but contacted and informed of the fact by none other than the Secretary General of The Yewnited Nations!'

Like many, when roused, McIver slipped into the accent of his upbringing.

'I'm afraid there wasn't time to inform you, you see..?'

'Wasn't time?' McIver thundered.

'No, you see, the President..' Douglas then clammed up in mid-sentence.

'Go on, Mr Douglas, you were saying... about the President?'

'Yes, the President was unavailable, and as you know, he likes to be consulted before political decisions are passed to the, er, the..military.'

'To *me*, you mean?' rasped McIver prodding his own bemedalled chest.

'Douglas nodded, almost imperceptibly, then shook his small balding, head uncertainly.

'Oh, I see,' McIver replied, with heavy sarcasm, 'So, the next world war can be initiated and the Chief of the United States Forces is informed only after the political button has been pressed?'

'Oh no, General, nothing was *decided*. No forces were alerted, or would be, without your consent. This was merely a political......'

'Ploy? Is that the word you're looking for Mr Douglas?'

'Well..'

McIver stood up. 'That's mighty reassuring, Mr Douglas. A real vote of confidence in my abilities...' He put both enormous arms on Douglas's desk and looked deep into the little man's eyes, '*and* my *loyalties*.' And with that he turned, picked up his impressive service cap, with its silver oak leaves and bald eagle badge, and made for the door. On opening it, he turned, and spoke clearly and menacingly.

'I should be grateful if you would have Secretary Scottdale call me at my office at the Pentagon – as soon as he can spare the time. Good day, Mr Douglas!'

He put on his cap, turned on his heel and strode out, his thunderous step shaking the filing cabinets and causing a number of aides and secretaries to pause in their work and mutter among themselves.

That evening, McIver was about to leave, when an aide told him White House Chief of Staff, Michael Denver, was on the scrambler.

19

'The hardest thing to learn in Life,
is which bridge to cross
and which to burn.'

(David Russell)

The Cotswolds, England.

Before the Event.

Although Goodchild was pleased to receive Julia's call, he had to suppress his natural impression that he was, perhaps, being used. For whereas his intelligence clearly knew it, his heart would have none of it.

However, not for the first time Julia's greeting expunged (temporarily at least) any such ungallant, lingering thoughts.

He was rather taken by surprise when she met him on her driveway – something she had never done before. He hardly had time to get out of his car before he was overwhelmed by the most effusive welcome yet experienced in their relationship. Not so overwhelmed, however, that his trained peripheral vision failed to miss the blue and white police panda car, parked conveniently behind the rose bushes.

'Robin! Mmmm,' Julia proffered a perfumed cheek for him to kiss,' thanks for coming at such short notice..'

'What is it, Julia...?' Goodchild began, 'are you in trouble?'

'No, no... just some silly misunderstanding,' Julia replied, truthfully. After all, she only knew Payne socially and her better instincts had already decided that their association must end.

Before crossing Julia's threshold, Goodchild had been appraised by her as to what was expected of him. It seemed to amount to this: that he should provide, not only moral support, but a character reference to the police, and soconvince them that Julia "could not possibly be connected" in any way, with the happenings at a certain Ford Cottage;

the death of a Mrs Amy Prince (whoever she might be) and the disappearance of her husband Jack, and a Mr Marcus Payne, whose distinctive car had been seen parked outside Ford Cottage, by Jacqui Strakes, probably after the time of death.

However, the local police sergeant, who "was making preliminary enquiries" (presumably before the CID invaded his patch), remained unconvinced.

Julia, who had a horror of police stations, was doing all she could to influence the conversation to prevent the sergeant uttering those fateful words involving "statements" and "coming down to the station."

However, it soon became clear to Goodchild that Julia was making things worse for herself. Her evasive answers to the sergeant's questions about her association with Marcus Payne were increasing his suspicion.

'When did you last see Mr Payne, Miss McMahon?'

'Well, now let me see, that would be..'

Julia turned to Jacqui, 'When would it be, Jacqui?'

But Jacqui just went pink and shrugged.

'Oh, I know,' Julia went on.., then suddenly remembered the last time was when Marcus had taken her out for dinner and that such a revelation was not ideal in Robin Goodchild's presence.

'Do you have a diary, Miss?' enquired the policeman patiently.

'Well, yes, but...' Julia was not enamoured of the idea of having her innermost secrets open to official scrutiny.

A little later when she managed to slip out to the kitchen once more, she was able to hiss in Goodchild's ear, in reply to his concern about her answers, 'This will look very bad for me at work. My job involves national security at a very sensitive level.'

Goodchild was inclined to reply that she should have thought of this before, but thought better of it.

'Just tell them the facts, Julia. I'm sure you've got nothing to..., well, reproach yourself for...'

'Haven't I?' said Julia unexpectedly.

Goodchild felt a bolt of concern run through him, but realized it had more to do with jealousy than Julia's well being.

'Look, Julia,' said Goodchild, in what he hoped was a masterful tone, 'all you've got to say is that you didn't know Payne very well; you only had the vaguest notion of how he earned his bread – we all did – and that you have no idea where he is now. That's true isn't it?'

'Well, yes...' replied Julia, uncertainly, nibbling a biscuit.

Goodchild was beginning to get a little annoyed.

'Is there something you're not telling me Julia?'

'Oh God, your not going to get all possessive and self righteous on me, are you? That's the last thing I need.'

'You asked me to come over, Julia,' retorted Goodchild evenly.

'Yes, and I'm beginning to wish I hadn't.'

'You two having a row?'

It was Jacqui.

'Jules, the Sergeant's told me to tell you he's leaving...'

'Oh, ...I see...,' said Julia, trying not to openly express the relief she felt inside. Then shutting the kitchen door carefully behind Jacqui and whispering out loud, 'Is that, er... it, then?'

'He says, you're not to leave the country,' quipped her friend, helping herself to a biscuit.

'This is no joking matter, Jacqueline..!'

'You're telling me, and Robin's not laughing either..'

Goodchild frowned and looked at his watch. 'Look, I'd better be going. The immediate crisis appears to be over and I'm flying tomorrow morning.'

'You're always flying aren't you, Robin? In every sense of the word.' Julia sat on a work top and buried her head in her hands. The events of the past few hours appeared to have taken their toll. Goodchild had difficulty in judging her mood and felt a little out of his depth.

Inappropriately, at that moment, his eyes at least appreciated Julia's shapely thighs encased in the light blue, designer jeans.

'Yes, well, I must go. Give me a ring if there are any further developments..'

'Oh, you mean like a call from Holloway jail?' retorted Julia thickly, looking up. Her eyes were moist and the fine mascara slightly smudged. The look she gave him remained with him on his journey home.

*　　*　　*

When Marcus Payne arrived at Jack Prince's house, he was sweating profusely as the enormity of his predicament engulfed him. How was he to placate Jack? How was he to dispose of Amy Prince's body? How was he to carry on with what he had come to England to do, and how was he to escape? Above all, what was he to tell Julia – with whom he had fallen so unwisely in love?

He decided, quickly that the situation demanded that Prince and he must both leave the country by the quickest possible means. He needed Prince where he could keep an eye on him, but what to do with his wife's body? God! without a medical opinion, he didn't even know if she was dead! And how would he persuade Prince to leave her?

His brain responded to these vital questions with a jumble of information – in the form of dramatic visual imagery.

The first was the disposal of the Buick, it was far too distinctive. There was an old water-filled quarry, not far from Princes' place. The second was to drive to Kent in a hire car and charter an executive jet to Albania, a place where they did not ask too many questions as long as you had hard currency. Luckily he still had nearly ten thousand pounds worth of Swiss francs, and the equivalent in American dollars. Hope-Watson was not going to be very pleased at this misappropriation of funds, but his task was practically complete and this was an emergency. Thereafter, events would have to be managed by remote control, a little earlier than originally planned.

20

At the small Kent airport, Payne had to charter a Gates Lear Jet 35 as it was the only aircraft immediately available.

At over £1,000 per flying hour, it was the most expensive aircraft in the fleet.

With its twin rear-mounted turbojets and six to eight seats, it was faster than a commercial jet, but more importantly, it could land at small airports – in poor weather, if necessary. It had the range to reach Cyprus or Tunis in one hop; so Albania could be reached in a little over two hours.

He was able to convince the operators that he was a South African diamond merchant and that Prince was a diamond cutter. As far as customs were concerned, they knew the aircraft to be empty and Payne and Prince had little more than they stood up in. They did not even search their small overnight bags, apart from letting a listless sniffer dog run its muzzle over them, in case of drugs.

They had buried Amy on the edge of a beauty spot where through tear stained sentences, Prince had told him he and his wife had first made love, soon after they had met. It had taken Payne all his powers of persuasion to prevent Prince from giving himself up to the police. Clearly, Payne could not allow that. He had on more than one occasion during that fraught period, fingered the solid metal of the small Beretta – which he later disposed of in anticipation of a possible customs search at the airfield. Prince was a lucky man in that he saw sense in time, otherwise he might have joined his wife in her unofficial grave. At all events Payne's troubles were far from over. For although chartering an aircraft allowed them to reach their rather unusual destination quickly, it did not obviate the possibility of the pilot being alerted by radio, should the inevitable hue and cry overtake the period of their flight. However, Payne had contingency plans.

Having already tackled a series of traumatic events in the preceding twenty four hours, he was, if necessary, prepared to take command of the aircraft in the final stages of their flight. Concealed in his luggage was a CS gas spray, disguised as a deodorant, which he would have little hesitation in using, should the need arise.

He knew he could handle a Lear jet, although the landing might be tricky, especially if the weather was bad. He might even get something for the aircraft from their friends in Albania,

Although that would be a bonus. In any event he must radio ahead to alert the cell in Tirâna, which was paid by Hope-Watson to handle traffic to and from Britain and Singapore and all their paymasters in Switzerland and Bermuda.

Take-off was uneventful on a perfect autumn afternoon, into an azure sky lightly adorned with wispy strato-cumulus clouds. Payne watched the pilot from behind, enjoying the sensation and the improved light that flying always seems to impart as one rises above all former vision impairing obstruction.

'Unusual destination, Albania. We were lucky to get clearance at such short notice,' remarked their pilot crisply.

'Yes, well I do have some limited influence there,' Payne replied, raising his voice above the whine of the twin jet engines, on full power behind them.

'Mm, we would normally go via Brindisi with a quick hop across the Adriatic to Tirana, although we seldom go there. Not a very hospitable place is it?'

'Oh, I think it's improving,' replied Payne, his mind racing.

This guy is too chatty for my liking, he told himself, and went to grasp the butt of the Beretta, in its usual place in his inside jacket pocket, but of course, it was no longer there.

'I wonder,' he said loudly to the pilot, 'might we fix

ourselves a drink?' They had scarcely taken any refreshment since dumping the Buick.

'Of course!' replied the pilot, jovially over his right shoulder, 'help yourselves. I'm sorry there was no stewardess available at such short notice, but you'll find everything you need in the galley, aft. If you need something stronger, it's in the lower locker.'

Payne helped himself to a generous gin and tonic and began to relax, only to be mildly irritated by Jack Prince, who complained that there was no beer. This caused Payne's ever active brain to begin to wonder what he was going to do with Prince; after all, he had little use for him now and he felt sure that Hope-Watson was hardly likely to welcome him. But while it was true that he had killed before, it had always been at long range, never close up and in cold blood. Now he had to consider that this might become necessary, and all too soon, for his rather delicate stomach – which heaved slightly at the thought of it. But then again, perhaps it was just the motion of the plane.

These dark thoughts were interspersed with the occasional wistful vision of Julia and their last night together. It had been bliss, but probably unwise. If necessary, he could justify their association because of Julia's role at GCHQ, but in reality, he had got little out of her on that score and to have pressed her further would only have aroused her suspicions.

Casting his mind back to the event that had led up to his present situation, he knew that he had taken the only possible course of action, for he knew that he had probably been seen at Prince's place and that it would not be long before people would begin asking questions about Amy. In any case, time was short before the culminating event, the planning and part-implementation of which, had brought him to England in the first place.

His reverie was interrupted by the pilot again, who informed him that they were now crossing the English Channel, and depending on Air Traffic Control delays in the Mediterranean region, their ETA at Tiräna would be in a little over two hours.

Once again, Payne's busy brain began to process his options. He concluded that he had little time to decide whether to take control. It would all depend on whether or not the pilot was alerted as to their true identity. (Payne had called himself Forbes because he had a Scottish grandmother of that name – and Prince 'Baker' because he was so unlucky!)

The problem was, how would Payne know if the pilot was informed; the man was wearing ear phones and the plane's radio loudspeaker turned off or down. Moreover, he knew that modern aircraft such as this, carried radar transponders which could respond to any ground radar station by simply pressing a switch, which would then display a code of small bars on the receiving radar screen, thus covertly answering any question the controller cared to ask - including did he (the pilot) have men of their description on board!

*   *   *

'The President asked me to call you, George. He said to say, he is sorry about what happened.'

As White House Chief of Staff, Michael Denver acted as a go between for the various factions of the Thomas Administration.

McIver made no reply.

'Are you still there, George?'

'I'm listening Michael.'

'Yes, we needed to test the Russians out on this one...'

'Test them out?'

'Sure, and the UN too.'

'Oh?'

'Yes.'

'Well now, how did they both make out?' replied McIver cynically.

'How's that, George?'

'Exactly!'

'I'm not reading you General.' said Denver, changing tone.

'I may not be a world class politician, Michael, but I sure know one thing...'

'What's that, General?'

'That, as Chairman of the Chiefs of Staff, I should be consulted on any point, however political, which may commit the forces at my command to any conflict, especially one which could have started World War Three!'

There was a silence at the other end of the line.

'And there's another thing...?'

But Denver interrupted him.

'Deputy Secretary Douglas would have appraised you of the facts had you given him the opportunity, General...'

'It's *me* who should have been given the opportunity, Michael,' rejoined McIver, 'and at the appropriate time. Not presented with a *fait accompli*!' And with that he replaced the receiver firmly and left his office.

21

Washington
30th November 1998

After the Event

At one of the now steady sequences of press briefings on *Broken Arrow*, a bald headed and rather lack lustre Pentagon spokesman made the following statement, the dramatic nature of which, perhaps deserved a more distinguished delivery.

"Secretary Scottdale, in consultation with the Chiefs of Staff, can now associate themselves with an - as yet unconfirmed report - (the one concession to McIver's latest protests) that the destruction of the infrastructure of England, part of Great Britain, and many of its citizens and government, was probably accidental, and caused by a Russian experimental intercontinental missile which exceeded its orbit, due to a malfunctioning propellent. Consequently the missile took up a more northerly orbit that passed over the United Kingdom. An attempt to destroy the missile remotely, unfortunately caused an explosion, which in turn, damaged a Chinese satellite, in a higher orbit. This satellite, which was carrying an experimental kind of neutron power source and other chemical agents, plunged from its orbit and on contact with the atmosphere, caused the widespread damage and extensive loss of life, of which we are all painfully aware. For reasons yet to be explained, the Chinese authorities have not yet admitted to this accident. That is all."

*   *   *

In Albania, set beside the Adriatic with Serbia to the North, Macedonia to the East and Greece to the South, the capital Tiräna with a relatively modest population of some three and a half million souls, presides over a modest economy based on fairly primitive agriculture, together with textiles and oil products. It is a nation with a chequered history. Invaded in the 14th century by the Turks and but for a brief period when a national hero, Alexander Skanderberg, drove them out, it remained under the Ottoman Empire for more than four centuries. After a long intervening period following independence in 1912, Albania veered from republic to monarchy up to the outbreak of World War II. After the war, the rule was Stalinist, the nation becoming isolated from the rest of the world community. Although a tacit return to democracy was signalled by elections in the early nineties, one influence remained strong: that of Communist China.

*   *   *

Inbound from the Adriatic, North West of Tiräna, the Lear Jet flew erratically at eight thousand feet with Payne at the controls. At that altitude the pressure in the cabin and outside were nearly equal and with the auto-pilot heading lock set on 105 degrees, he had helped Jack Prince open the main door enough to pitch the unfortunate and comatose pilot out into the cold slipstream, and watch his body fall into the distant blue of that exotic sea.

Now he had to overcome several obstacles. Firstly, convincing Prince that he would not be next! Secondly, landing a plane with which he was only barely familiar. Thirdly, avoiding the Albanian authorities by (if necessary) naming the senior official whom Hope-Watson had bribed so expensively. Finally, he had to dispose of the plane at a price which would boost his own operational fund!

Sweating at the controls, Payne had managed to contact the cell who would manage their arrival on a pre-arranged frequency. However, it took some time for him to speak to someone with good enough English and sufficient authority, to name a suitable landing field and even longer to establish its co-ordinates so that he could punch them into his satellite navigator. Having done so, he set the autopilot once more and had a rare cigarette.

'Ere, where the bloody hell're we going?' whined Prince from behind him.

The aircraft, having settled once more, relieved of Payne's clumsiness at the control yoke, whistled along contentedly at 430 knots. Payne had set the altitude lock to 6,000 feet and the altimeter unwound slowly as they descended gently to that height.

'You know very well, where we're going, Jack... Albania,' Payne replied equitably, 'I've told you a dozen times already...'

'Yeah? Well I've never bloody erd of it,' Prince complained.

*   *   *

Singapore
October 1998

Before the Event.

Officially, diplomat and international peace co-ordinator, Rear Admiral Lloyd Hope-Watson (RN Retd); Her Majesty's Ambassador resident in Singapore.

Unofficially, he was rallying point for right wing ex-patriots in the Far East, Australasia and beyond. He coordinated the views and efforts of those disillusioned by Britain's gently declining industrial performance – compared with those emerging economic giants of the Pacific Basin. He also advised (covertly of course) on the setting up of funds which might be used to assuage this growing body of disillusionment and transmute their unfashionable hopes into reality. It was a reality which drew ever nearer with the addition of yet another millionaire who wanted Britain, or perhaps more specifically England, to be as she used to be as they remem-

133

bered her in their salad days - up to the late nineteen fifties. Indeed, such was this sentiment among his growing and far flung band, that Hope-Watson had toyed briefly with the notion of styling it the *Nineteen Fifties Club!* But on more mature reflection he decided that this trivialised such an ambitious endeavour.

He was also remembered as a skilled negotiator with the Chinese, and had advised on Hong Kong's recent stormy transition to full ownership by that great and growing power.

Hope-Watson was assisted in his official duties by his wife, Li Chan, and in his extramural activities by his step daughter, Mi Ling, a willing twenty two year old, who was raised in the astringent political climate of Lee Kuan Yew's Singapore, and therefore culturally amenable to her step-father's political philosophy, unlike most students of her age, in other, particularly Western, societies.

On the other hand, she had not quite yet faced up to the radical aims of her mentor and their consequences, in spite of the fact that she had become an essential part of the process.

Occasionally, they would have mild economic arguments, where Mi Ling, an economics undergraduate, would play devil's advocate.

'Oh that's all part of the same thing,' Hope-Watson was saying airily, seated in his white wicker chair on his favourite spot on the veranda, 'companies producing more and more of the things that their perceived customers don't really need, or can actually afford. Wasteful manufactured surpluses..'

'Why wasteful?' Mi Ling interrupted him.

'Why? Because it's the natural and fundamental things that are in short supply now...'

'Such as?' enquired Mi-Ling, warming to the argument.

'Such as, fresh air and clean water,' sniffed Hope-Watson, inclining his large aquiline nose toward the balustrade, where the Straits surged turgidly below, 'and space, and silence, an increasingly rare commodity these days. Then there are raw materials, timber, plants, wildlife and peace of mind - you name it.'

'A rather abstract view. You sound more like an environmentalist, Uncle Lloyd.'

She had always called him uncle, since he had married her mother when she was only two years old.

'OK,' she continued, 'give me an example of a manufacturer's surplus.'

Hope-Watson took a deep breath then exhaled ostentatiously.

'The world motor car industry. Too many manufacturers, too many makes, too many new cars, chasing a reducing number of customers. The market is reaching, or *has* already reached, saturation point. In many nations, notably the UK, gridlock has either arrived or is just round the corner.'

'So, what's your answer?' asked Mi Ling, studying him intently with dark, beautiful eyes.

'Tax the damn things out of existence,' replied Hope-Watson expansively, 'and put the money into more wholesome projects.'

'Projects or products?'

'Both!' said Hope-Watson, half laughing. He enjoyed these exchanges. They helped him unwind after a day of dry official diplomacy.

'Such inconsistency!' giggled Mi Ling. 'Anyway, hang on, what happens to all those employed in the motor industries. Where are they going to work?'

'You could have made the same argument for fox hunting in the eighties,' roared Hope-Watson, reaching for a cigar.

'When fox hunting began to be curtailed, those employed in it had to find other employment.'

'Hardly a realistic comparison, surely?' remarked Mi Ling seriously. 'Consider the difference in scale?'

'Look,' said Hope-Watson, earnestly, waving the unlighted cigar, 'you know that the multinational companies, which dominate motor manufacturing in the late nineties, do not care about people, countries or local communities. They only care about profits. As soon as one location becomes unprofitable they simply move to another and take their capital with them. There have been numerous examples of this. Anyway, the whole industry is an environmental menace. Together with the oil industry, they have resisted all attempts to clean up their act.'

'How can you say that?' pealed his step-daughter with great emphasis, and yet in tones that reminded Hope-Watson of a wind chime, 'What about catalytic converters – and unleaded fuel, to name but two?'

'Just tinkers with the problem,' retorted Hope-Watson relaxing back in his chair, causing it to creak in protest at his bulk,'and merely swaps one form of pollution for another. More than one quite *fundamental* invention ...' he paused to ignite the large Havana, drawing the flame to the fine tobacco, then puffing audibly,'has been *bought up* - or suppressed! Whereas... had they been encouraged, they might have obviated the use of petrol altogether! Mmm.. mmm...'

He drew on the cigar and watched the stiff breeze whip the aromatic smoke across the balustrade and out to sea.

Now in full flow, he continued. 'Today there are few technical reasons *remaining* to prevent most vehicles running on liquid gas. Or even extracting the hydrogen from water! Why hasn't it happened? I'll give you three guesses.'

'You really are a terrible old cynic, Uncle,' Mi Ling giggled.

'Listen girl,' said Hope-Watson, leaning forward and suddenly becoming deadly serious, simultaneously wiping the smile from Mi Ling's face, 'I'm not joking here. Things are getting worse there all the time; the society is on the verge of moral collapse. Children are murdering other children. Doctors are being attacked and fear to visit their patients in the cities. The whole place is grinding to a halt, and foreigners are taking the very fish from our fishermen's nets. Why, we're even taking lessons from the Taiwanese on how to teach our children maths!'

He paused in his tirade to cough, then turned on her and to her, till she felt the very force of his formidable personality.

'Look,' he said quietly, but with a hint of menace, 'I need

to know whether you're with me, or against me. The latter would not be a good position to be in.'

Having finished, he took a deep draft on his cigar and regarded her intently, awaiting her response, like a spider viewing its prey.

But Mi Ling was not easily intimidated and she studied her step-father's face carefully for several seconds.

'Uncle,' she said at length, reaching out and touching his hand, 'you shouldn't get upset. On the whole I agree with what has to be done. But I'm not just playing devil's advocate. I need to learn and to be sure.'

Hope-Watson's craggy face broke into a smile,

'Child, you are older than your years. I knew I could count on you, but I have to be sure, there's a great deal at stake. When a lot of people are going to die, one really has to believe in what one is doing – and have the support of one's family.' He enunciated the last part of his sentence slowly and deliberately.

A question then leapt to Mi Ling's lips, but she did not ask it. It was, what did her mother think about it all. But in reality she already knew the answer. Her mother would not question what ever her husband did. Perhaps it was this above all that made Mi Ling uneasy.

'I know,' she said carefully, sitting back and regarding a potted palm distractedly. 'It's an awful course of action in the full sense of the word, but it has at last, I think, become necessary.'

She looked him straight in the eyes again with a frank and honest expression which almost moved him.

'I'll continue to help all I can, Uncle Lloyd.'

'And you'll see it through to the end, girl? It won't be easy on any level, I promise you...'

Mi Ling nodded, her expression had suddenly become very grave, and had a more sensitive witness been present, they could not have failed to notice the sadness in her eyes – and not a little fear. 'To the end, Uncle,' she said at length. Then, after a short pause, 'and God help us ...all.'

'Amen to that!'

Hope-Watson patted her on the head gently as he stood up,

'But remember, we're not alone... Many great minds are joining us, and more with every passing week.'

But as a sudden gust of warm air bore away his words, Mi Ling glanced toward the end of the long veranda, to the small tropical garden, where her mother busied herself among the exotic flora that grew in profusion there. When Hope-Watson noticed her sudden tears, she was quickly able to dismiss them as grit in the wind.

22

Albania

Before the Event

As Payne wrestled with the control yoke of the Lear Jet, Jack Prince clung to the back of his seat whimpering with fear, for even he could tell that Payne was not entirely up to the task. The airfield to which he had been directed at last, after considerable delay, was in a remote rural area away from prying eyes. The delay had forced Payne to circle – for which he had had to disengage the auto-pilot. This, together with the occasional large drifting clouds, had been a disorienting and somewhat frightening experience, as there were some rather large hills – not to say mountains – in the vicinity, which he had been unaware of when he had settled on their descent to six thousand feet.

They were now on their final approach and descending through thinning cloud at around 4,000 feet. The aircraft was bucking and yawing in moderate turbulence, which once again Payne had not bargained for. If that was not enough, the delay, unscheduled low altitude flying, and Payne's clumsiness with the throttles, had caused them to use much of their diversion fuel, the safety margin all planes carry in case they are unable land at their planned destination. Payne knew he had only one, or two at most attempts, at getting down.

'Ere, you *sure* yer knows what yer doin..?' asked Prince fearfully, his bad breath coursing hotly past Payne's ears.

Mercifully, the cabin air conditioning had mainly dispersed it by the time it reached his sensitive nostrils. But to be sure, Payne lent forward in his straps to adjust his cabin air vent. However, in doing so, his sweating palm slipped from the yoke and as he had failed to trim the aircraft properly, the Lear Jet bounded wildly to one side.

Prince yelped behind him, 'Watch it – can't yer! My Gawd, where did you ever learn to fly a plane?'

'Sit down and shut up,' barked Payne firmly, as he wrestled to regain control.

Once again Payne began to wish he had pushed Prince out with the unfortunate pilot, but he might just need the cretin yet, he thought, as he fought to bring the brown horizon back to the horizontal. He knew any major heading errors on the final approach could either be disastrous, or would mean, at the very least, going round and trying again, for which he might not have sufficient fuel. It was therefore, with some satisfaction and great relief that he saw the little plane icon on the Altitude Indicator settle once more and the real world align with his silver wing tips outside.

Payne recalled the words of his instructor back in his sunny, salad days in the Cape: 'Use the control yoke to aim at the runway threshold and avoid major banking on the approach.' But where was the runway? All he could see was a dusty valley, lined with unfriendly looking boulders!

'Get the gear down and check it.' He fumbled for the lever and a satisfying whirr and final clunk ensued as the under-carriage locked into place. He was relieved to see the three small green lights which confirmed this. The aircraft slowed noticeably with the added drag.

'Gradually decrease approach speed.' He gripped the twin throttle levers with his right hand, slippery with sweat, and wished he had those neat white kid leather gloves that some professional pilots wore.

'Select stage one flap...' He reached frantically for the flap lever, failed to find it and because he had not yet found the electric trim switch, the Lear Jet suddenly rose and yawed alarmingly. Prince squealed from behind him, choked and then Payne smelt the sour odour of vomit.

Cursing Prince loudly, he sweated and fought the silver beast he tried to tame so clumsily.

Still too fast for the approach! Of course! a Lear Jet has *speed brakes* – erectile vertical surfaces on the aircraft's wing. After a quick and frantic search, he located the lever, marked *speed brake,* and nervously engaged it. The aircraft slowed very suddenly, and the nose tipped below the dusty horizon, throwing him forward in his blue nylon straps. He heard Prince gagging again behind him.

He could see what passed for the runway now. It was paved, but looked dirty, cracked and pitted concrete. 'Flaps!' He still needed those, and finding the lever, selected "full flap." Instinctively, Payne hauled gently on the yoke to get the nose up as the Lear Jet slowed again but inclined its elegant nose earthward.

Peering ahead, a startling bolt of fear went through him as he saw a *vehicle* moving down the runway centre, raising a cloud of red dust, which rose, lingered mockingly, then languidly dispersed.

From behind him, Prince had recovered enough to yell at him.., 'There... there. Look! There's a bloody wagon on the runway..!' Payne hit him then, with a powerful, backward punch.

There was a squeal from behind, just audible above the sonorous whine of engines, then a soft, almost imperceptible thump. When he withdrew his smarting fist, it had blood, spittle and vomit on it. With no time for niceties, he quickly wiped it on the empty co-pilot's seat to his right.

From the mortal silence behind him – apart from the fluctuating whine of the twin General Electrics – he must have knocked Prince out – or killed him! At that moment he did not care.

The runway was coming up at him at an alarming speed now.

Thank God! The vehicle and its dust, had moved off to the side, but remained concealed in the reddish brown cloud that now drifted over half the length of the runway – his half!

His old instructor's words penetrated his panic, 'Gradually decrease to an approach speed of...'

But an approach speed of...what? He had learnt in a Cessna..!

He would try 100 knots and trust to luck, if he had any left.

Payne eased back the twin engine thrust levers. Too far! The stall warning buzzer engaged noisily at 99 knots and distracting lights flashed at him angrily. He pushed the levers very slightly forward again and lowered the nose fractionally. The noise and lights stopped as abruptly as they had begun.

The mental commentary in broad South African returned, 'Keep the runway in sight. Point at the threshold, control speed with power and trim. Hell! Where was the Trim Switch? Ah, there it was – no wonder the aircraft had been difficult to control. He had been flying it out of trim.

'Keep the runway in sight.' That was fine, in theory, but the brown barren strip kept disappearing!

But yes, yes...

At last, he could see the runway numbers now, and what passed for a centre line, dirty, white and rutted.

'Remember to "'flare'" at 10-20 feet above the runway...'

Payne hauled back on the yoke as the Air Speed Indicator needle backed to 100 knots.

'Throttle to idle before touch down ...'

He pulled all the way back on the two thrust levers.

The twin engines' whine died away.

'Fly along the runway and let the air speed bleed off...'

Payne recalled that if an aircraft's sink rate above touch down, was too high, they would hit the runway hard... It was, and they did!'

The shock as the undercarriage oleos bottomed jarred his teeth.

For a moment he thought they might come through the wings and puncture the tanks – then they really would be for it!

The Lear Jet bounced jauntily back into the air and yawed

to the left.

Instinctively, Payne hauled back on the yoke and prodded the big rudder pedals, but dimly he remembered that extra rotation of the yoke so near the runway would only stall the jet and not influence its ultimate direction.

'Fly the aircraft onto the runway..!'

Bang! They were on the runway again, but heading crabwise toward the boundary scrub – then out of the freshly whirling dust loomed...*the vehicle they had seen on the approach!*

He was acutely aware of two men throwing themselves out and away from the Russian made jeep – for that was what it was – before there was a metallic crunch, and the Lear Jet's elegant silver nose rode up over the vehicle and largely demolished it.

By this time Payne's face had contacted the padded control yoke and dallied briefly with the perspex wind shield – until his shoulder harness finally restrained him. He just had time to see two wheels roll off in different directions, and the jeep's hood rise up before him, with the words 'Policia' painted in white on its battered green metal.

'Once on the runway, control yoke back, brake to a stop.' His exhausted brain echoed redundantly, and dizzily, before he finally passed out.

*   *   *

In late nineteen-ninety seven, soon after Britain's 99 year lease from China of the Hong Kong New Territories expired, and so was restored to China, the following letter to the London *Times*, was "leaked" from the Diplomatic Bag – ostensibly to the higher echelons within the Foreign Office, to whom (it was wrongly supposed) its acerbic passages referred. The letter was never published, but it was from then on that Hope-Watson's career began to dry up:

'*Sir,*

One can't quite comprehend   the motivations, or

indeed sanity, of the current leading liberalistic, (one hesitates to say ruling classes!) or the "great and the good" – as the media sycophantically describe them.

They pontificate on TV, or the Radio (the BBC!) , or write hypocritical and fatuous articles in the newspapers, about how the countryside is being despoiled – and how wildlife is dying, species by species; or how the sea and rivers are being polluted; or how crime is out of control. And yet it is they who are responsible for the entire, sick scenario.

These hypocrisies are legion, but a foremost example is tacit collusion with the polluting, commercial forces and interests, such as the agro-chemical industry, in their deadly despoilation, through the support of unsound farming practices, and "dead hand" support of the Common Agricultural policy of the EC.

More fundamentally, they are culpable by refusing to devise fiscal measures to put any realistic brake on increasing population, (the root cause of most environmental ills) despite the obvious fact that people are living longer; or that large numbers of workers are no longer required to man huge factories, (didn't we administrate over a third of the globe with 9 million souls? So where is the need for a current population of fifty-six million, and rising?). Fine, if we had the room, but as any visiting tourist will testify, we plainly haven't, and we're all paying the price for it in a rapidly descending quality of life. Examples of this are too many to list here.

While Far Eastern competition has all but eclipsed British industry in the making of most things useful, we have become lick-spittle, lap dogs to our former enemies (in all continents!) Yet still they (the Great and the Good) insist in abetting access, residence and ownership by almost any from abroad, allowing mass entry to a very restricted and once beautiful place – confusing the population with alien cultures and laying waste the land with development, a plethora of motorways and supermarkets, supplied by an agricultural wasteland, which supports fewer species of bird and pollinating insect than is currently found in London itself!

Meanwhile, in the old Commonwealth, the shutters have gone up against British immigrants. They now have to queue for entry with the rest of the world. Yet where is our immigrant points system – for age, qualifications, job experience, health, linguistic ability and clean police record – so widely demanded elsewhere?'

Later it was judged that what establishment figures – including his peers – could not forgive, was the notion that his letter noxiously implied that there was no such thing as democracy in Britain in the late nineties!

Be that as it may, the letter neatly codified the foundation of Hope-Watson's "policy" toward his native country, and it was from this seed of discontent that he - together with a growing band of wealthy and influential internationals – began to scheme and coalesce. They were a disparate group. Some nobly motivated, if misguided, others scheming and disingenuous. It was on the fringes of this gathering group that, as can be imagined, eccentrics abounded.

Hope-Watson was aware of this and although he was never so presumptuous as to call the group his "Flock", in many ways his role could be likened to that of a relentless sheep dog.

Most, but by no means all, lived outside the United Kingdom and even those who did not, travelled – often extensively – for both pleasure and business. Some of their number, suffered from what Hope-Watson dubbed the "Tchaikovsky Syndrome".

This was based on an anecdote about the great Russian Master who, it seems, was in the habit of taking his vacations in Italy, to escape, *inter alia,* what he considered a boorish insensitivity in Russian officialdom. (In addition, of course, he wished to imbibe the kinder

Mediterranean climate). However, it was said, that on arrival in Italy, or shortly afterward, Piotr Ilyich would begin to complain of the inefficiencies and lackadaisical manner of his Neapolitan hosts and wished himself back in the Homeland, where he might receive more consistent service and have himself, and his many requirements the better understood.

In short, some people are never quite satisfied with where they are at any particular time, and frequently wish themselves elsewhere. Even if they complained of that 'elsewhere' quite recently!

Hope-Watson was almost certain that this was the case with many of his more elderly supporters, but in the early stages of his campaign, he could ill afford to alienate a single one, for he needed every penny, every dollar, pound and franc – and each supporter alive, be they eloquent or banal, to assist him in his audacious and dangerous plan: the destruction of late nineties Britain as she was – and to start again in a manner of his own design and choosing.

But this was only the first trick, preposterous though it might sound.

The next was not to reveal his hand in any part of the debacle, and what led up to it, but indeed to condemn it openly on the world stage – at the appropriate time, and to get himself elected to lead the brave new administration – which would rise politically, like a phoenix , from the dust!

But it was more important to be funded by many nations international bodies and foundations, who if aware of the cause of the downfall of the old nation, and the intention of the leadership of the new, would do more than heartily disapprove, but intervene, which (in Hope-Watson's judgment) would give rise to the same, misguided liberalistic mess that existed before.

But how could he keep all those who must know of his involvement – for he had kept the list as short as practicable – from spilling the beans, when it was time for him to ascend the pyrrhic throne? The only way he knew was to have something on each and every one of them! And this, he had at least, set out to do!

There was one more anecdote with which Hope-Watson entertained his friends, both before and after his diplomatic career was unofficially beyond repair.

Apparently, there was a foreign tourist walking uncertainly down Whitehall. He approached a bowler hatted gentleman (in the days when they were to be found!) and asked: 'Excuse me sir, which side is the Foreign Office on?' To which the bowler hatted gent replied, without breaking his stride, 'Ours, I hope – but then one is never *quite* sure , these days!'

For it was to prove that even in the darkest moments of his campaign, Hope-Watson was not completely without a sense of humour. Friends and enemies alike, confirmed this.

23

When Payne came round, he knew not only physical pain but fear.

He was lying on rush matting covering the stone floor of a draughty room. Prince was lying some distance away. The toe of a long shiny leather boot was leisurely exploring his ribs. Payne, raising himself on one sore elbow, gazed upward into the hazy void of his returning consciousness to identify the boot's owner.

His reward was to have the heel of the boot contact his aching forehead, forcing him back onto the matting. It had not been a blow but a powerful push. In any event, it left him in little doubt as to his status as a guest!

At length, the boot's owner spoke – presumably Payne guessed – to him, but at first he could not understand the language in which he was being addressed, until his tired brain made the connection. Of course! His oppressor was speaking Mandarin – not Albanian. Their captor was Chinese.

A bark of command brought two unshaven soldiers of slavic appearance into the room and both Payne and Prince were dragged across the floor. This terse treatment caused Prince to cry out, complaining of an injured arm, but his protests were unheeded and they finished up gasping and groaning in a smaller interrogation room, where they were both tied by leather thongs to rough hewn chairs.

Although it was now dark, except for a dustily recessed wall lamp, Payne could see that their chief captor was a Chinese Major, who now lit three cigarettes expertly at once. Payne feared the worst but the Major merely thrust them in turn, between Prince's cracked lips, causing him to gasp and splutter (he did not smoke) and then Payne's. Finally, to Payne's considerable relief, the Major placed the last cigarette between his own lips, drew on it deeply and regarded them thoughtfully.

A jumble of thoughts and protests came to Payne as he warily eyed the Chinaman, but something told him to remain silent. The butt of a handgun protruded from the Major's unbuttoned holster and the Slavs lolled in the corners of the room, the lamp glinting dully on their battered Kalashnikovs, the distinctive forward curving magazines, wound with dirty elastic tape.

Obviously some kind of interrogation was to follow. Payne decided he would stick to the same story. However, he had two prime concerns. Firstly, he had to quickly determine what exactly the Chinese wanted from them and why? Secondly, Prince might incriminate him through weakness. Here, his only defence would be to deny anything Prince might impute.

At last the Major spoke in English, of a sort, 'Why you here and from where you come?'

Payne thought hard before answering. Surely the Chinaman must know the answer to at least the second question, namely that they had flown from England. As to the first, well... He decided to stall.

'Look Major,' he began, reasoning that the man might appreciate mention of his rank, 'We're very tired and hungry, and my friend is hurt. Do you think we might rest and have some food, before we...'

But the response was swift and impatient.

'You answer questions first, then you rest..., and eat ...maybe,' the Major added hesitantly but with menace.

Payne groaned and rubbed his aching stomach. He caught sight of Prince looking at him wild-eyed and desperate in the dim light, his face filthy and streaked with sweat.

And so began a long night.

Through this interrogation, Payne learned that they were hostages to fortune, for it became achingly clear to his befuddled brain, that the Albanian cell which they had contacted had either been infiltrated by the Chinese military intelligence, or it had been set up with their collusion – and possibly their money. Of course, it hit him like a lightning bolt! Hope-Watson had arranged all these nominated foreign cells to which his "ground forces" might flee. But they were no more than traps run by the Chinese, where "operative refugees'" (or "deserters?") such as himself and Prince might be interrogated, processed and probably eliminated. Except, perhaps, where live scapegoats might be needed – following Hope-Watson's planned, controlled and now imminent destruction of Britain.

Not for the first time in the past twenty four hours, Payne had to think fast to ensure that he gave the answers this man wanted without endangering his own life or person. He would also shield Prince – at least for as long as he might prove useful.

So it was that the interrogation subtly became a two way process as Payne, seemingly innocuously, slipped in almost as many questions as his Chinese captor.

At last he began to get the gist of it.

The Chinese needed scapegoats to help incriminate the US by providing eye witnesses and evidence to prove that US Forces or the CIA, had people on the ground before and during the Event. Clearly, such revelations, if convincing, would have a devastating effect on US diplomacy and standing in the world community.

As the ghastly evening wore on, with the Chinaman losing his temper on more than one occasion, Payne used his limited Mandarin to lull the Major into admitting that Beijing would also like to incriminate the Russians for being in collusion with the US. The background to this must haave been be the Chinese rearmament that followed events in 1996, when US Admiral Kearns had led a powerful and intimidating US Naval task force to Taiwan, to compromise the communist military exercises there. Now, China was making it clear that the United States was her enemy and taking any opportunity to discredit America on the world stage.

Payne had to decide whether the Chinese Major's revelations were genuine or mere propaganda ravings. Yet having regard to the fact that he had had to elicit much of the information (luckily the Major's character was not particularly strong) added credibility to what he had said.

If these things were true he had to admit to being somewhat shocked. For although he had never really trusted Hope-Watson – and knew that he must have powerful backers, he had not realised just how powerful! For himself, he had agreed to arrange the commando preparations for *Counter Strike! for* three reasons: firstly, for the money (Hope-Watson had promised to make him a dollar millionaire); secondly, for the excitement; and thirdly, because he hated what the flabby liberalisers had done to the social fabric and image of the Britain he had looked up to as a boy in South Africa.

In the early days, he had connections through South African UNITA and through them this had opened up a shadowy world of international right wing terrorism. When he first met Hope-Watson through his father, who had been a senior South African diplomat, they had many long conversations into the small hours about the diminution of white Anglo-Saxon values and traditions and how Britain's economy and influence were being undermined by socialist and liberal forces.

He recalled that once (after too much gin) he had suggested that a post cold war, practice missile attack, from the Ukraine toward Western China, might cause the Chinese to react by adopting a harder policy toward democratised Russia and the Americans (who were their perceived paymasters). In any event, there had certainly been manifestations of the latter, culminating in the Chinese military exercises off Taiwan, and the official promotion of anti-American literature.

In the small hours, when Payne (and his interrogator) were at the lowest ebb, a piece of paper was thrust before him, together with a pen. It was made clear, with much shouting and waving of weaponry that unless he signed a statement and agreed to record on video (the next day when he had been suitably cleaned up) an admission to his clandestine work for the Americans, he would not leave that place alive.

It was at that point, when the imperatives of escape began to take precedence in his brain, he blacked out from sheer exhaustion.

When he awoke, he was lying on a bunk in an extremely itchy pair of pyjamas, otherwise apparently clean. He hoped that the discomfort was due to the texture of the material and not to any co-habitants!

The room was small and he was lying on a single wooden cot. It was early morning and the sun was sending reddish rays, diffused with dust, into the room. Apart from the bed there was only a dark wooden table on which stood a jug of water and a heavy table lamp. An incongruous item in such a bare room. Looking at it gave him an idea. He was lying facing the door, which he presumed was locked. In its upper part was a slatted window devoid of glass. Through this came a noise, low and burbling. It was a man snoring. It must be his guard! Payne levered his aching joints from the simple mattress, but before putting his feet to the stone flagged floor, paused and looked beneath the bed. There on a furled blanket lay his clothes, neatly folded. Silently he slipped into them and advanced toward the door.

*   *   *

Hope-Watson needed to work hard on his cabal of wealthy sentimental expatriates, and even harder on the less sentimental international brokers, and financiers. For both he and they, needed not only a respectable cover and rigid security, but ultimately, credible scapegoats – be they individuals, organizations or powerful nations!

At the beginning of their association, when they had been on better terms, Hope-Watson and Payne had done considerable work on laying trails which might lead post-Event investigations away from them and the cabal. However, when Payne's resolve began to falter, and his dalliance with Julia

McMahon produced nothing other than his own self-gratification – together with his increasing enjoyment of the more decadent aspects of modern Britain – Hope-Watson decided he was no longer completely reliable. Someone with Payne's knowledge was clearly dangerous and would have to be dealt with, but not before every ounce of usefulness had been wrung from him.

*   *   *

Ostensibly based in Madeira, where many of Hope-Watson's Macao Portuguese old colonial friends had settled, the Cabal had a respectable front as the Funchal Far Eastern Club, where international bankers (and their proxies), old colonials, soldiers and retired diplomats, arranged periodic *soirées* at Reid's Hotel, nominally to reminisce on past glories. However, halfway through these evenings, the "gentlemen" (whose covert collective power was awesome) would retire to a discreet terrace where they would ensure, by way of generous tips to the staff, that they would not be disturbed or overheard and they could discuss "tactics." In spite of the high average age of the gathering, they had embraced modern technology – to the extent of toting digital, as opposed to analogue, mobile telephones, thereby making eavesdropping difficult. Also, the latest in laptop computers was easily concealed under a generous panama hat! These machines could both send, and receive facsimiles by satellite – and much of the traffic was to and from Singapore!

24

Albania

Before the Event

When Payne reached the heavy wooden door of his cell, he first ascertained that his guard was still asleep. He was, and deeply too, judging by the tenure of his snoring. A faint aroma of alcohol drifted up. This confirmed Payne's confidence in what he was about to do.

Peering between the wooden slats of the vent in the upper door, he could see a length of the passage beyond, lit by the rising sun from some unseen window and a faltering kerosene pressure lamp on a low table opposite. Also on this table, much to Payne's considerable delight, were two British Passports, his and Prince's. This spurred him on.

He began by banging fiercely on the door with his fists. There was no response other than a slight break in the rhythm of the man's snoring. He looked round and saw what he took to be the slop bucket in the corner, a third full with some fetid liquid. He took it up and deposited most of it through the vent in the door. There was no immediate response, then a ghastly choking and spluttering and what he took to be Albanian curses. Suddenly, a large puce, unshaven face appeared in the aperture, its head soaked with liquid and reeking gently, the mouth uttering obscenities at him through short, broken, blackened teeth. Payne could not believe his luck, for a short length of the guard's red kerchief was sticking through the slats of the door. Payne lost no time but seized the material immediately, causing the man to sink to his knees increasing the stricture at his throat. A ghastly wheezing ensued as Payne hung on grimly, hoping the material would hold.

This commotion eventually brought the other guard to the door. Unwisely he unlocked it, at the same time trying to brandish his Kalishnikov. But Payne was ready for him. He took up the heavy table lamp and crashed it heavily across the man's shoulders, for he was taller than Payne had expected. This sent the second guard sprawling, dropping the assault rifle with a clatter in the process. Payne caught it, and grateful for its short length in the confined room, swung the weapon upward crashing it down on the man's skull – killing him instantly.

The first guard, on his knees in the open doorway, was choking and pleading for his life. Payne grabbed his keys, and baulking at another killing, bound the Albanian tightly with his own belt, then gagged him with one of the man's evil-smelling socks, held in place with the red kerchief that had been his undoing.

This done, Payne dragged him writhing and wheezing, back into the cell, to join his dead compatriot.

Payne stepped shakily out into the partial freedom of the passageway, locking the rough hewn door behind him with trembling fingers. Finally, he seized the passports from the table near the door and lumbered off up the passageway, seeking an outside door in the next stage of his quest for freedom.

Meanwhile, in a more generously appointed room at the end of the passage, the Chinese major awoke suddenly, and was for a moment unsure of where he was, a sensation heightened by the fact that he had re-arranged his room before retiring, to embody the principles of *Feng Shui*, thereby ensuring the promotion of positive energy and good fortune. However, on this occasion his oriental art was to let him down badly.

Hearing untoward noises and remembering that he had "guests", he dressed quickly and buckled on his holstered automatic. On stepping out into the corridor he came face to face with the fleeing Payne. It was difficult to know which man was the more surprised.

The Chinaman went for his gun but fumbled it. Payne, startled and acting on impulse, kicked him heavily in the testicles. As the major doubled in agony, Payne finished him off with a risky single shot to the ear – the part of the oriental's anatomy which happened to be closest to the Kalishnikov's muzzle at that moment. The bullet passed through the Major's brain and left a significant part of it on the greasy stone wall, together with copious quantities of blood.

Payne, tripping and retching, stumbled toward the end of the passageway, where he paused, momentarily, outside the door of another cell. Jack Prince's frightened face was framed unexpectedly in its aperture.

*   *   *

"Nothing in fine print is ever good news."

(A.Rooney)

Singapore March 31st 1998

Before the Event

After dinner, Hope–Watson retreated into the comparative coolness of his study for a post–prandial cognac and to escape his wife's and stepdaughter's chatter. However, on entering this male-orientated sanctuary, (Mi–Ling called it the "House of Commons" on account of its decor, dominated by green leather chairs and brass wall fittings) he immediately noticed that his new facsimile machine had delivered a substantial message which meandered across the pale green carpet.

Having determined its origin, Hope–Watson sighed expressing mixed feelings, for before reading any communication from the Funchal Far Eastern Club, it was currently necessary to refer to an anonymous code book which was replaced monthly. At first glance the initial reply to Hope-Watson's proposals, might have been interpreted as a rebuff. However...

From FFEC, Funchal Madeira, March 31st 1998

To: Rear Admiral Lloyd Hope–Watson (RN Retd) Singapore.

Thank you for your presentation concerning membership.

While we, the undersigned, look to you to provide the initial rallying point, the momentousness of what you suggest has never been tested before, not even by HAWKER and SIDDELEY – neither of whose philosophies, by the way, do we share. What you suggest is perhaps more Wellsian. (H.G.Wells was after all a closet Eugenicist and was in favour of PR and a NRD in spite of his brief dalliance with the FBS) .

Our agreed concerns are set out in *FFEC Memorandum of the 3rd January 98.*

If these concerns can be rectified within a reasonable timescale, then what you are suggesting *may be* justified.

As to the means, we leave this up to you and the SPECTOCOM you are assembling. We realise that LOLITA is unavoidable, indeed, germane to this process. We nevertheless regret it.

However, at this and indeed every stage of the process, our concern is that SOPWITH must be HOPE & CROSBY. For, although we are sure that you are already aware of this, it cannot be over-emphasised. If CARLA is ever CHAPERONED, we shall adopt DENISE and if necessary, join the ROYAL YACHT SQUADRON.

Remember that all those with P&O and a ROYAL WED-DING INVITATION, and who take the TRIPOS and have

TRAN-SUBTERRANEAN experience, BETEC must be SUSPENDED if RECOURSE remain.

Yours faithfully,

Secretary to the Joint Committee FFEC
From FFEC, Funchal Madeira, March 31st 1998.

Hope–Watson grimaced, put down the coded fax message and opened a small, discreet wall safe concealed behind a brass, marine clock. Having carefully unlocked and hinged the clock forward, he spun the combination wheel of the safe and quickly took out the Memorandum referred to in the FFEC fax. He had hammered out its highly controversial (and questionable) provisions on a visit to the FFEC earlier that year.

This document was in plain language (except for some key words and acronyms) so needed to be kept under lock and key. However, he made an urgent mental note to "do something" about the FFEC's communication security, for he considered the code employed in the faxes recently received, increasingly ludicrous. They would certainly not fool the CIA, or indeed any other competent intelligence service.

Peering imperiously into the inner reaches of the safe's green baize interior once more, Hope-Watson fished out the dog-eared FFEC code book for that month and with much grimacing and grumbling, translated the coded elements of the fax message. Having done so, it read thus:

To: Rear Admiral Lloyd Hope–Watson (RN Retd) Singapore.

Thank you for your presentation concerning membership.

While we look to you to provide the initial rallying point, the momentousness of your proposal has never been tested before, not even by Hitler or Stalin – neither of whose philosophies by the way, do we share.

What you suggest is perhaps more Wellsian. (H.G.Wells was after all a closet Eugenicist and was in favour of Population Reduction and a New Order, in spite of his brief dalliance with the Fabian Society.)

Our agreed concerns are set out in FFEC Memorandum of the 3rd January 98.

If these concerns can be rectified within a reasonable timescale, then your plan may be justified.

The means, we leave to you and the specialist team of experts and commandos you are assembling. We realise that loss of life is unavoidable, indeed, germane to this process. We nevertheless regret it.

However, at this and indeed every stage of the process, our concern is that security must be paramount! For although we are sure that you are already aware of this, it cannot be overemphasised. If Counter Strike! is ever compromised we shall Deny all knowledge of it and if necessary, renounce you.

Remember that all those with power and influence and a right wing inclination and who take the prolonged trips abroad and have transferred substantial sums overseas, before the EVENT commences, must be suspect if records remain.

Yours faithfully,

Secretary to the Joint Committee

FFEC Funchal, Maderia, March 31st 1998

Helping himself to a Cognac and a Havana, Hope–Watson turned to the Memorandum mentioned in the coded facsimile message.

FFEC Memorandum of the 3rd January 98.ALHW (Hope–Watson) to take command of COALMAN(Counter Strike!) and receive SAPPER (Financial Support) until 3 months after completion of:

The EVENT

The simultaneous, selective destruction of all installations, establishments, executive personnel and supporters (and where unavoidable, the employees) of allentities who uphold, or would be likely to prolong,the present moral, spiritual, environmental and comparative economic and social decline of Great Britain.

This operation to concentrate on the areas where such necessary destruction will have the greatest effect to achieve its purpose.

Any physical conflict with HM Forces should be minimised as the EVENT must take place without prior warning of any kind , and thereafter their role should mainly be rescue and coordination.

The help of other nations in the rescue phases shouldbe encouraged, and indeed will becomenecessary.However, political leadership will need to be retained at all costs, together with the fostering and preservation of Britain's international presence & influence. In particular, the United Nations Security Council.

Justification

1. It is regretted that the oldest democracy has now become so discredited and politically, economically and environmentally, corrupt, that it has finally become necessary to arrest its decline and moral disintegration from the Monarchy downwards. With the millennium approaching, the timing of this historical, yet necessarily painful event, is particularly appropriate.

On reading this passage, Hope–Watson recalled the words of his speech which had so obviously persuaded the powerful decision makers within the FFEC.

"The corruption of the very fabric of society has reached such a point that it is almost certainly irreversible by normal means. The people have lost faith in the politicians – as to the Monarchy they have become a media bauble and any example they might have provided to the populace has been lost in a series of sordid exposés..."

Hope–Watson sighed at the recollection of this minor triumph and returned to the memorandum before him.

2. To terminate increasing crime and lawlessness, drug abuse and the promulgation of gratuitous immorality via modern communications media, including the exploitation of children.

3. Unchecked traffic growth, threatening to destroy the environment and quality of life.

4. The usurping of 300 years of Parliamentary rule by our former enemies and their quislings.

5. Unchecked population growth, the source of all environmental and many other problems, such as public health, quality of life, crime, mental health, increasing twenty-four hour noise, pollution of land, sea, air and waterways.

The greatest danger of these maladies is that they are are self-perpetuating and never admitted by the media or government, for fear of alienating readers, advertisers, viewers, voters, compromising short term, vested interests.

Meanwhile, the planned environmental destruction of Southern England continues unchecked, where rural land equal in area to Greater London is due to disappear by 2016, and one fifth of England will be under concrete by 2050.

6. Profligate use of the motorcar by a large proportion of the population – with adverse affects on matters already mentioned and the persistent national neglect of an efficient and reliable public transport system – is a scenario which is unlikely to be checked by any effective political action, other than the highly drastic event you propose.

7 Regrettably, denigration of the stock market to the point of being a mere "funds casino", instead of serving its original purpose of long term funding for industry and commerce, and thereby providing an alternative to the greed and short termism of the banks. In any event, EEC Monetary Union has severely curtailed the City's competitiveness in world financial markets and this may well be in accordance with the wishes of a number of large EEC member states.

8 The sale of indigenous parts of the national economy and infrastructure, e.g. water, power, electricity and gas, which, while barely reducing government borrowing, has exposed vital services to foreign ownership and done little, if anything, to reduce monopoly.

9 The threat to free speech - one of the tenets on which the nation was founded - by the insidious cant of political correctness, which originated on undistinguished American University campuses as a joke!

10 The dilution of native British culture by low grade influences from the USA, manifesting itself in poor speech patterns, appalling dress sense, assinine TV programmes, films and junk food. (Unfortunately, the best of American culture does not survive the journey across the North Atlantic).

11 Also, it must be noted, that little, if any, Continental culture has managed to cross the English Channel. Any that exists was probably already part of UK society before the Treaty of Rome. This might be argued as a fairly damning indictment on the wider social concept of the EEC.

Hope–Watson did not finish reading the document. He would do that tomorrow when he was fresh. The important thing was that the Rubicon had now been crossed, and, because of that, tomorrow would be a big day – a historic day. What a pity there were so few with whom he could share the moment.

25

*"The truth
will ouch!"*

(Arnold H.Glasgow)

The Cotswolds, England
September 1998

Before the Event

'Julia! Your bloody boyfriend's a killer. It's here in the paper!' Jacqui Strakes was standing in Julia McMahon's chinzy lounge waiting for her friend to finish dressing.

There were sounds of muffled protest from above. Eventually Julia's shapely calves appeared as she delicately descended the narrow stairs.

'Jacqui, whatever are you raving about? And I do wish you wouldn't swear!'

Jacqui handed her the newspaper.

Julia put her Prada handbag on the coffee table and took the proffered newspaper. As she began to read she turned pale. It was a fairly small item on an inside page.

Missing Charter Jet Pilot Drama

The body of Brian James, the pilot of a Charter executive jet from Hawkfield Charter Company, Kent was recovered from the Adriatic Sea off South East Italy yesterday by Italian fishermen. According to the Italian coastguard, the body had been in the water for several days. There was no sign of his aircraft, a Gates Lear Jet, which left Hawkfield, Kent, last Friday morning.

A company spokesman said that Captain James, a senior pilot with the company for ten years, was taking a Mr Melvin Forbes, a South African Diamond dealer and his cutter, John Arthur Baker, to Albania. However, the Albanian authorities are reported as having no knowledge of the flight apart from a flight plan received last Friday, and that no one answering to the description of Forbes or Baker, has entered the country.

163

Gloucestershire police are anxious to interview Marcus Payne, a
South African citizen, and John Alan Prince, a self-employed
general dealer, in connection with the disappearance of Mr Princes'
wife, Mrs Amy Prince. Neither of the men has been seen since last
Thursday morning.

'My God!' exclaimed Julia, dropping the paper and
applying a delicate open hand to her chest. She sat heavily
in an armchair.

'Do you think he's dead?' enquired Jacqui.

'Who?' replied Julia, lifting a tousled head from her hands
and looking up.

'Well, Marcus,' said Jacqui uncertainly.

'Probably,' whispered Julia huskily. Then, as an afterthought, 'How should I know?'

'The newspaper's not very helpful,' Jacqui went on,'I mean
it doesn't say the plane, well...'

'Crashed?' moaned Julia, finishing the sentence for her.

'Well, yes.'

'Jacqueline,' retorted Julia with exaggerated patience,
'How do you suppose the plane could fly without a pilot?'

'I dunno...' There was a moment's rare silence between
them.

'Hang on...' Jacqui pealed excitedly, 'but Marcus could
fly...'

'What?' said Julia sharply, sounding more like her old
self.

'Yes. He told me one evening,.... in the club...'

'Did he, now?' Julia gave her one of her withering looks 'I
need a drink.' She got up abruptly.

'Golly. It's a bit early isn't it?'

Julia ignored this reproof, and having taken a bottle of
Tio Pepe and a small crystal glass from the sideboard, poured
herself an ample measure.

'Just a minute,' Julia said quickly, after sipping the sherry,
'What do you mean Marcus is a killer?'

Her friend was no fool, although few gave her credit for it.
As a junior school teacher, she had a good analytical mind,
and her favourite TV programme was Inspector Morse!

164

'I think it's quite obvious,' Jacqui answered boldly, as Julia, seated once more, watched her, wide-eyed and incredulous. 'Marcus must have dumped the pilot...'

'You're mad!' spluttered Julia, interrupting, 'How can you say that?'

'There was no sign of the plane...' Jacqui announced, dangerously confident.

'Is that surprising?' Julia almost screamed,'in two hundred feet of water!'

'No sign, Jules' Jacqui explained patiently, 'If the plane had gone down there would have been *something* – some floating objects, or traces...'

Julia snorted, 'You've been watching too much TV; since when have you been an expert on...?'

But Jacqui was in her stride now, and unabashed, rasped dramatically, 'Oil, seat cushions, plastic – anything buoyant...'

Julia calmed and began to look thoughtful.

'Don't tell me,' said Jacqui, pausing, hands on ample hips, a resigned expression replacing her excited flush, 'you're going to call Robin?'

Her moment centre stage had been brief.

*　　*　　*

> "If opportunity doesn't knock,
> build a door."
>
> (Milton Berle)

Payne was suffering from shock now, as well as fatigue. Three killings in thirty six hours! The little boy in him told him he wasn't really a killer – just a soldier, compromised. The man knew differently. What would Julia say? Part of him formulated the excuses he would make to her, the other knew that he would never see her again.

Seeing Prince's face grimly framed in the cell door had been unexpected. It was too soon. It forced a decision.

It was made. He aimed the Kalishnikov at the door and fired an ultra-short burst.

The lock shattered. He grabbed Prince's arm. The man shrieked, Prince's luck dictated that, of course. It was his injured limb!

They stumbled toward the outer door, just as an Albanian guard urged on by a vociferous Chinese officer, drew its bolts from outside. Payne raised the Kalishnikov once more and winced as its shattering roar, in the confined space, dispensed with the two men and much of the door.

Taking a deep breath of shock and relief, Payne coughed wretchedly in the lingering cordite smoke and tripped on the spent cartridges rolling at his feet.

Outside, he gazed wildly round, blinking in the bright sunlight. Like a trapped animal, Payne's first instinct was escape – instant escape – and for this he searched desperately for some sign of the airfield. Their luck was in, for there, above a belt of low trees, fluttered a ragged, dirty wind-sock.

*   *   *

*"Common sense
is genius dressed in its working clothes."*

(Ralph Waldo Emerson)

Robin Goodchild sat and tried to listen dispassionately, first to Jacqui Strakes and then to Julia, trying not to be distracted, for the skirt of her designer suit was short, and made shorter by the embrace of the soft armchair.

As he listened, his mind was on two tracks. Firstly, he began to agree with Jacqui's analysis. This was the first time he had been impressed by her disguised mental ability. Secondly, he wrestled with the blinding physical effect Julia still had upon him, and the resentful instincts aroused by the unfolding story they obliquely examined between them. For it revealed the extent of her association with Marcus Payne, and made hitherto unspoken facts, difficult to disguise.

Once again, he saw himself summoned to be the unpaid adviser in a difficult situation, which was none of his doing. While his better nature told him not to be churlish, his ego was bruised and demanded reward. In any event, the immediate question, having reviewed the probable facts, was what to do next.

'I think we should tell the police,' announced Jacqui, rather tactlessly.

'And tell them what, exactly?' demanded Julia, eyes blazing.

'What we have discussed, that we have reason to believe Marcus Payne and Jack Prince have left the country...'

'Well, they already *know* that don't they?' said Julia testily.

'I was *going* to say,' Jacqui went on resignedly, 'that they dumped the pilot and commandeered the plane. The authorities probably think that the plane crashed, with all hands – so to speak...'

'I wonder,' interjected Goodchild, thoughtfully.

Both the women looked at him, but in very different ways. Jacqui merely waited politely for his next word, having recently changed her opinion of him, while Julia... was weighing him up, appraising.

'As far as we know, there has been no prolonged search for the plane. I believe that it may have been tracked on radar, or was picked up on radio, after it left the area...'

'It's a pretty big area, Robin,' Jacqui interrupted. As a teacher, her geography was quite good! 'The pilot's body might have drifted for miles.'

'Yes, probably, but even so. If your hunch is correct, I think they landed in Albania as planned.'

'But they denied it,' said Julia.

'*They* might have good reason to,' Goodchild explained. 'After all, for one thing, it's a pretty valuable plane.'

'How valuable?' asked Jacqui, somewhat irrelevantly.

'At least a million,' replied Goodchild, matter-of-factly.

'Blimey!' exclaimed Jacqui.

'Yes, yes, alright,' huffed Julia impatiently, 'so they landed in Albania. What of it?'

'Well... ' began Goodchild, treading carefully, 'I think we owe it to the relatives of the pilot, and the owners of the plane, to ...'

'You're not going to *tell* them...' shrieked Julia, unexpectedly alarmed.

'Well, yes...' replied Goodchild, lamely.

'And why *not*?' demanded Jacqui, secretly gratified at seeing Julia discomforted by her own doing.

'The police... They'll want to know everything ...'

'I expect,' retorted Jacqui, briefly and mischievously.

'Oh do shut up, Jacqui!' Then turning to Robin, 'You've got to *do* something!' Julia's wide eyes were moist and appealing.

'I thought I *was*,' replied Goodchild, inadequately, regretting the words almost before they left his mouth.

26

Washington
December 1998

After the Event

In his pre-occupation to find out who was responsible for the destruction of Britain as a functioning nation, by the effective neutralisation of England, its industrial and political core, McIver was increasingly aware that he was being kept in unwarranted ignorance by the CIA, and by his political masters.

In self-examination, his mind went back to a report by a West Point instructor on his leadership qualities:

"I question whether Cadet McIver is quite ruthless enough in character to achieve high command."

If there had not been an unfortunate fire in that particular instructor's office – which destroyed many of his students' records, including McIver's, he doubted if he would be where he was today!

Clearly, he knew that at this point in his career, he must retain some promise of a political future himself, and to this end, it was essential not to allow anyone to align him as scapegoat. Yet he must also safeguard his friends and family. He needed to confide, but to do so could be dangerous, not merely from a breach of confidence, but because all who might share his suspicions would do so at their own risk. McIver was old-fashioned, he thought of others.

Meanwhile, officially, he must be prepared to take responsibility, militarily at least, for an effective and appropriate response to the devastating attack on Britain. But first must come the political initiative predicated on his, and his senior staff's advice. But how to advise the inadvisable, a body politic that knew something more than him? Yet it was also true that he almost certainly knew something that others did not – but to expound it in an unsatisfactory way or inappropriate time, might end his career by giving the excuse needed.

To tackle this dilemma, McIver needed more information, both militarily and politically covert in character. For this he had turned to Barry Hartog, close friend and undoubted expert in his particular field.

*   *   *

Hearing shouts from behind the hutted complex, Payne urged Prince into a run. Stumbling, the two fugitives made off across uneven sandy ground, covered by coarse grass, concealing they knew not what hazard. They had just gained a small hollow, when Payne heard a zipping sound, followed by another. Ahead a fountain of dust and sand, spurted. Abruptly, the Kalishnikov was ripped from his grasp. A lucky shot had contacted the weapon and it now lay half buried, some yards distant. Payne pulled Prince down, and both men crawled, panting and desperate, to regain the weapon, their mechanical salvation.

Time was short.

The shouts were coming closer. Payne at last reached the assault rifle. He tugged, but it would not budge, held embedded in its sandy resting place. By the time he had released it from an emerging strand of rusty barbed wire, snagging the curved magazine, their captors were almost upon them.

Prince panicked.

'Get down you fool!' hissed Payne through clenched teeth. But in a scenario which lasted seconds, but seemed like minutes, Prince half stood, wincing as he tried to support himself with his injured arm.

'I can't go on, I'm goin' t'see if...' He never finished the sentence, but spun round sharply, facing the kneeling Payne, a look of extreme surprise on his rotund face. 'A-m-y!' he cried, uttering his late wife's name for the last time, and fell face down, inches from Payne's grubby, outstretched hand.

'Christ!' moaned Payne, experiencing unexpected remorse. He was at once, very much alone.

The shouts were immediately above him then, and he knew fear. Looking up wildly, he saw a Chinese officer and three Albanians, the first of whom released a large, dark German Shepherd dog – at first panting heavily, then leaping, teeth bared, toward him. The Chinese officer brandished a murderous looking handgun and was shouting something in Mandarin.

Payne raised the now-battered Kalishnikov for the last time. He pulled the trigger and heard that sickening, dull click that signifies an empty gun.

'Hell, this is *it!*' he rasped out loud, and feeling strangely detached from the events about to overwhelm him, thought vividly of Julia.

Just then the ground gave way and Payne fell...

Darkness. Falling, falling, tumbling. Sand gritting his hair, blocking his ears and nostrils..

Was this hell? Payne panicked. Better the dog – or the Chinaman's bullet than to be buried alive!

Those who have said to have experienced the near threshold of death, and yet returned, just in time, to life – all speak of glimpsing, or entering, *a tunnel filled with a bright light, shining from its end.* Payne now found himself in that tunnel!

'Was he dead?' he asked himself in initial painful terror. No, this one was *real* – it stank of diesel oil and Avgas!

Lying choking and spitting the sand from his mouth, he found himself at last, at the very edge of his goal – the airfield! And there, framed in the tunnel entrance, the dull metal of a single engined plane, glinted – invitingly.

Bermuda

Before the Event.

In the spring of 1998, Hope-Watson, was on leave from his official duties.

Travelling and posing incognito, he blended well with the rich clientele of the Grand Ocean Hotel in Hamilton. He was a man whose tastes inclined toward Patek Philippe, rather than Rolex, his dress distinguished by those discreet touches of wealth, four buttons at his jacket sleeve, rather than the plebeian three, the exact shade and weave of his lightweight suits, and the fullness or silk finesse of his ties, depending on the hour and the occasion. However, whenever possible, discreet dark glasses were *de rigeur*, which presented no difficulty since, as might be expected, most people wore them in sub-tropical Bermuda, nearly all the year round – even when it rained!

Retiring from the public terrace to the privacy of his room, Hope-Watson was trying out the first of his speeches to be presented to the Malthusian, Syndicate Bermuda, a select, collusive and vitally important, fund-raising element for the cause.

However, his attention span was curtailed by the humidity, and his gaze wandered to the two day old copy of the pink Financial Times blending well with the counterpane! What caught his eye was a news item concerning Liverpool, a city of which he originally had fond memories from his early naval cadet days. But things had changed, and so had his opinion of that boisterous metropolis.

...12 shootings in 13 weeks adding up to 43 in the year...

Betting shop shooting almost certainly drugs related. ...Police chief worried that drug dealers were infiltrating the Civic structure of the city to feign respectability.

The prospect of an ex -(or indeed active!) drug baron, as a future Chairman of the Police Committee could not be ruled out!

Hope-Watson's first reaction to such news was predictable, and reflected in the tone of the speech he was now rehearsing – and in his later life's work. Nevertheless, always the opportunist – where his prime cause was concerned – his devious and productive mind began to establish a possible linkage, encapsulated in the truisim his old training captain had instilled in him when Hope-Watson was a naval cadet, 'Always try to turn a disadvantage into an advantage!'.

*   *   *

The next evening he gave his presentation to Syndicate Bermuda in their palatial and panoramic clubhouse, near Great Bermuda's highest point, Gibbs Hill – all of 256 feet above the turquoise Atlantic. Security was especially tight, numbers limited and all present heavily vetted and sworn to secrecy – on pain of even more tangible constraints!

Its finale began with the following rousing declarations:

'It's the clean slate syndrome, gentlemen!

Our aim, is to replace all the present day centres of power, most of which are clearly misguided – not only regarding the benefit of the individual citizen but the nation as a whole.

All the finest elements, which formerly set Britain aside as a leader, economically, morally and spiritually, have been, and are being, eroded.

The Monarchy has become degraded and a focus for sleazy speculation. If no suitable inheritant is found, to continue the Royal line – and maintain the respect of the people, I am afraid it may have to be replaced.'

Hope-Watson paused here, inadvertently allowing an interjection from a member of the audience, whose face he could not see because of the spotlights illuminating the dais. However, the heckler was distinguishable by the fact that he was wearing evening dress, or at least a bow tie.

'Yes, but how many of the people will be left to maintain the respect you mention?'

Hope-Watson paused to take a sip of water, before he replied,

'I'm afraid *that* is the nettle we must all grasp, if we are to take this daunting and urgent matter, forward.

In fact, it pinpoints the essence of the great dichotomy of human existence: namely that *human lives* are both the *most precious*, and at the same time, often, the *cheapest* commodity – in economic terms – and sadly, in the wider environmental sense also.

Illustrations of this are many, but just two will suffice. Widescale unemployment and rigid employment selection (where most are discarded) are dependent on the simple balance of labour, supply and demand, at a moment in time. Those unsuccessful must fend for themselves, and...'

But the man with the bow tie, boldly interrupted, and all eyes were upon him:

'Yes, but not to be *murdered!* Can there really be no warning, so that people can leave, or at least protect themselves...?'

Hope-Watson replied patiently enough,

'Unfortunately, it is simply not possible to issue advance warnings, for paramount security reasons, of which you should already be aware. To do so would jeopardise the whole movement and alert defensive forces. Complete surprise is essential.'

The heckler then replied in steady clear high tones, lending untruth to the later rumour that he had surely been drunk.

'I'm just rather concerned that you might be *enjoying* this,' he retorted, unwisely. 'After all, most despots bear a grudge. Is this not merely another case of "throwing all your toys out of the pram", on a fearful and irremediable scale?'

(Assembled gasps at this)

Catcalls and shouts of "shame", ensued, and many other mutterings besides.

But Hope-Watson could not help smiling. This showed, and the audience warmed to him because of it.

'Well, let me say that I feel I should be annoyed by what has just been said, but I, genuinely, am not, and I'll tell you why. These are valid points which need examining, and history will judge us on them – or something similar. So I am grateful to the gentleman and I also believe that his colourful language was necessary to highlight the matter. We are indebted to him!

I shall be happy to explain matters further, *after* this meeting, if he will kindly leave his name with the secretary...'

However, the man in the bow tie, his person still obscured in shadow, replied with rising emotion:

'But these matters need discussion – in *open meeting ...now!*'

Yet this was *not* an open meeting, and so he was shouted down, and quickly left the meeting – followed by several of the ushers, an ample number of whom, stood at various points about the edge of the large, darkened room. Immediately afterwards, a transient waft of welcome night air entered the forum, momentarily lowering the tension and the temperature; a little visiting goodness, soon to be overwhelmed by the baneful atmosphere within.

After a brief pause, during which the hubbub quickly fell to an acceptable level, Hope-Watson continued with his *prepared* speech – once more:

'... *the very fabric of our home society is being destroyed and replaced with, the banal, the worst excesses of commercialism, coupled with moral and spiritual decline.*'

'*This last point brings me to the moral influence of the Church in Britain, or what remains of it!*'

This remark was greeted with nervous laughter.

'*Ladies and Gentlemen, moral leadership based on Judeo Christian principles is being replaced by a lemming-like course of pandering to every human deviation, including, homosexuality, feminism, disingenuousness, and the very denial of the Resurrection – and even God,*

175

as a being - the very rock on which Christianity, the Church and spiritual England was founded.

We need not mention Catholicism, except to say that it continues to advocate the internationally irresponsible message of free birth, without any reliable means of contraception, a recipe, Gentleman, for famine, disease, over-crowding, crime, wars and environmental destruction..., perpetuating its dogma through the influence of ancient Bablyonic practices,'

'Shame!' shouted yet another single dissenter, a member of the small Irish Catholic contingent, and he noisily prepared to leave. Once again, the man was followed, and this time Hope-Watson did not bother to reply, but continued, unabashed.

'...An increasing section of the media is promulgat-ing sex and pornography. Our children and grandchil-dren are being corrupted as we speak, by violent videos and films.'

Meanwhile, in the wings of the small stage, which Hope-Watson now dominated so effectively, two senior members of Syndicate Bermuda – conversed confidentially, in lowered tones tinged with concern.

'My God, George, he's certainly got the bit between his teeth...'

'I know,' said his companion, 'I get the feeling I'm on a rollercoaster that's increasingly out of control!'

'I hope you're not getting cold feet, old chap. The walls have ears you know.'

'Quite, and what can one do, at this late stage?'

'Let's go and have a drink,' replied his comrade, ducking the import of the question, and they made their way slowly to the bar, Hope-Watson's diatribe ringing in their ears, but fading slightly, as they went.

'The British countryside: one of the last and finest managed landscapes in the world, is being beset by misguided road building, with every increase in its area, an increase in polluting filth, and a corresponding decrease in greenery, freshness and beauty ...'

Where now are the fragrant pastures and meadows through which we used to run as children?'

As the two erstwhile members reached the rather intimidating, sound proof glass doors of the bar, they lingered, listening, before going through, coincident with Hope-Watson's on-stage pause for dramatic effect.

Then...

'Grubbed up, gentlemen! for some monstrous motorway, or agro-wilderness, where no larks sing – all advocated by Brussels!'

They nodded wryly to each other, in mock agreement at this last gruff cadence, before the big, brass bar handles and the heavy plate glass wooshed and swung to behind them, as they entered a, temporarily, more convivial, domain.

*   *   *

The next morning, the sun awoke Bermuda's coral sand shores with a pinkish kiss – illuminating its islets, causeways and bridges, in soft focus, between Hamilton Town and Great Sound, up to Port Royal Bay. At the clear, murmuring water's edge of the gently washed beach, a darkish, linear and recumbent shape, moved back and forth in unison with the subdued and sparkling surf. The bow tie seemed incongruous at that hour, and the crimson that oozed beneath it spoiled the, otherwise idyllic, wholesomeness of the spot.

Later, on the terrace of the Grand Ocean Hotel at Hamilton, Hope-Watson had breakfast, served from silver dishes. Afterwards, he breathed in the fine clear air and sighed contentedly. For the moment, he did not miss the Straits at all!

Whether it was for reasons of diligence or vanity, next to the Frank Cooper's Oxford marmalade, in its glinting dish, a small black Olympus Pearlcorder played softly, delivering metallically, the closing stages of his speech:

'And what of employment? The young are idle on the streets, taking drugs and other noxious substances. A lost generation!

While those over forty-five or fifty are cast out from their careers, yes careers gentlemen, not just jobs. For they will never be employed in their homeland again. Twenty and thirty years experience and knowledge disregarded and taken from an economy starved of long term wisdom and that all so rare commodity – common sense!

To be replaced by what or whom? A machine? Or a teenage girl who knows nothing – except perhaps, where her next packet of drugs may be had? Or when her next period is due!

We have experienced the spectacle of an Italian woman from the EEC, telling our fishermen, that they can no longer carry on their trade, which their fore-fathers have plied for 600 years, because there is not enough fish in our coastal waters for the rest of Europe! Britain has found to its cost that it has an entirely different economy from those on the European continent. The UK is still a dollar-based economy, whereas continental economies are based on the German Mark. The ERM debâcle was characterized by the UK joining while in recession at far too high a rate against the Deutsche Mark, while Germany was in a post unification boom. Consequently many UK homes and businesses were sacrificed in paying for that boom.'

A muffled thumping, then came the finale – a repetitious piece de resistance!....

'No more drug addicts
No more unchecked crime
No more delinquency
No more ram raiders
No more lefty BBC
No more Liberal 'Reward the Criminal' judiciary

No more persecution of the old by the young
No more TV watching infants
It's the new Jerusalem, gentlemen!'

As the clapping that had preceded a standing ovation began, together with the first bars of Parry's *"Jerusalem"*, Hope-Watson leaned over, and switched off the machine, leaving no sound but the slapping of the wavelets on the beach below and the chink of expensive crockery behind.

27

Albania

Before the Event

The plane was a single-engined Yak aerobatic aircraft, a type not uncommon in air displays in South Africa, before Payne had left his native country in the late nineteen-eighties. The sight of it brought forth a welter of mixed feelings: nostalgia, relief, and finally, anxiety – which begged the vital questions. Could he fly it? Was it fit to fly? At least, as far as Payne could tell from his present location, it remained unattended.

Emerging from the smelly tunnel, he walked watchfully but quickly toward the plane, bending forward as he went. On reaching the protection of its wings, he inspected the machine cautiously. An old refuelling truck stood some way off, apparently deserted. With any luck, thought Payne, the aircraft had just been refuelled.

He realised that he had precious little time before his pursuers found him. For although it was unlikely that they would take his unorthodox route into the tunnel, they would have vehicles, and having deduced his whereabouts, converge on their quarry and entrap him. However, for the moment...

Surveying the airfield horizon, Payne could detect no immediate signs of life or movement, apart from some circling birds. The sun was up in an almost cloudless sky...

Good flying weather!

It was strangely silent. But in these quite, clear conditions, sound carried...

Off to the East – Payne judged according to the position of the sun – at the very periphery of the vast area of yellow concrete and dusty grass – the faintest sound of a motor vehicle engine could be heard – or perhaps more than one – far off, and not yet in sight.

Were they coming for him?

He approached the Yak with fear and purpose now. He climbed – a little painfully – onto the wing. The canopy was open. He reached into the compact cockpit, lifted the straps of the safety harness from the pilot's seat and clambered in. The plane seemed to fit him like a glove. It was a good and reassuring feeling.

With the stick between his knees and his aching feet resting lightly on the worn metal rudder pedals, his tired eyes searched quickly across the chipped black paint of the instrument panel.

The notation was in Russian.

First, with the starting sequence urgently in mind, Payne hunted for the ignition switches, fuel gauge and battery switch...

He hesitated, and nervously surveyed the silent airfield. Then, of necessity, he struggled to recall a distant conversation in the bar of his local flying club. A visiting pilot, having arrived in a similar Russian machine, had described a starting sequence that involved a compressed air starter system...

With this in mind, and with sweat beginning to bead on his forehead and his heart pounding, Payne searched the little cockpit for the main pneumatic valve. During this quest he located the air intake shutter control and the starter switch. Then, at last, he found what could only be the main air valve!

However, before starting the big, radial piston engine, he needed to know if the small aircraft had sufficient fuel for a flight to Larissa, in Greece – some one hundred and fifty miles to the South East. From there, Payne reasoned, he might get a scheduled flight from Athens to Singapore, where he was determined to confront Hope–Watson. Crossing into

Greek airspace and landing at Larissa might be problematical, but he would have to deal with those difficulties as they arose. Anywhere was safer than where he was right now!

Pressing his foot on the right-hand rudder pedal and balancing its weight with the left, he felt the hard reassurance of the American Express Card, still secured under his right instep by sticking plaster. Thankfully, it had not been removed or detected by his former captives.

Having found the fuel gauge and the battery master switch, Payne watched the white indicator lights climb slowly toward three quarter full, just as the roar of approaching vehicle engines became ominously more distinct. Looking up, he could just make out two square dots on the horizon – their images apparently dancing – suspended above terra-firma in the shimmering heat haze...

Time was short before the first bullet. It came soon enough...

A resounding clang startled him as the first round struck the cab of the refuelling truck. Either they were poor shots or cleverer than he had given them credit for – if they hit the tanker, both he, and the plane, would probably go up with it!

The indicator lights on the main tank fuel gauge were still, mercifully, climbing, but Payne could wait no longer. Briefly checking that the elevator trim was neutral, and the brakes were applied, he turned the main air valve to "on," set the throttle a few centimetres open and pressed the starter. The engine turned and coughed and a plume of acrid blue smoke blew past the cockpit, before the big piston engine clanked to a stubborn halt. A jolt of horror hit him. Radial engines would often refuse to start without pulling the propeller through several revolutions, *by hand!* He had a stark choice: either to keep gunning the starter and risk exhausting the reservoir of compressed air, or to get out and turn the big propeller. Considering his present position – a highly risky, and time-consuming manoeuvre!

Payne began to release his straps, but decided it was too late. The choice was made for him by a further two bullets striking the refueller. It was now clear that either the vehicle was interposed between his pursuers and the Yak, or it was their intended target. But although at first, Payne prayed for the former situation, his fatigued brain quickly acknowledged that in either case, his chances were poor without some means to defend himself.

For the moment, there was nothing for it but to try the starter once more and hope the engine would fire, and *keep running*, before the plane's pneumatic starting system gave out.

He pressed the starter button again as another bullet sang over the canopy. They were getting his range. He closed the canopy with a reflex action, hoping vainly that the thin plexiglass might give him at least some protection.

The engine coughed once more and stuttered, as the two blade propeller arced before him; a black hesitating shape across the brilliant blue of the sky then stopped mockingly in the vertical position.

Keeping low, and perspiring freely in the rapidly heating cockpit, Payne pushed the starter button again, rewarded by a wheezing sound and an inconsequential circulation of the airscrew.

Panic gripped him.

Suddenly he remembered... What a fool he had been to overlook the obvious! There must be a cockpit activated engine primer pump! After several panic–stricken seconds, he found the primer and gave it six good squirts – hoping that it would be good enough.

He pressed the air starter once more...

Crack...!

An incoming bullet starred the upper canopy glass, concurrent with a throaty roar from the engine and a bone-tingling vibration. The propeller ahead of him transformed from an accusing dark digit against the bright blue sky, to a semi–circular transparent blur.

Gasping with relief, Payne released the brakes – giving vent to the hiss of escaping air. Then, easing the throttle forward, the Yak hesitated, then trundled forward with a jerk. Throttling back slightly, Payne shielded his sweat–smarting eyes against the dazzling sun, as he sought a safe path to the runway; taking a direction he hoped might simultaneously distance himself from his pursuers.

Fortunately, such a light plane was not restricted to the defined concrete taxiways, and he turned sharp left, setting the throttle to give as fast a taxiing speed as he dare. He was aiming instinctively for the threshold of the runway which would allow an Easterly take–off direction, merely to take him away from the men in the jeeps. As there was little or no wind, any runway would suffice.

Payne could plainly see his pursuers now, and his mouth went dry. The two jeeps quickly changed direction toward him from the South East. He eased the throttle forward a little more, but in spite of the fact that he had the stick back to prevent the little plane nosing over on the bumpy terrain, the tail began to lift alarmingly above the uneven surface, making steering difficult. Keeping his head low, he glanced wildly round the cramped, unfamiliar cockpit for some answer to his looming problem, when there, protruding from a socket in the floor, was the shiny black butt of a hand–gun. It was a large bore, signal pistol.

*   *   *

Robin Goodchild decided early one Sunday morning that it was time to force the pace and take Julia away for the weekend. With Payne out of the way, it was not only an opportunity for him but would provide a much-needed change of scene for her.

There was only one restriction as far as he was concerned. It would have to be Brussels, as his work took him there most weekdays, but next weekend was his first Friday night stopover, returning Sunday evening trip. After all Julia might appreciate the novelty of him piloting the plane which conveyed her there and back. As to whether or not to book a single or double room, he thought it on the safe side to book singles and see what developed! In any event, he thought it better to hurry and get it arranged before the popular Miss McMahon's social calendar was booked up.

'Why yes, Robin, that would be nice. I've never been to Brussels and I've heard so much about it!'

And so it was that this somewhat disparate couple left Birmingham International Airport on the Friday night flight to Brussels with Goodchild as second officer at the controls on the flight deck, and Julia McMahon not far behind him, in the curtained off Business Class. The date was the 23rd October, 1998.

*   *   *

'What about this GCHQ?' Hartog enquired.

McIver got up and drew back the the blinds and looked down on the Potomac River – it was almost morning. It had been a long session.

'What about it?' he said stretching.

'Well, I understand the Brits spend – or used to spend – over one and a half billion dollars on security services,' Hartog replied, looking up blearily, from his pile of notes.

'Yes, that's right,' McIver yawned. 'Je–sus, I need some coffee.'

'Of what exactly, did that expenditure comprise?' Hartog persisted, peering over his reading glasses.

'Oh, MI5, MI6 and GCHQ, I guess,' replied McIver, sitting opposite with his hands behind his head.

'Can you explain those components, George, I'm a little weak on foreign security services...'

McIver stepped up to a wallboard and taking a marker, drew a simple block diagram, revealing the main components of the British Security system – or as it had been. He explained with some irony, that *he* did not yet know which elements had survived, but he guessed they would all be overseas.

He explained wearily, 'The Prime Minister is – er, was – in overall control, but MI6, the foreign and military intelligence element, came under the Foreign Secretary, whereas...'

McIver pointed to the right of the diagram, 'MI5, the domestic element, came under the Home Secretary.'

'And GCHQ...?' enquired Hartog, looking up red-eyed but alert.

'Controlled by joint Ministry of Defence and Foreign Office Liaison,

There are – were – intelligence controllers for the UK, Europe, Western Hemisphere and the Middle East.'

'How did they pick up on the Middle East?' Hartog queried.

'OK, let me think,' McIver hesitated, rubbing his head and looking down, eyes momentarily closed, 'Oh yeah, there's a SIGNIT listening post in the Troodos Mountains..., in Cyprus, which incidentally – as you might expect, is still intact.'

'You mean Cyprus?' Smiled Hartog mischievously, picking up on McIver's slight grammatical error.

McIver half-heartedly threw the plastic top of a marker pen at him and smiled ruefully.

'OK..., I guess it would be,' mumbled Hartog, thoughtfully rubbing his eyes, and tossing his pencil on the table with a clatter. 'We need to look at that, but right now, let's go and have breakfast!'

28

*"Modern Western life
is like a ship wreck –
it's every man for himself!'*

(R.T.T)

———

Albania

Before the Event

Payne reached down and tugged on the black butt of the signal pistol, praying that it was loaded, for at first glance round the little cockpit he could see no spare cartridges. The pistol freed from its location in the cockpit floor and he took it up in his right hand while steadying the control column with his left. He managed to snap open the breech. There, nestling in the one and a half inch barrel, was the brass base of a fat signal cartridge.

The two jeeps were approaching fast from his right, one behind the other. That was their mistake. Payne opened the canopy of the bouncing plane enough to aim the big pistol at the leading jeep. With difficulty, from the bucking aircraft, he pointed the snub barrel slightly above the driver's windscreen and squeezed the trigger. There was a loud crack and a *woosh* as the projectile struck the dusty windscreen and exploded with a deafening bang and cloud of greyish white smoke and windscreen shards. Luckily for Payne, the round was a white smoke puff – the most powerful and long ranged of all signal ordnance. The leading jeep at once veered sharply to the right, and – hitting a patch of rough ground with its front wheels at an acute angle, promptly turned over, spilling its driver and armed passengers out onto the rough ground like rag dolls. The following jeep, going too fast to take avoiding action, struck the first vehicle and rode up and over it with a resounding clang, at once emitting a cloud of steam from its ruptured radiator.

All this happened in a instant, and Payne in the bucking, roaring Yak was soon past the scene. In his mirror, through the brown, swirling dust, he glimpsed broken, runway approach lights, and realised that at last, he was approaching the runway threshold. Turning the machine to the right, he found himself on the black and dirty white, vertical bars of tarmac, that marked the threshold itself. The large dirty white letters, 07, denoted the runway heading of 070 degrees – North East. He ran the Yak straight onto the runway proper, pausing only to check the trim, and with the rudder almost fully left to counteract the engine take–off torque, he opened the throttle to maximum boost.

The powerful little plane roared down the runway, raising an enormous dust cloud. Payne could see no distance markers, but after only a little more than ten seconds at full power, the aircraft seemed to want to get airborne. He glanced at the air speed indicator and at 120 kph, eased gingerly back on the stick. He was rewarded by what he could see of the airfield below from either side of the small cockpit, fall away. He was airborne! Forward visibility was nil! The only view here was the Yak's sharply upward sloping, squat rounded nose, vibrating slightly under full power and filling the sky before and above him. After gaining height and exhilarated by his escape, Payne eased stick and rudder, turning cautiously to starboard, until the bubble compass read 135 degrees. He was on his way to Greece!

*   *   *

'How about dinner in the *Grand Place?*' Goodchild blurted out impulsively as Julia was unpacking.

'Er – fine,'replied Julia looking over her shoulder, not quite sure where, or what the *Grand Place* was, but not wishing to display her ignorance.

Goodchild had prudently booked separate rooms and had just looked in to finalise the evening's arrangements. Then Julia said something charming, followed by something mildly perplexing.

'Well, don't you look sexy in your uniform?' she remarked with a delicious giggle.

Goodchild who had not had time to change, flushed. Then Julia said:

'Will you be a darling and excuse me a while? I need to make an urgent phone call. I'll see you in the lobby at what, 7.30?'

'Fine,' said Goodchild, 'I'll book a table for 8.00.'

When he had closed the door, Julia paused, before opening her personal organiser, which never left her. Then she crossed to the bedside telephone and asked, in perfect French, for an outside line

*　　*　　*

The Grand Place at the very centre of old Brussels, originally the town's *Nedermerct*, or lower market place, is dominated by the elaborate Gothic Town Hall. Although the medieval, cobbled square is flanked by impressive ancient guild houses, and warmly-lit and inviting restaurants, the town hall remains its focal point. Its gables and cornices, softly illuminated at night, in gentle coloured lights – giving it an almost magical and ethereal appearance. A strangely reassuring link with the past, looking benevolently down on a sometimes soulless present.

Seated in one of the most elegant hostelries, *Maison du Cygne*, and satiated with good food and wine, Robin Goodchild and Julia McMahon were enjoying the delightful music and light show centred on the Town Hall.

Goodchild was at the nearest point to happiness in his thirty seven years.

Suddenly Julia leaned forward and gazed at him intently, delicate wafts of Chanel emanating from the low cut neck of her silky black dress. The miniature diamonds in her fine gold necklet, sparkled in the soft candlelight. A shapely knee brushed his.

'Robin,' she announced coquettishly, emboldened by the fine burgundy in her crystal glass, reflecting its soft red fire on to the crisp white tablecloth, 'You're wondering, aren't you?'

Goodchild was taken unawares. Her charming enquiry lent piquancy to the warm glow which presently enveloped him.

'Er – wondering what, Julia.' His thoughts raced through the possibilities of his supposed wonderment.

He had hoped he had suppressed any outward clue as to his thoughts, but evidently not, for Julia drew back from him, taking away the slender hand, and the delicate elbow that had supported it, remarking with mock indignation, 'And I don't mean *that* either, you naughty boy!'

Goodchild flushed, 'I really didn't mean...'

But she interrupted him, leaning forward again, large eyes gazing into his, making his head spin.

'I mean,' she began, 'you've been wondering whom I rang at the hotel – before we came out..?'

'Well, it's none of my business...'

'Yes it *is*, Robin...' She reached out, again and placed her hand over his, together on the pristine tablecloth. He looked down at this most innocent of physical coupling, and in spite of himself, dared to hope for more.

'It was Jacqui,' Julia went on, her voice acquiring a delicious subdued huskiness.

'Oh,' said Goodchild, mildly relieved, 'what did she say?'

'She said,' Julia almost whispered, 'that I should give you a chance.'

Goodchild gulped, the muscles in his neck tightening.

'I can't think *what* she meant.' Julia cooed, leaning back and taking up her glass once more – eyeing him wickedly.

Back at the Novotel Hotel near the airport, they made love – and Goodchild's happiness was complete. It was short lived, for shortly afterwards the bedside telephone rang.

It was the airline handling agent. Their aircraft had developed a fault in Birmingham and would not be available for the Sunday evening Brussels turn–round. A great deal of telephoning to the Captain of the aircraft (who was staying in another hotel), to the handling agent, and to their

Birmingham base, signalled the end of the social aspect of their weekend.

Eventually, they learned that their flight was delayed from Sunday evening and would take off at 7.30 am on Monday morning from Brussels National Airport at Zaventem.

*   *   *

> *"And now abideth faith, hope, love...,*
> *these three;*
> *but the greatest of these is...*
> *love."*
>
> (From St Paul's Letter to the Corinthians)

'Marcus, where are we going?'

'It's time to leave, Julia. Please trust me. There's not too much time to waste.'

'Why? I don't understand.'

'Please Julia, get in the car.'

'I should call Robin and Jacqui..., I...'

'There's no time for that now.' Marcus was insistent.

'I've never seen you like this, before. Where are we going?'

'To the airport.'

'But at this hour. There'll be no flights. Anyway, where to?'

'I have a private plane waiting. I'll explain on the way.'

Julia stared at him, and then took one despairing look at her cosy home, its lights warmly blazing, and feared she would never see it again.

She awoke with a start. Her mobile phone was ringing, its tone muffled slightly. Goodchild breathed peacefully beside her. His unremembered presence was a shock – especially after her dream!

She eventually located her diminutive telephone, buried in her handbag.

The call was from Jacqui. Julia glanced, eyes smarting,

head spinning from the previous evening's reverie, at the illuminated bedside digital clock. It was early, *5.10am, Monday, 26th October, 1998.*

'Jacqui, what the ...? Whatever is it..?'

'Jules, something, something...,' Jacqui sobbed, 'something awful's happening here... I can't understand it!' There were muffled rumbling sounds in the background and the line crackled.

Then, Jacqui Strakes voice changed, strange, shrill and rising on a growing cadence.

'I... I *love* you, Jules...!' the transmission faltered and wavered ethereally. Then a final awful sound Julia wished she had been spared – the sound of her dearest, and most stalwart friend, dying!

The phone went dead.

Julia screamed into the small, lifeless black instrument, 'Jacqui, *love*, what is it? What *is* it!'

Goodchild woke with a start to find Julia in hysterics, exhorting him to, *do something!* before falling, distraught, prostrate and unyielding, into his bare, cold, aching arms.

It was the beginning of a terrible day.

29

*"Necessity is the mother
of taking chances."*

(Mark Twain)

Athens, Greece

Before the Event

Payne flew low across the Albanian countryside leaving the coast behind him with its hundreds of ruined bunkers and pill boxes, a legacy from its troubled past, mixing with the beauty of the last unspoilt coastline in the Mediterranean. Looking down he saw white sandy beaches and islands with trees and, turning inland, citrus and olive groves among the stark shells of unfinished and unregulated building.

He would liked to have flown over the Byzantine ruins of Butrint, further South, but this would be an indulgence which would cost valuable time and fuel. Crossing the Greek border would be a hazard. If Greek air defences should spot him... He decided he must keep low, very low.

He was beginning to have second thoughts about Larissa as he vaguely remembered that it might still be a Greek Air Force station. He had no maps, apart from those in his *International Travellers* diary. As his ultimate destination was Athens, it made sense to get as near to it as possible. Accordingly, he changed to a more southerly course. He was fairly sure he could land the Yak on any smooth flat surface and could therefore forego the facilities and official dangers of an established airfield. The less people who saw him enter the country – and by what means, the better.

Seven hundred feet felt dangerously low, especially as the terrain became increasingly hilly. It was also very hot and sweaty under the plexiglass canopy, and Payne struggled to open it a little. His single armed struggle was

193

rewarded by warm blasts of air which buffetted him and refreshed him marginally, as the little plane bucked and twisted in the rising air currents.

He had only been to Athens once before with his father, and that had been some ten years earlier. He remembered the coast road near Nea Makri and decided to head for it as the coast would give him a good bearing.

So it was that, a little over an hour and fifteen minutes later, he glimpsed the blue of the sea beyond his port wing tip. The terrain beneath him was undulating and brown, but the occasional glimpse of the sea was uplifting. Eventually a fair-sized town came into view which he hoped was Marathon, but might be Nea Makri, five or six miles further South. In either event, it was time to turn inland again. He was halfway through a 90 degree turn to starboard when the engine coughed, spluttered and assumed sonorous full song again. Payne panicked. Of course, he was almost at the limit of his endurance! The turn must have temporarily starved the motor of fuel. It was time to get down; he could not be much more than twelve or fifteen miles from Athens.

In the hazy distance to port, he could just see a large road with the sun glinting on the windscreens of cars and endless streams of trucks. It must be the Rafina-Pikermi-Athens main road. Ahead he searched frantically for a suitable landing site, before it was chosen for him by his near empty fuel tank!

Below him the dusty hilly terrain swept by remorselessly, the countryside giving way to the first signs of Athenian suburbia. He must get down, but where?

Two basic choices occurred to him: they were, land on a little used road – if he could find one straight and wide enough – they all seemed windy, hilly, or they were occupied by streams of trucks; the other choice was of course, the land itself, rapidly being taken up by villas and industrial or farm buildings. There was a third choice, land in water, the sea – or perhaps the foreshore. He remembered a beach, of sorts, at the small seaside resort of Mati, on the coast road South of Marathon. If he failed to get down there, then there was always the great plain of Marathon itself.

The decision was made.

Payne turned the Yak 180 degrees, away from the impending fume-filled, hazy sprawl of Athens, and back toward the coast, and hoped desperately that the fuel would hold out long enough for a controlled landing.

* * *

Brussels

After the Event

At breakfast Julia was still very upset. The news from across the English Channel was consistently confusing and increasingly grave.

Both she and Goodchild sat in silence in the big impersonal hotel restaurant, the predominant colour scheme of which appeared to be cream and brown. The gloomy continental lighting arrangements seemed, on this unique occasion, to be particularly appropriate. They sat at one of the many dark polished wooden tables scattered with white napkins and nickel silver serving sets, their continental breakfast of assorted bread rolls and cheeses, almost untouched. Surprisingly the big room was half empty. Julia remarked that it must be because the stranded were all under sedation in their rooms – nursing their private grief.

They both wanted desperately to go home but all flights, including theirs, were cancelled. The most disturbing thing was the complete communications blackout. No telephone lines or cellnet channels, no TV or radio broadcasts seemed to emanate from that former beacon of news, music, drama, information and opinion – the United Kingdom.

Looking round at their immediate surroundings, she found them unbearably banal and passive. She wanted to do something about the situation. The normality and ambience of their environment appeared to mock them and their predicament.

'I can well understand why people take drugs,' remarked Julia bitterly, toying with her coffee cup. 'To suspend reality would be very attractive, right now.'

Goodchild nodded glumly, head bowed, his normally fine features, pale, drawn and even haggard, in sharp contrast to the Prince of Love he had been the evening before.

'He looks awful,' thought Julia, unreasonably. But then she caught sight of herself in the polished silver plate breakfast tray before her, and decided she looked very far from her best, her hair scragged back, dark shadows under the large dark eyes. She looked up and the adjacent wall mirror confirmed it, mockingly.

She excused herself and made her way to the Dames cloakroom. After repairing her make up and brushing her hair, to her horror she noticed tears begin to trickle down her newly-groomed cheeks.

She stifled an involuntary sob.

'Can I be of any assistance,' asked a soft female voice behind her. Julia's automatic reaction was embarrassment and an instant rejection of this impertinent stranger's offer. However, when she saw the kind eyes and the dog collar above the sober black dress, she hesitated.

The Deaconess spoke quietly and sympathetically in perfect English, 'Would you like to talk, outside...?'

Julia was about to decline, when the woman extended her hand, and to Julia's own amazement, she took it.

Outside, in the corner of the large lounge, they settled on a quiet corner shielded by large potted fica plants. Once seated on the black squashy leather sofas, the Deaconess, introduced herself, 'My name is Bryony,' she said, 'May I know yours?'

'Julia,' said Julia simply, dabbing her eyes with a tissue.

'With this awful news from England I am trying to bring a little comfort to the English guests, stranded here. May I ask if... you're sure you have suffered bereavement?'

'I'm sure,' replied Julia, a little coldly, looking up. She wore an expression which bordered on defiance. She was beginning to regret this encounter, and Robin would be wondering where she was.

The woman opposite her had quite hypnotic, almost violet eyes, which could not be ignored, and although Julia had started to get up, when Bryony spoke she felt compelled to listen and she sat back again, although not totally receptive.

'Life is full of change.' Bryony began, 'We need to change throughout our lives in order to grow. Changes are hard to cope with, unexpected ones are harder still. We have been forced into a change which was unexpected; it was uncharted and therefore – scary. We cannot change what has already happened, any more than we might have prevented it. But changes lead to a new way of life. Pain is often a route that can lead into the very essence of life...!'

'I have to go,' Julia said suddenly, jumping up, 'my friend is waiting...I...'

'I am glad that you have a friend,' said the Deaconess, without reproach. 'God bless you for listening.' Julia walked away quickly. She felt a little better, even decisive.

'Robin,' she announced loudly, joining him at their table, making Goodchild jump, and the nearest listless guests, stare in her direction, 'we've got to *do* something!'

Twenty minutes later saw them in a taxi, grim-faced and ashen, driving along the misty motorway – away from the Airport, back towards the Brussels Ring and NATO Headquarters. When at last, the large bronze four star sculpture, standing before their destination, came into view, Julia grabbed the roof strap of the Mercedes as it swung into the driveway, and rehearsed what she would say to gain admission. As the car drew up at the barrier, she took her GCHQ pass from her handbag and hoped it would do.

30

*"This was the century that dreamed the impossible
and invented the everyday;
the century that searched for knowledge
but struggled for understanding;
that longed for love, but found relationships;
that longed for peace, but plunged into
indescribable slaughter."*

(John Tusa, British Journalist,
Director of The Barbican Centre, London)

"Two women protesters in black wetsuits and snorkels boarded a Royal Navy nuclear-powered submarine yesterday after swimming up the Clyde into a top security base.

The action by peace campaigners was viewed as one of the most serious breaches of security at the Faslane submarine base, where the Navy's new Trident ballistic missile boats are based. Ministry of Defence police began an investigation immediately after the women were arrested, soon after they entered *HMS Revenge*. Both women, from the Faslane peace camp, entered through the submarine's main hatch and climbed down the ladder into the control room. The RN was reticent about confirming a claim by the women that they wandered around the control room and Captain's cabin before being apprehended by a sailor.

Five years previously, a man gained access to *HMS Renown*, a Polaris missile submarine, at Faslane and in 1988 three protesters were found in the control room of *HMS Repulse*, another Polaris boat.

HMS Revenge, nuclear-powered, but not armed with nuclear missiles, was undergoing maintenance.

The swimmers were able to avoid patrol launches and searchlights as well as the submarine's night watch. They were amazed how easy it was to get inside the submarine. They swam from the beach to a pontoon which acts as a buffer between the jetty and the submarine. Then they scrambled aboard and walked to a hatchway. It was over five minutes before a sailor appeared. An officer was called and they were escorted off the submarine. The Faslane peace camp has now closed after a 14 year vigil."

*   *   *

HMS Revenge

The North Atlantic

One Month Before the Event

Many hundreds of feet below the choppy Atlantic surface, the huge submarine interior was darkened, except for the dim operational lighting, designed to aid night vision in the unlikely event of having to surface.

In the Captain's cabin, the light was normal, and as far as anybody on board knew, the ship was about her normal occasions.

Except, perhaps, one of the two temporary members of her company....

Within the comparative comfort of the cabin, with its bright, almost homely, furnishings – chair and bunk coverlets and other subtle trappings afforded to the Commanding Officer, two senior officers of unequal rank... talked quietly together and drank coffee from plain white cups.

Exceptionally, on one of Her Majesty's ships, the two officers wore the uniform of the United States' Navy. On their cap badges, the bright Bald Eagle featured, where the King Edward's Crown should have been. Their conversation was spasmodic and subdued, but one had the greater clarity and imperiousness of higher command.

The unnatural light delineated the maturity of the men's faces, dark shadows emphasized the intensity of their eyes, and worry lines were deeply etched around their mouths.

'This guy's one of the few I've met who genuinely seems not interested in solutions. He holds on to his personal problems and grievances as if guarding them, possessively – like a dog with a bone!'

The other man whistled softly and looked concerned.

'Not a good attitude for a WEO on a Trident Missile submarine, Sir.' The last speaker blinked frequently in the subdued light, his squat face all attention, like a frightened rabbit, the demeanour obsequious in the presence of his superior.

'No, it's sure not,' agreed his superior, leaning back, toying with his sugar spoon, 'and we're going to have to do something about it.'

They were discussing the ship's Royal Navy Weapons Engineer Officer, an increasingly disgruntled Lieutenant Commander, who had discovered, with ill-timing for the purposes of that particular mission, that he was on a service career redundancy list.

The senior of the two men threw down his spoon with a clatter making the other man jump.

He had three immediate problems.

Firstly, how to inform the Lieutenant Commander, that all such redundancy lists would soon be – well, redundant!

Secondly, that *they* were not supposed to *know* that the Lieutenant Commander had discovered he was on the list.

And thirdly, not to divulge the ultimate purpose of this particular voyage, and the Lieutenant Commander's crucial role within it! For he was a substantial reason why the two senior Americans were on board.

If this was not enough, Captain Wade Brannigan, USN, the junior of the two Americans, was also unaware of the *ultimate* purpose of the voyage, for which this mission was only a rehearsal.

The truism, then, concerning the loneliness of command, strongly applied – for *this* command was not only unique, but had hidden and delayed intent.

At all events, it was too late now. The one hour countdown to the final firing sequence had already begun.

As far as the crew were concerned, it was just another

practice firing, except that on this voyage, all 14 missiles were due to be fired, the first time this had been done. Considerable expense was involved, with each missile costing several hundred thousand pounds. The United States Navy Department had made an exceptional and generous contribution to this mission, which was yet another reason for the looming senior American's presence on board. Apart from assessing the crew on the ultimate stage of their training cycle, he was, with few exceptions, the most senior of examiners in this procedure.

A series of complex codes controlled the arming and fusing of all nuclear weapons, to protect against unauthorized firing. These codes were normally changed daily. If the wrong numbers were keyed in several times the weapon locked and disabled itself – so completely that it could not be fired until repaired.

In addition.... there was an array of somewhat bizarre, last ditch security arrangements, preventing unauthorized firing of any one of the 14 Trident missiles. These comprised two fireproof safes, each holding the two firing keys – unremarkable in appearance, considering the power and mayhem they could unleash.

On an adjacent bulkhead, under separate lock and key, were a loaded handgun, and a hickory baseball bat, with the somewhat unrealistic purpose of restraining renegade individuals attempting an unauthorised launch of any of the eleven thousand mile range missiles. The missiles' potential power was awesome, each carried five independently targeted Multiple Re-entry Vehicles, capable of delivering a multi-megaton yield, nuclear device – or a variety of other subtle weapon combinations.

Shortly after sailing, the regular Captain of *HMS Revenge,* Commander Geoffrey Halstead RN, had suddenly been taken ill and was receiving attention in the sick bay.

Hasty high level communication ensued. This was rated a highly important voyage by all concerned, not least of all MOD (Navy), as it embraced the sole purpose of many months of expensive training. Therefore, to ensure its continuance, last minute high level dispensation had been given to Brannigan to take command, and to proceed with the full firing exercise of 14 Trident dummy warheads on to widely dispersed safe target areas, in the Atlantic .

Accordingly, the two assigned key holders on this voyage were, for this mission only, to be the two senior officers on board: firstly, Captain Brannigan USN – Trident Technical Information Liaison Officer with the Royal Navy for the previous two years – (eight years after the first handover of the Trident D5 to the British) and shortly to be given command of the nuclear aircraft carrier, *USS Lexington.*

And the second key holder...

Admiral Edward J Kearns – Senior Trident Training Assessment Officer (a post he was shortly to vacate, following promotion to the highest achievable rank: that of Chief of the United States Navy, on the personal recommendation of Secretary of State for Defense, Richard Scottdale).

The reprogramming and re-targeting of the Trident launch computers was based on a test scenario, the object being to pinpoint highly selected targets, down to an accuracy of a few hundred yards, in the event that a friendly NATO country was occupied by a determined, and otherwise irremovable enemy. It was not generally known that obsolete Polaris Missiles could be primed with a variety of warheads, other than nuclear, or indeed a mix of conventional and tactical nuclear bomblets.

Kearns and Brannigan were acknowledged experts in this procedure, but it had never been done before with Trident. It was this unique knowledge coupled with their high rank and training roles, which afforded them the privilege of effectively commanding one of the Royal Navy's potentially most potent ships.

Brannigan recalled the first of many long briefings attended by himself, Admiral Kearns and the Lieutenant Commander Weapons Engineer Officer. Kearns was responsible for target planning, Brannigan would assist and the Lieutenant Commander would be responsible for the synchronised multiple launch.

202

'These targets...where are they exactly...?' enquired Brannigan, a little nervously.

'They're only virtual targets, we're not actually going to drop anything on them. It's all really an interactive computer model. The missiles will fire but their multiple warheads will contain only radio beacons so that we can track them, some small explosive charges, marker smoke and fluorescent dyes....'

'I see, so that aircraft can confirm where they fall...'

'Exactly, but the computer simulation will show trajectories and fall of shot on the reciprocal headings...'

'I get it, so if the computer targets England to the East, the actual dummy missiles will fly and fall to the West, in pre-determined positions in the Atlantic...'

'That's it. That way we get the best of both worlds without doing any damage!'

'OK,' said Brannigan, getting interested at last. 'Where's the first virtual target..?'

'Baldonnel...'

'What's that?'

'It's an Air Force Base...'

'What!... A British Air Force Base?'

'Irish'

'I don't get it,' said Brannigan

'You will.'

They all three leaned over and looked at the marked chart which Kearns had unrolled.

'What's this... Aberforth?'

'Oh, it's just an old missile testing station...'

'And where's that... Wales?'

'West Wales.'

'Uh ha...' said Brannigan,

'The first thing you do need to know is that this is a top secret operation. It's to test the ultimate war scenario.., when things go wrong! A kind of self destruct operation, on a very grand scale.'

'But do the British know we're using one of *their* submarines to carry this out ...?

'Well, of course they do – what a question?' his superior

expostulated, interrupting with a timely splatter of incredulity. He consoled his conscience with the thought that 'The British', in this context, had a wide meaning!

And now, as the countdown continued, the emphasis was on meticulous preparation, and at the appointed time, both Kearns and Brannigan inserted their keys. Then Brannigan gave the order to fire... to the Royal Navy Lieutenant Commander, Weapons Executive Officer.

* * *

Marathon

Before the Event

While Payne's mind swung darkly between landing alternatives, he had a sudden feeling of *déja vu!* Then the Yak's motor coughed and immediately stopped.

As the ground rushed up to meet him, he fumbled desperately with throttle, mixture control and fuel tank valve, when, to his enormous relief, the big engine burst into life once more... just in time...

The Great Plain of Marathon was not as sparse as it had been in classical times, nor even as he remembered it ten years earlier, but was now covered in trees and dotted with houses. Payne turned the round snub nose of the Yak hopefully toward the south of the Plain – and the somewhat diminutive, but possibly clearer, beaches, of the small seaside town of Mati.

Aiming at a clear stretch of beach, well North of the town, he throttled back to 150 kph at the top of his final approach for landing .

He was still going far too fast...!

Easing the machine to starboard, which took him briefly out over the sea, Payne began a desperate side slip to port, to reduce speed. Glancing at the air speed indicator, its needle fell mercifully to an indicated 130 kph At this point, he felt confident enough to level out and commit himself to land, his speed falling away to 110 kph for the final approach.

With a trembling hand, he gently backed the throttle. The Yak appeared to float.., then *fall,* approximately 100 metres for every 10 kph reduction in speed, above the propitiously smooth sand.

Suddenly, a bolt of fear hit him, almost paralysing him. He'd forgotten to lower the wheels!

Too late...!

The Yak hit the beach skidding, prop bending, motor stopped. Wet sand plastered the wind shield and canopy until he could see almost nothing. He had no control. The plane slewed in a movement which seemed to last and last... But was actually over in seconds.

Abruptly, there was a splash and an awful, distant sloshing sound...

He was in the sea!

Fumbling, in a panic, he tried to unfasten his straps. He felt suddenly cold, in spite of the high ambient temperature in the cockpit. His hands would not respond, still failing to undo his safety harness. Finally, his straps fell away. Now for the canopy... it wouldn't budge. Had it been damaged in the forced landing? He groped wildly for the canopy release....it seemed an eternity before he managed to unlatch it. Finally, he was able to breathe fresh sea air.... But he must get out...!

There was an ominous creaking, bubbling and churning outside as the waves slewed the aircraft back and forth.

Was he sinking?

Then, at last he was free...! Blinking and panting in the bright sunshine... he hauled his aching body on to the metal wing, just as it wallowed, and began to gently submerge, the water frothing white at the leading edge, then sinking, sinking gently..., into the blue grey, salty waters of the Aegean sea...

31

*"Perseverance is not a long race;
it is many short races
one after another."*

(Walter Elliot)

Singapore

Before the Event

When Payne finally arrived at Changi Airport, Singapore, at 0730 in the morning, he was comparatively refreshed, having caught the Singapore Airways 15.20 Saturday over-night direct flight from Athens. He had managed to sleep well during the long journey, largely from sheer exhaustion. Most of his cash had been confiscated during the Albanian debacle, but the concealed American Express Card had paid for his flight and seen to his many other needs – including a much needed replacement, lightweight, wardrobe and luggage, purchased at Athens airport. This was urgently needed after his ducking in the Aegean off the Marathon Plain.

He had been fortunate that no one had been around to witness his dramatic entry into Greece! Landing in the sea had been a net benefit as it had neatly disposed of the plane, and so avoided some awkward questions and possible arrest. Being a strong swimmer he had been able to make the hundred or so yards to the beach without too much difficulty. Having thumbed a lift to the airport and purchased his new clothes and luggage, his only remaining slight difficulty had been his partially water-logged passport!

Once outside the terminal building, he stood in the warm sunshine and sniffed the air. Some of the old familiar smells of Singapore were just discernible in the sultry breeze. Or perhaps, he almost imagined them: the traces of incense, sandalwood, meat cooking in coconut oil and frangipani –

among the wafts of jet kerosene from the airport behind him.

He felt, now, fit in all respects to confront Hope-Watson, although he had to concede to a tremor of concern. For one thing the formidable ex-admiral would not be best pleased at the loss of his cash! Yet, after what he had gone through and overcome, Payne told himself that this was absurd.

Once again using his American Express Card, he took a taxi not to the Embassy near Tanglin, but to Hope-Watson's private address, near the Marina Bay Golf and Country Club, off the East Coast Parkway, between Katong and Singapore City's eastern boundary.

During the drive along the coast road, he recalled memories of his first visit to Singapore with his father. He remembered a place of contrast: wide avenues, lawns, monolithic government buildings, luxurious department stores and the marmoreal dignity of its commercial banks. Things had changed...

He was struck by the all pervading influence of Mammon; tall towers with shaded glass windows, and huge advertising signs, proclaiming Japanese and other Far Eastern electronic products – glimpsed above and beyond the large trees lining the wide road. However, the huge purple sign proclaiming the native product, *Tiger Balm,* he remembered from his youthful first visit to the island, was no more, much like the eponymous and regal animal from which the product took its name.

At 8.45am Payne paid off the taxi in a pleasant tree-lined road near Marina Bay, opposite Ambassador Hope-Watson's private residence. Here the family had made their home – eschewing the official residence in Tanglin – now used only for formal receptions.

He was kept waiting for nearly an hour. The sergeant in the small street level reception hall apologised but was unable to confirm if the Ambassador was at home, or at the Embassy.

Payne was about to leave in disgust, and find a hotel, when the sergeant suggested he should go and have some breakfast, and return at 11.30am, by which time he was sure he could contact the Ambassador, or a member of his family, who would then receive him.

As he walked away from the residence, something made him pause and look back at it. It was a magnificent colonial house, dating back 90 years or more. A colonnade of broad white pillars supported its upper balcony with two winding stone staircases descending from either end of its portico, spilling out on either side, resembling curdling cream from the edge of some gigantic cream cake, giving the building a neo-classical or judicial appearance. Before he turned away, he glimpsed a large vivid splash of colour. It was a butterfly as big as a man's hand, and, as it floated erratically upward, it took his eye to one end of the balcony, where a slim young Chinese or Malay girl, dressed in a short white shift, stood briefly, among the profusion of foliage, looking down at him. He thought she smiled at him before turning away, but he could not be sure.

When he returned some hours later, he had but a short wait this time before being ushered into the cool entrance hall, where he was immediately greeted by Lloyd Hope-Watson, still Her Majesty's Ambassador to Singapore, but exuding a presence even beyond that exalted rank, that was nascently independent.

'Why, Payne! How are you?' said Hope-Watson, smiling broadly, resplendent in a white linen tropical suit, extending his hand. With that Marcus Payne's long-awaited audience with his powerful mentor, and hopefully *former* controller, had begun – and Payne was ready for him. Or so he thought...

Ushered into the empty lounge, the call of a distant peacock was just audible from the gardens below; jagged waves of reflected sunlight played on the half open, tall, white shutters that extended from floor to high ceiling, across one end of the large, elegant room.

Payne was strangely intimidated, which was most unwelcome. He had never been to the house before, although it had been described to him well enough, but he had seen photographs, even a video, when his relationship with Hope-

Watson had been warmer. For he knew the ex-admiral's present, surface *bonhomie* would not and could not last.

He was right.

So was it the house or the man that intimidated him? No, it was the *two* together, that gave the present situation its slowly gathering malevolent strength. Payne knew he would need all his stamina – and perhaps more than his total powers of persuasion – to deflect this behemoth of a man, from his chosen course.

Hope-Watson sat heavily on the cream silk brocade sofa and ushered Payne to take a seat opposite. Then he took out the obligatory cigar and ordered cool drinks.

A Chinese boy, in a short white jacket and black trousers, brought a silver tray with ice cubes clinking in crystal glasses. He had returned with the drinks in an astonishingly short time. He was so obsequious in Hope-Watson's presence that Payne thought he was going to *back* out of the room!

'So, Marcus,' Hope-Watson said at length, 'what's been happening?'

Payne felt like a fifth-former being interviewed by his housemaster. Before he could answer, Hope-Watson cut him short. Leaning forward solicitously, he enquired, 'Did you have a good journey?'

'It was somewhat unconventional,' Payne replied flatly, with enormous understatement, sipping his drink.

'Oh dear, how was that?' said his host, with mock concern, immediately leaning back among the cream silk cushions and puffing on his cigar.

'I imagine you've read the papers?' replied Payne, testing what his adversary, knew.

'Which ones?' said Hope-Watson, simply. There was an annoying twinkle in his eye and he oozed the confidence displayed by many powerful men.

'Perhaps I didn't quite make the *The Times*,' replied Payne obliquely, gazing round at the rich, but simple decor.

'Dear me, you sound peeved...,' teased Hope-Watson, not unkindly.

'Look, let's stop playing games, Lloyd, we both know why I'm here.'

'Well now..., to give me a successful report on your highly expensive activities – I hope,' said Hope-Watson, sounding almost hurt.

'Not at all...' Payne, began, but Hope-Watson interrupted him a second time – a simple, but unnerving ploy.

The big man leaned forward once more,'You *will* stay to dinner, I hope..? It will be just you and me. I'm afraid the girls have prior engagements...' And before Payne could answer, 'Stay the night, please do...' Hope-Watson offered, touching Payne's sleeve with old fashioned familiarity. 'You *do* have a dinner jacket...?' he added, quite seriously.

'No,' said Payne without expression,' but I accept your offer...'

'Is that to dinner, or to stay...?' enquired the admiral, teasing him again.

'Both,' said Payne, with mounting annoyance.

During the afternoon, Payne circumspectly reported that he had completed his set up of ground agents, who would operate immediately before, during and after the Event.

Throughout his report Hope-Watson nodded sagely. His manner almost avuncular. Then he said abruptly, 'I suppose what I'd really like to know, is what precisely you're doing here? I don't recall a face to face report in Singapore featuring in our plans.'

At last, the crisis had come. From now on he must be *very* careful.

'The best laid plans... and all that Lloyd,' replied Payne quietly, in an almost conciliatory tone.

'Quite.' agreed Hope-Watson, with thinly disguised menace. 'Why exactly did you leave England? By what means and under what circumstances?'

'I was coming to that....,' stalled Payne.

'I hoped you might.' Hope-Watson was peering at him imperiously rather as if he was reproving a naughty child.

Payne was also aware that the man likely as not knew exactly what he had been up to, but was waiting for him either to lie, or to confirm his behaviour. In either case, he was possibly a dead man, *unless*, he could convince Hope-Watson that there were others who knew the *whole situation*, outside this room, and this house... and yes, even outside the Ambassador admiral's collegiate power centre: the Funchal Far Eastern Club cabal.

'I'm afraid things didn't go *quite* according to plan....,' began Payne, rather lamely.

'I think I'm aware of *that* much,' glowered his host.

Payne suddenly thought of Julia – and the possibilities of escape began to enter his mind – but it was probably too late now. He must stick to his purpose, which was to turn this megalomaniac – or kill him. And to delay, or cancel, *Counter Strike!*

'One of my operatives...'

'Which one?'

'A man called Prince, Jack Prince...'

'What of him?'

'His wife had an unfortunate accident...'

'What kind of accident?'

'I'm afraid she was using the diesel fuel for domestic purposes.'

'What? – You fool!' roared Hope-Watson, slamming down his glass and spilling the contents.

Payne looked down and watched the liquid being absorbed by the expensive Indian carpet. From this point on the gloves would be off! He decided to go on the offensive.

'It's no good you ranting and raving. You didn't allow sufficient funds to recruit enough skilled and reliable people...'

Hope-Watson assumed a state of controlled apoplexy...

'If you hadn't spent so much time – and my money on socialising....' he enunciated the word as if it was something obscene, 'you might have...'

'It was necessary, to find out the lie of the land, and to assess people's attitudes. People who might be useful...'

'Oh, and we all know what kind of people, socialites with long hair and short skirts..'

Payne had difficulty in controlling his temper, but he knew he must, or lose the argument and much more besides.

'If you are referring to Julia MacMahon,' he said quitely, and with as much dignity as he could muster, she happened to be a senior officer at GCHQ....'

'Oh, and what precisely did you get out of her – apart from the obvious?' scoffed Hope-Watson.

'My God, what a cheap remark!' shouted Payne, forgetting his former resolution.

'All right, all right,' said Hope-Watson standing up, and holding up his hands in a conciliatory gesture, 'recriminations will get us nowhere. We need to look at damage limitation and yes, damn it... determine your commitment to the whole process...!'

So, Hope-Watson had finally reached the nub; the reason Payne was in Singapore. The reason for his dalliance with Julia. The reason why Hope-Watson was so angry and distrustful of him, the reason why Jack Prince had died – and all those others too, the memory of which made him feel sick.

Or was it just the memory....?

Amazingly, Hope-Watson did not press this key point, which Payne would have been hard pressed to answer, but was ranting on about the current state of late nineties' Britain, presumably in justification for his grandiose scheme...

"Faith in the judiciary is seriously undermined in the public's perception, by their consistent lack of common sense, when dealing with issues and cases where the populace, middle classes and community, feel aggrieved by their bizarre judgments concerning the rights of wayward and irresponsible individuals – many of whom have made no tangible contribution to society. In this context, it is difficult to see just whose interests, they, and other factions of the ruling establishment, actually represent... Except perhaps, the powerful liberal Fabian elite..."

As he listened glumly, Payne, knew that with dinner yet to come, he would not elude being brought to account, and begun to wish he had never made this madcap journey, which had been started by the simple impetus and daring imperatives of escape.

*   *   *

"Crabbed age and youth cannot live together:
youth is full of pleasance, age is full of care;
youth is full of sport, age's breath is short.
Age, I do abhor thee; youth I do adore thee,
O sweet shepherd! hie thee,
For methinks thou stay'st too long."

from

The Passionate Pilgrim

(William Shakespeare)

When Payne awoke he felt awful and he could not determine where he was. He was only aware of a throbbing head and a pain-racked body. He felt as if a lifetime's hangovers had been visited upon him all at once.

It was dark. Very dark.

A faint smell of mildew was in the air, which, though cool, was very humid. A not unfamiliar sound was just perceptible above the roaring in his skull, the slap, slap of water.

Once again, he was near the sea, but a very different one from the Aegean.

Painfully he began to recall the events leading up to his present predicament. He remembered ruefully, what must have been the previous evening's meeting with an implacable Hope-Watson; the discussion that had become the inevitable argument – or verbal confrontation.

Now, he cursed himself for not being more subtle in effecting his purpose; which was to try and reason with his former mentor and persuade him to abort what Payne had come to recognise was a monstrous and unwarranted scheme of destruction. However, Hope-Watson had been adamant that the end justified the savage means, and that

213

too much treasure, time, effort and reputation had been expended to stop now. This was an unaccountably inadequate excuse when matched against the terrible outcome.

Although Payne had barely been a match for Hope-Watson's towering presence and intellect, he could nevertheless see through the altruism justifying *Counter Strike!* and realise that like so many lesser schemes throughout history, it was really a matter of personal power, or megalomania dressed up as magnanimity.

The timing of the Event, was obviously of particular importance to Hope-Watson, on two counts: operationally and historically – with the approaching Millennium, Britain would certainly have a dramatic new start to the new century!

Payne's more immediate concern was what Hope-Watson had done to him physically.

He felt feebly for broken bones. There seemed to be none, but his mouth was unbearably dry and had a foul taste. To his further horror and distress, he experienced recurring nausea, dizziness and bouts of unconsciousness, the extent of which were difficult to judge as his Rolex was missing from his aching wrist. However, before passing out, he was aware of a vision.

The figure, or apparition, appeared slight, female and predominantly white. She seemed blessed with luxuriant black hair, possibly long, because it was secured in a chignon.

When this being reached out to him with slender hands, his first reaction was to draw back. But her touch, when it came, was soft and cool, and, before passing out again, he experienced an overwhelming feeling of great tenderness, and a delicate flower-like perfume – reminiscent of the white South African Chincherinchees of his childhood.

When he awoke, it was as if he was floating, but he felt better. As his eyes began to focus properly, he saw that he was no longer in darkness, but bathed in a diffused green light and was aware of a variety of natural fragrances. A serene woman in her fifties, with delicate oriental features, was bending over him.

'Who are you?' he managed to croak. The woman reached out and bathed his forehead with a cool scented towel and gave him some much needed water, the best he had tasted in his entire existence – or so it seemed to him.

'My name is Li Chan, but you must rest,' said Hope-Watson's wife.

*   *   *

He was concerned about the fragmentation and a perceived weakening of purpose in the FFEC cabal. He was concerned about Li Chan's long absence. It was most unlike her. But above all, he was concerned about Payne. Not for his welfare, because he believed him to be dead. Regrettable? Yes, after all he had first met him when he was little more than a boy. He had liked his father too – on brief acquaintance. But he had been disappointed in the boy. He had become a threat. He may already have compromised *Counter Strike!* which, thanks to him – and other waverers– would have to be brought forward.

He would have to get someone to dispose of Payne's remains before they were discovered. The basement, where he had had him taken the previous evening, was not entirely secure. Pity though – they had shared some dreams together, but there was no room for weakness in an enterprise of this magnitude. No point in conceiving it otherwise.

He had to admit that Payne's unannounced visit had been something of a shock. He didn't think he'd get this far! The man's odyssey had been foolhardy, but impressive, and he had to admit to a grudging admiration for his persistence. It was a pity he had not devoted that talent to the planned cause. However...

'Have you seen your mother?' he enquired, looking in on Mi Ling in her airy office overlooking Marina Bay.

She looked up at him quizzically, over her large reading glasses, 'No, I thought she was with you.'

'Damn the woman,' retorted Hope-Watson, testily.

'Uncle!' pealed Mi Ling in a hurt tone.

'I'm sorry,' he said briefly, propping open her door, his large frame filling the doorway, 'but it's very inconvenient..'

'Oh dear,' replied his stepdaughter, rather mockingly. 'What did you want her for?'

'I just like to know where she is... Always disappearing...'

'Uncle, you're so possessive. She's her own person after all.'

'Yes, that's the problem,' he rasped, turning to go.

'You might try the garden....,' Mi Ling suggested, giggling slightly.

'Of course, why didn't I think of it? Spends half her life there. Wonder she doesn't take her bed there.'

'Perhaps you've got too much on your mind,' Mi Ling suggested pointedly.

'I'll see *you* later,' he said, and left.

* * *

At either end of the great terrace balcony which ran the whole length of the Hope-Watson private residence, two long winding sets of stone steps ran down from either end, to the big terrace garden, set splendidly, less than twenty feet above the sea.

It was toward one of these elaborate stone stairways that Hope-Watson now strode, purposefully...

Half-way down, shielding his eyes from the sun, emerging unexpectedly from behind a cloud bank, he called out his wife's name.

Below, hidden among the myriad palm fronds – an area for which Li Chan's gardener had eschewed the somewhat brooding native vegetation, for Mediterranean, oleander and bougainvilleas – both Li Chan and Payne heard Hope-Watson's call, and knew fear. His intrusive bellowing, incongruous above the fine tinkling of the fountains, that surrounded the central bathing pool.

Indeed, it happened that from that fearful moment, their

lives were to change irrevocably, because it was then that Li Chan decided to deceive her husband – for the first time, and Payne gained an ally in the enemy camp!

'Rest here,' whispered Li Chan,' Soon, I'll get my gardener to take you back to safety. Now I must lead my husband away from here.'

With that, she was gone, leaving Payne looking up into a shady pili nut tree, and attempting to raise himself up on to one elbow – which he painfully failed to do. Much hope and light went with her; and as he passed in and out of consciousness, he could no longer sense the many fragrances there. But Hope-Watson's phrases from the night before coursed through his turbulent mind...

'...Democracy itself is already under siege, and has been for some years! It's just that no one will openly admit it..'

In his delirium, he began to wonder if Hope-Watson was right after all. Was there any real democracy left in the Western World – or any justice? But this only fired yet another synapse in his befuddled brain and Hope-Watson's words returned – like the demons of childhood nightmares. But there was no mother to comfort him here... or was there?

'I want to return to England to end my days – you can have too much sun – but I want the England that I knew. Not a desert of supermarkets, ugly modern motor cars and seven days a week traffic jams... ill dressed youths... polluted air and water... even in the countryside... I want my wife and daughter to walk safely anywhere... as they can here, without being attacked by some alien culture rapist.'

All was unreal, but again Julia's face returned to him. That at least was almost real...something to hold on to – or for?

'What the British Establishment forgot, to their lasting cost, was that truly rich men, left to their own devices, do not need to play by the rules if they are blackballed from the club...!'

'Did you find mother?' Mi Ling was locking her office as Hope-Watson swept past in a cloud of cigar smoke.

He turned, hardly breaking his stride as he continued along the corridor that ran the length of the house, 'Yes, yes, my dear, she was in the garden, as you said...' Suddenly he stopped. 'Look here, will you do something for me?'

'If I can.'

'I have to go out. Take my calls if they're urgent. I might not be back until after nightfall. Then we can all have drinks on the terrace. Delay dinner, if your mother will allow it... until, say 8.45....'

'That's very late, uncle,' chided Mi Ling.

'Please do it child.' Hope-Watson threw the command over his shoulder and was off down the passageway, humming tunelessly to himself.

Mi Ling, sighed. Sometimes, her stepfather could be a little hard to take!

A short time later, in a narrow alleyway at the back of the house, a light van pulled up under the palm fronds. It was getting dark. Two Chinese men got out of the van and conversed softly in Mandarin. One took a bunch of keys from the other and they descended down a half concealed flight of steps. With some difficulty they opened a rather rusty steel door. Then they both disappeared inside, but reappeared five minutes later. Once again there was a muffled conversation in Mandarin, and one returned to the van and emerged with a small mobile phone.

Meanwhile, in the members' bar of the nearby Marina Bay and Country Club, Hope-Watson was enjoying an unfashionable Singapore Sling when the telephone on the end of the deserted bar rang.

The barman answered it, then holding up the receiver, called to Hope-Watson, 'It is for you, Sir....'

32

Singapore

Before the Event

Li Chan found her daughter reading the *Straits Times* in the cool lounge, the big ceiling fans whispering above, sonorously and gently rustling the large window blinds. A fine strand of ebony hair had fallen across her narrow, fine featured face. The large eyes were accentuated by small underlying shadows and the sable brown irises wide and bright with concern.

'Where is your stepfather?' she enquired, brushing back the hair.

'*Pada pukul tujoh dia keluar rumah,*' replied Mi Ling in Malay, without looking up.

'He went out of the house at seven o' clock?' repeated Li Chan in English, 'But where has he gone? I have to give instructions for dinner.'

'Oh yes, I am sorry,' said Mi Ling, looking up at last,' he said to delay dinner until 8.45.'

'But that is very late,' said Li Chan.

'That is what I said,' replied Mi Ling, smiling up at her mother kindly and balancing the newspaper on her bare knees.

'That dress is too short,' chided her mother, looking flummoxed.

'Why mother, whatever is it? You look worried,' said her daughter perceptively.

Li Chan stared at her, searching her face hesitantly.

'You must tell me what is troubling you mother,' Mi Ling

219

said holding out her hand. Eventually, Li Chan took her hand and sat beside her.

'It's your stepfather,' she began. Then pulling her small hand away, she clutched her thin neck above the severe collar of her long silk dress and sniffed, as if about to cry. Abruptly, she turned and looked at her daughter. 'Can I trust you?'

'Why mother?' replied Mi Ling, genuinely shocked, 'But what a question, I am...'

'But you work with him....,' Li Chan interrupted.

'Yes, I do... But...,' Mi Ling began, her tone slightly defensive.

'*Belum. Dia lambat..?*' said her mother, intently, ringing her hands, until her thin jade bracelets chinked.

'No, mother, he is not ill,' said Mi Ling translating, 'what makes you say this?'

'You must promise to say nothing of what I tell you... or what I must show you...'

'What must you show me...?' replied Mi Ling more interested in the showing than the telling.

'Come with me, now,' said her mother getting to her feet, 'We don't have much time...' And a bewildered Mi Ling followed her mother out onto the darkening veranda and down the winding stone steps at one end.

*   *   *

'What do you mean, it's not there?' demanded Hope-Watson experiencing a rare frisson of panic.

'Stay there, I'm coming down.' He handed the phone back to the barman, paid and left the club hurriedly.

When he arrived at the back of the house, it was dark except for a dim wall lamp. The two Chinese were lolling against the small van and smoking. When Hope-Watson approached on foot, they extinguished their cigarettes and stood up, languidly.

He addressed them, gruffly but softly, in Mandarin. Then they followed him down the steps to the steel door.

They searched the basement and garages thoroughly, but Marcus Payne, alive or dead, was nowhere to be found.

*   *   *

'He should be taken to the hospital, but it is too risky. They will ask many questions,' said Li Chan, as they hurried along.

'But *who* is it that is sick, mother?' Mi Ling insisted as they hailed a taxi.

'You will see, soon enough,' replied her mother anxiously.

Ten minutes later they arrived at a small private clinic, off the Central Expressway. They were ushered in and immediately taken to a private ward, where they found Payne, asleep but with a dreadful pallor.

'He has been drugged,' said a white coated Indian doctor, coming up behind them. He lifted the clipboard containing the temperature chart at the foot of Payne's bed, 'It is a wonder he is not dead,' he continued in a strong Indian accent. 'He must have... how you say it? The constitution of the ox!' he ended brightly, bringing faint smiles to the strained faces of both mother and daughter.

'Who is he?' whispered Mi Ling to her mother.

'He has no identification,' said the doctor overhearing. 'This should be registered. An offence, or attempted suicide has been committed.'

But Li Chan took his arm, and took him to one side. The Indian began to shake his head, but Mi Ling saw her mother open her handbag and press something into the doctor's hand. He nodded briefly, sighed and went away.

Li Chan looked round cautiously, 'I have his passport...' she hissed. 'He is a South African, called Marcus Payne.'

'But where did you find him?'

'He was a guest of your father, last evening. He arrived unexpectedly. Your father knew him, knew him well, but he was not welcome. I could tell that...'

'But what happened? Where did you find him?' Mi Ling repeated.

'I found him in the basement, this morning – unconscious. I thought he was *dead!*'

Mi Ling's delicate hand went to her own full lips, 'My God,' she whispered... 'Are you saying..?'

'Yes, your stepfather did this. Or had it done to him... for whatever reason.' The tenor of her voice fell, in sadness, on the last phrase. Then turning suddenly, accusing, she hissed darkly,

'Did you know about this?'

'*Bapa tidak beri tahu.*' Mi Ling stuttered involuntarily in Malay, saying that her father did *not* tell her.

Her small elegant head bowed, Mi Ling stared blankly at the floor, for she was shocked by her mother's implied accusation,

'*Benar, tidak?* ' Li Chan enquired sharply if she spoke the truth.

'You know it is the truth I'm telling you,' replied Mi Ling with tears starting in her large almond eyes.

Then the two women embraced briefly, looked down at the unconscious Payne, and wondered what would become of their lives.

As mother and daughter contemplated their return to the house, with great fear and trepidation, Mi Ling, for one, faced a great dilemma: to stand by her mother and her rehabilitation of Payne – with all that entailed. Or, to carry on with her support and assistance for her awesome "uncle" in his ambitious and cataclysmic adventure. Here indeed, her mettle was tested, because a little of the import and effect of what he planned had been brought to her very door – and invaded her closest family relationships.

For Li Chan, her relationship with the man she had loved, and supported in his career, including his high profile public life as a senior diplomat – despite her naturally retiring nature – would be at an end, and probably her continuing status as an Ambassador's wife. Her life would be in ruins, and so why was she contemplating such a course of action? It was not just to save the young South African, however personable he may be. It was not just that her husband had attempted to kill someone. No, it was that he had felt unable to confide in her; the fact that he had done it in her household. The changes she had observed in him over, recent months, suggested an obsession, but not with his diplomatic career – for she sensed that was failing. No, it was his neglect of her, combined with whatever plans he was hatching with Mi Ling, which were driving a wedge between them. All these things had now brought matters to a head. A decision, long postponed through her own passiveness, now had to be made.

Who knows, she thought, perhaps I shall be able to reclaim my daughter and if providence allows, return to Hong Kong?

They had decided to walk slowly back to the house together, to give them more time to think. They trudged the first humid, palm-lined suburban streets in silence, each mulling over the consequences of a great decision they had both made, yet not yet enunciated – even to each other.

Over the next few days, while Payne recovered from protracted detoxification treatment, the two women alternately returned to his bedside, slipping away from the house on the pretext of a joint shopping trip. Sometimes, when Hope-Watson was away at the Embassy, they went together, rebuilding their relationship in the time they shared, through their mutual concern.

Although he grew fond of Li Chan, appreciating the kindness and steadfastness that masked her growing sacrifice, it was Mi Ling's solo visits which Payne really enjoyed – and anticipated with growing pleasure!

It was there, in the curtained off cubicle in the little clinic, that Payne had told them his story, and there also, that their lives were changed irrevocably. For he explained that time was desperately short and that he had a plan which would expose Hope-Watson and hopefully save the imminent destruction of England. For he was probably the only one who knew as much as Hope-Watson himself, and could therefore make public, or reverse, the situation before it was too late. Payne realised, of course, that both women, in spite of their close family ties, might be in jeopardy, should Hope-Watson discover that they had helped him. He therefore proposed that they leave Singapore soon after they had helped him in the execution of his last ditch plan, to save many lives and divert from millions more a revolutionary catastrophe.

Perhaps Mi Ling's turmoil made her vulnerable, but although she would never admit as much, she was subconsciously influenced in her decision to betray her stepfather, by her growing attraction to the young South African. It had begun when she first saw him from the balcony, as he walked slowly and a little uncertainly, away from the house. She remembered him looking up at her, which had prompted her involuntary smile.

Many momentous events begin with an upward glance, but a smile can add mystery.

* * *

Hope-Watson was also in crisis. He was grappling with problems and developing situations which would have swiftly defeated a weaker man.

His most immediate concern was the disappearance of Payne. But if this was not enough, he felt increasingly threatened and assailed by the internal politics in his own organization. There were urgent coded faxes, which expressed doubts about logistics, and the political, economic and social control of the recovery of the UK, after the Event. But the main pressure concerned security. Adverse references were made to incidents and disappearances during the earlier Bermuda Conference.

Some members' comments, reported to him, went as far as suggesting that England was beyond redemption and probably not worth saving!

This last point made him particularly angry, and served to strengthen his resolve!

He was determined to impose the authority of a renewed moral code. Someone had to do it! He maintained that consensus was, and had proved to be, quite useless, and only produced a lower common denominator promoting downward moral drift.

He had always maintained that people would invariably take the easy and selfish way. After *Counter Strike!* he was committed to restating ancient truths, and applying them forcibly to modern conditions. People had lost the habit of discussing moral things and the Church had abdicated its moral responsibility by capitulating to modern liberalising fads, and thinly disguised personal self-gratification.

He decided to give the order to bring *Counter Strike!* forward before it could be stopped. This was all the more important now that Payne had disappeared – which almost certainly meant that he was still alive, in spite of the fact that the dose he had given him should have killed a donkey! What a very physically strong but philosophically tiresome, young man he had turned out to be!

Hope-Watson had had to delegate more and more of his official diplomatic duties. He contrived to convince his First Secretary that it was good for his career – all that experience and decision-making and honing of his language skills! However, the man had not unreasonably, begun to complain – obliquely of course – which was as close to complaining that a senior diplomat could get, at least where his ambassador was concerned. Of course, the occasional diplomatic reception was unavoidable, as were the really major decisions affecting the running of the Embassy. All matters regarding China for example, (including trade links) were reserved for his attention.

*   *   *

Mi Ling was finding it increasingly distressing to work for Hope-Watson knowing what she did. However, it had been impressed on her by Payne that if she continued to co-operate with her "uncle", she would learn his latest plans and movements. More vitally, (where her own and her mother's self-preservation were concerned) acting normally would allay his immediate suspicions.

Naturally, her heart was no longer in the work, and she had difficulty in concealing her reticence. Moreover, the thought of spying on someone like her stepfather, who had been such a powerful mentor, was against her normally light-hearted and generous nature.

Not surprisingly, as their normal life resumed, she began to view the prospect of his inevitable downfall with some misgivings. Yet the hidden trauma was still there; the thought that her beloved "uncle" had actually tried to kill a guest in this house – their home! Apart from the obvious, it was the gravest possible violation of hospitality – something which was deeply ingrained in her culture and upbringing. And yet, there was her own naivety – and yes, hypocrisy, to ponder, for had she not co-operated with him on plans that would lead to the deaths of countless millions, many of whom – probably most – were completely innocent?

Day to day, maintaining her smile was the most tiring feature of the whole nightmare. Hope-Watson was beginning to give her strange glances, and asked more than once if there was anything wrong, a bad sign in one so normally unsolicitous.

One evening, after a particularly trying day, she retired to the comparative coolness of her room and changed into white cotton shorts and top, when the bedside phone rang. It was Payne! She caught her breath. 'You should not be calling me here!' she gasped.

'I need your help urgently, and time is getting very short.'

'Why, are you ill again?'

'No, no. Look, I'm staying in the Pasir Panjang Hotel, it's on the coast... near the Ayer Rajah Expressway...'

'Yes, I know it..,' replied Mi Ling, trembling, 'that's awfully near..'

'Don't worry, I'm in disguise,' said Payne, fingering his itchy, newly grown beard. 'Besides, I don't think it's near any of your uncle's watering holes..'

'What do you want me to do?' answered Mi Ling anxiously, growing hoarse and slightly weak in her shapely knees.

'Better not discuss it on the phone. Can you meet me?'

'Er, yes, OK,' replied Mi Ling, her heart leaping involuntarily.

'Can you come to the hotel?'

'No, better not do that. I'll meet you at the Haw Par Villa Dragon World. It's just along the coast road from the hotel. I'll be in my car in the car park..., a red Mazda sports. When my top is down, it's quite distinctive...'

'I'll bet...' said Payne, smiling.

Mi Ling, flushed and quickly hung up.

Payne found the Chinese Mythological Theme Park, after a longish walk East, along the Pasir Panjang coast road. The offshore evening breeze helped drive away the humidity, while his newly grown "hospital beard", and Panama hat, gave him the degree of anonymity he needed.

He quickly spotted the red Mazda, and he experienced an involuntary pang of desire, when he caught sight of Mi Ling, coolly elegant in white chiffon head scarf and dark glasses, seated at the wheel.

It was clear that she did not recognise him as he approached. Indeed, she began to look somewhat alarmed, until he waved and took off his hat.

'Oh... your disguise is... impressive,' she said, laughing nervously, as he got in the car.

'Yes, I thought so,' he replied smiling easily.

'We must not be seen here together, we had better go for a drive.'

'Fine, but don't go too fast. We need to talk, very seriously.'

'Oh dear,' she said, starting the motor. It was the first thing that came into her head. His proximity made her realise that the attraction between them was mutual, and very strong.

During the drive West, back along the coast road, he outlined what he wanted her to do. She drove carefully, the breeze whipping occasionally at her scarf and hair, listening intently but tight-lipped. Although her body was alive to him, her mind was appalled by the peril implicit in his plan.

Eventually, she pulled off the West Coast Highway and crossed the bridge to Ming Village. There she stopped at the end of Pandan Road, and switched off the engine, gazing fixedly, out to sea.

'Something wrong,' said Payne, laconically, enjoying the sight of her smooth brown thighs.

'What you ask is quite impossible,' she said stiffly.

Payne shifted uneasily in his seat, 'I know it's difficult for you, but...'

'Difficult! It is suicidal!'

Oh dear, thought Payne, they were having their first row.

'You are asking me to give *you*, you...a...a... '

'Fugitive,' volunteered Payne helpfully.

'Yes, fugitive..., an Embassy technician's pass, to the, the...'

'The cipher room?'

'Yes, cipher room. The most secret part of the building!'

'But you're the Ambassador's daughter...You can do it...'

'I think you have inflated idea of my importance...' stormed Mi Ling, flashing a good deal of eye white, having removed her large Raybans.

'I think...'

'What? What you think?' She turned toward him, the large eyes now mainly almond, but blazing wildly.

'I think, you're *very* beautiful...,' said Payne, sincerely.

Mi Ling flushed.

'And *I* think, you watch too many American films...! I suppose you say next that it is only when I'm angry?'

'Well yes. That too,' replied Payne defensively, but with a hint of a smile behind his beard.

'Your beard...It is awful!' she fumed.

'Come on Mi...'

'Do not call me that!'

'I was going to say,' Payne went on calmly, 'that we're beginning to sound like an old married couple.'

'You presume too much... altogether...'

'Mmm, perhaps you're right,' he said, lighting a rare cigarette, 'But right now I..., we..., your mother... and England.., don't have much choice..'

There was a brief silence between them, during which Payne admired the girl's gently heaving bosom and smoked casually, watching the exhaled smoke, whipped by the breeze out to sea.

At length she spoke, 'Very well I *will* get you the cipher code for one day only. You must not go there. And the broadcast must not be made from the Embassy, or indeed even from Singapore..'

'Good thinking.' acknowledged Payne.

'And one more thing...,'

'What's that?'

'Stop looking at my legs!' she shrilled, and with the very faintest of smiles, she donned her glasses and started the engine.

*   *   *

And so, Payne – knowing something about the international intelligence communications network, from his association with Julia – made a coded broadcast to the intelligence world.

At Mi Ling's suggestion, he transmitted the message from a light aircraft, hired from Changi Flying Club, at the limit of its range at sea, just south of Vietnam.

It very briefly detailed Hope-Watson's core intention to selectively target the United Kingdom and his motives behind the attack. It was naturally difficult to cite the precise methods, but gave warning that the authorities should prepare the population and take a whole range of precautions. He was about to transmit the code for *Counter Strike!* when he realised that by so doing, he might actually trigger some of the detonating receivers, the installation of which he had arranged! Strangely, at that point, the plane's transmitter had broken down!

He then pondered about the integrity of the entire message. He had done what he could, but doubted if it was enough. He had already sent a more direct warning in plain language to the international news agencies, via the Internet, using a hired laptop computer with a satellite link, but he doubted if it would be believed, for he was painfully aware that they received hundreds of hoax warnings, almost every working day!

On the international long range, high frequency wave length, there were many receiving stations, some professional, but mostly amateur. However, few stations were capable of breaking the daily changed diplomatic code. It was a double-edged sword, for in one way it gave the message credibility, but in another, it limited its reception drastically. Most who received it, would ignore it as some whimsical code within a code, and so not take it seriously. But Payne knew that if the integrity of transmission was not compromised or jammed, it *would* be received by British GCHQ at Cheltenham, England, and that the Chief Cipher Officer there, would take it seriously enough to refer it upward. Moreover, even if the message was ignored by that officer's superiors and government, it would still be re-coded, and repeated for later assessment, by selected diplomatic stations abroad. Especially those with an MI6 or CIA, presence.

The Chief Cipher Officer at GCHQ, at that time, happened to be one, Julia McMahon.

Confirmation of an earlier message was indeed received by the US Consul and the British Embassy in Brussels. The latter at first treated it as some diplomatic hoax, but the US Consul, a careful man, sent it to the Central Intelligence Agency in Washington. However, there were certain tensions in Anglo-American intelligence co-operation at that time, and so delays – even in the interpretation of electronic eavesdropping, were inevitable.

33

*"Hope deferred
maketh the heart sick."*

Anon

————

Brussels

Tuesday, October 27th 1998

After the Event

Julia McMahon returned to Goodchild who was waiting impatiently in the Mercedes taxi, outside NATO Headquarters where it was raining gently. He had not been admitted.

'Well, what happened?' he enquired, as she got in. 'You've been a very long time.' Although it registered with Goodchild that she looked very tired, he was impatient for news.

'I was interviewed by an RAF Group Captain,' sighed Julia, 'I have to come back in a couple of days. We'd better go back to the hotel.' She leaned forward to instruct the driver, with Goodchild tugging at her sleeve, 'Novotel, Zaventem, *S'il vous plaît.*'

On the way back to the Novotel, as the Mercedes hissed along the ever damp Brussels Ring, Julia told Goodchild what little she knew.

'Is it very bad? When can we go back?' He asked her intently.

'Robin,' replied Julia, passing her hand briefly across her forehead in a gesture of fatigue, 'I know very little. In fact, I doubt if *they* know much yet...'

'But what are they *doing* about it? How could this have happened?'

'We're not even sure exactly what has happened, yet,' she replied, gazing out of the window at the traffic, that looked so normal.

Goodchild felt excluded by her use of 'we're not... sure'.

She was very tired, and not just physically. It crossed her mind that crisis affected people in various ways. Some became stoic or rose to the occasion. Others were just a pain! Apart from her companion, the news, (or lack of it), a thousand unanswered questions – and most of all Jacqui's death – assailed her, adding to her incipient migraine.

She pondered sadly on the death of her friend and felt somehow responsible. Then she thought of her home, wondering if the cottage was still standing, and if she would ever see it again.

Some days later, she was interviewed again by the Group Captain, who was now attached to the British Overseas Service Contingent. This comprised specialist senior British officers from all three services, who had travelled to Brussels, from all over the globe. Essentially, they augmented those already stationed at NATO and so made it their natural headquarters.

'Miss McMahon,' said the Group Captain gazing at her intently, 'what you have told us is valuable. I think you should see Ambassador Taylour, who is co-ordinating the situation internationally, principally with the Americans, since he is our man in Washington,...'

'You mean I am to see the British Ambassador to Washington?' said Julia incredulously.

'I think so, yes. You can tell him what you have told us... Oh, by the way, you won't have to go to the States; he's coming here..., next Wednesday.'

'Oh, I see... Look, I know this might sound a bit wet,' she laughed nervously, 'but, well...'

'Yes,' said the Group Captain, kindly.

'When can I go home?' she replied simply.

The Group Captain stood up, signifying that the interview was at an end, 'All in good time. We don't know that it's safe yet.' He paused, and lowered his voice confidentially. 'As far as we can tell, Ireland, Scotland and Wales seem relatively unaffected. Unconfirmed of course.'

'Of course,' replied Julia. She seemed to have heard that

phrase somewhere before. As she rose from her seat she felt giddy and suppressed a yawn. She seemed to be continually tired and felt that she had suddenly aged.

'Perhaps you have relatives – or other interests in those countries?'

'I'm sorry...?' she enquired, having retreated into her own thoughts.

'Scotland, Ireland...' repeated the Group Captain 'I was saying perhaps you might consider going...?'

'Oh, no. I don't think so...' Julia shook her head, but at the same time wondered if Robin could be interested. It might be better for him than staying in a hotel in Brussels. She would remember to ask him.

*   *   *

Southern England

Late November 1998

After the Event

Rescue operations were proceeding with the US Marine Corps, British and UN troops, using Micro Impulse Radar. This micro-chip radar device largely replaced sniffer dogs by penetrating rubble and pinpointing respiration and heart-beats at a range of up to three metres. Where the wreckage was too unstable to support rescuers, the detectors were inserted into the debris from a safe distance to indicate signs of life.

Physical destruction appeared limited, mainly to the inner city areas, but occasional unseen dangers lingered for the unwary in rescue teams. Against orders, a number of men had removed their protective masks to smoke, or simply because they were hot, or uncomfortable. For this they were to pay a heavy price, for pockets of retained nerve gas and radiation were still in evidence. But after two weeks, the rescuers' detectors and Geiger counters told them that even these hazards had begun to disperse and fade.

With these few exceptions, as a body, the well-equipped troops, suffered few casualties from these agents, but the urban population had not been so lucky.

Collateral damage to the main services was keeping the technical restoration teams busy. Numerous gas lines were damaged, and these had kept fires burning, fires which would otherwise have long since been extinguished. Water flooded the streets from broken mains, and electricity supplies were only just being restored. Damage to power stations was limited, but some staff had perished from gas or had varying degrees of radiation sickness.

Problems with the electrical power system were mainly confined to transmission and distribution breaks. All nuclear plants were automatically shut down by safety systems when the attack began. Moreover, there was little urgency to restart them, as the base electrical load for the country had fallen by nearly two thirds. Although this would slowly rise as more supplies were connected, it would never again be much more than half of that previously consumed.

Communications on a national scale were still heavily disrupted, with most of the main telephone exchanges badly damaged and staff missing. The engineering regiments had managed to restore a number of the key cellnet transmitters, dotted about the country, because mobile phones were more useful than terrestrial lines in any emergency – particularly one as extensive as this.

A few hospitals were damaged, but most destruction was through fires, caused by staff affected by gas and radiation when smoking, and because of early electrical damage.

Unfortunately, as might be expected, the mortuaries were full, and teams of Marines, Pioneers and volunteers had brought in mini mechanical diggers, to excavate mass burial grounds on wasteland – of which there was an increasing amount, as city centre areas were bulldozed.

For example, there was hardly any major structure standing in greater South East London, from New Cross to Croydon, extending to Chatham in the East. And as reports came in from team leaders from all over the country, this appeared

234

to be the worst affected area, followed by West Central Birmingham, Wolverhampton, Liverpool, Manchester and Leeds. Bristol city centre had survived and Bath was untouched, together with Exeter. Parts of Plymouth, however, required almost as extensive a reconstruction effort as took place after the 1939–45 war.

The main university towns had taken only token damage; Oxford centre was intact, but Cowley, the motor manufacturing suburb, had been largely demolished. The worst affected of the southern coastal towns were Brighton, Bexhill and Portsmouth. Bournemouth however, was relatively unscathed, apart from the usual communications centres damage.

The following piece appeared in *New Britain Forward!* an embryo government broadsheet:

London

'It has emerged that overall physical damage has been surprisingly light, the exceptions being significant parts of some of the larger cities. For example, in London, certain South & East areas were wrecked — while the City, West and North remain structurally untouched.

The main London tourist areas remain intact: the Palace of Westminster, all the Royal Palaces, St Paul's, Trafalgar Square — even Greenwich, south of the river, and the old Naval College.

Casualties

Early US surveillance reports little evidence (photographic, electronic, or heat signature) of mobile wounded, in the normally populous areas. Indeed, all discernible casualties appear to be fatalities, whether in or out of vehicles — on all the thoroughfares and other public places surveyed.

Other cities and manufacturing centres

Among the regional cities, Liverpool is heavily damaged, as is most of Birmingham centre, Wolverhampton, Manchester, Sheffield, Leeds, and many of the ethnic areas. Whereas, some, but not all, of the industrial areas are almost intact. A major exception is motor manufacturing, reported to be at a virtual stand still at Dagenham, Derby,Cowley, Longbridge, Solihull, Swindon, Coventry and Ellsemere Port.Where Derby is concerned, one strange anomaly is that whereas theJapanese owned carplants have been destroyed or heavily damaged, the Rolls—Royce Aero Engine works appears unscathed, and work is reported to be continuing normally, following the restoration of power supplies.

Airports

London Heathrow and Gatwick have suffered minimal physical damage, with none of the runways or manoeuvring areas seriously affected. The exceptions are the communications centres, including the control towers, radio, radar and operations centres. Once again, this appears to be a recurring pattern throughout the land. However, efforts are being concentrated to restore these facilities.

The Countryside

In rural districts, there are obviously fewer fatalities per given area, and once again they are more concentrated around centres of communication, such as telephone exchanges, military installations and airfields, power and telephone lines and the like. There is also evidence that fewer have died from the gas or the effects of radiation, as from some other syndrome. This has begun to be related to diesel oil. However, not all diesel fuel is suspected, but it is sufficiently widespread to cause fatalities among a relatively large number. In particular, young men and youths, are particularly badly affected in places where they are known to have congregated: pubs, arcades, town and village centres. One village policeman, whose house was destroyed, commented that it was almost as if a par-ticular section of the younger, rural population had been "culled"!

Strange fatalities

However, fatalities among girls of this age group, appear to be restricted to those who were in the company of the unfortunate boys at the time. Overall, affected groups are small and widely distributed. Another surprising finding is that many of these youngsters died up to seven hours in advance of the main Event — which as the whole world now knows, began at 5am on Monday 26th October, 1998.

The diesel fuel, thought responsible, when tested, contained an, as yet unknown toxic ingredient, which takes from forty minutes to two hours to kill — depending on the concentration.'

* * *

The English Midlands

November, 1998

After the Event

Robin Goodchild's return to England was in the same manner as his departure – at the controls of the familiar, smallest Boeing, the 737 or "Pig", as it was affectionately known. What was not the same, was the country he had left, for it had changed, irrevocably.

On the aircraft's final approach to Birmingham International, things looked much the same, except for occasional strange blackened patches, which sometimes necessitated traffic diversions – even on the motorways. On closer inspection, Goodchild judged road traffic flow reduced to half normal, for a Friday in November. Acting as Captain for this flight – due to aircrew and other staff problems! – he was glad to have "Bob" Marley, as second officer. Bob, who was black, had been in the country during the Event – and lucky to escape with his life, had been giving him a vivid account of his experiences.

All too often, when Goodchild asked after a particular colleague, Marley's answer had been a sombre shaking of the head, and occasional rolling of the eyes.

'Man, I can tell you, I never hope to go through such an experience ever again. It was awesome...'

'I can imagine,' commented Goodchild, checking his height. Although in reality – he could not imagine.

'Them bangs were like the tumbrils of hell itself...' Marley went on..

'Really...?'

'Yeah, it being very early and nearly dark, see..., well, that didn't help... I can tell you. It sure ruined my breakfast...'

'Flaps, Bob,' Goodchild reminded him.

'Oh....., right.' Marley, leaned forward and applied the first flap setting, slowing the small airliner, perceptibly.

'But what's it like down there?' enquired Goodchild, 'Are there many changes?'

'Changes...? I'll say there are changes..,' replied Marley, easing the twin throttle levers back a fraction, as they continued their descent, '...you ain't got no ILS, for a start!'

'I know,' said Goodchild, stoically, 'but we'll manage, the visibility's quite good... ' He arced his head, back and forth, squinting slightly as he gazed out of the flight deck side windows.

'How's the airport, otherwise – reasonably normal?'

'Normal ain't the word,' replied Marley, flatly.

'No?'

'No..., I'm afraid a lot of guys... and babes, died...'

'Oh,' said Goodchild, on a down note, and he gripped the control column more tightly. 'Perhaps you'd like to tell the passengers what to expect then, since you know more than me...'

'OK,' responded Marley, twisting in his straps to switch

on the cabin address system. He enjoyed this little task; it appealed to the showman in him.

*　　*　　*

**"The price of selfishness
is loneliness."**

(R.T.T)

The Cotswolds, England

After the Event

Julia was glad to be back.

To her delight, her home and the village seemed normal – on the surface anyway, as far as she could tell. But the people appeared permanently changed by the experience. They had lost their spontaneity, and appeared hollow-eyed and withdrawn, nervous... and even strangely suspicious. For example, they started at any loudish sound, such as the passing of an aircraft overhead, or a motor cycle – although there were noticeably fewer of both of these former everyday phenomena. She noticed that the young children clung unnecessarily to their mothers in a manner, uncharacteristic of the nineties .

Robin had told her they would all get over it. While, proudly back in his old job, at first, he gave the impression of carrying on as if nothing had happened. But she was sensitive enough to know that was far from the actual truth.

In her pre-occupation with re-establishing her life, there were times when she almost forgot what had happened, but reminders occurred most days, and on most journeys, abrupt areas of devastation, greatly reduced traffic, a quietness and widespread air of melancholy – even in the bright November sunshine. An undeclared mourning was abroad – and yes, a quiet anger too.

She had decided, quite suddenly, to completely refurbish her home.

The carport had thankfully been demolished. She

decided to rip out the coloured bathroom suite and replace the outdated artex ceiling finishes, change the shagpile carpet and the mosaic tiles, to give away the goatskin rugs and venetian blinds. But most redolent of all – she wanted to get rid of all that chintz!

She had been given the new job of directing the restoration of communications at the devastated GCHQ.

Julia's past place of employment, more popularly known as the "spy centre", or GCHQ, was situated on the edge of the Cotswold spa town of Cheltenham, famous for its horse racing, Gold Cup, the splendour of its Regency buildings, a centre of variety in the arts, including literary and jazz festivals, home of Europe's largest school for girls.

The tree-lined avenues and pleasant parks seemed intact, as they shed their multi-coloured leaves in an occasionally breezy November.

The old GCHQ main building at Cheltenham told a more sombre story. It had been devastated. Many of Julia's old colleagues must have been on duty at the time, killed where they worked, or while taking a cup of coffee in the canteen; or perhaps when they were arriving for duty during the shift change, or sadly, leaving for home in their cars.

She had wondered about this. The timing of the Event meant that nearly all the management staff, who worked a normal 8.30am to 5.30pm day, would be absent from the building, and should therefore have survived. So why had they chosen her for such a key job, with so many more senior people available? She had found out later that they had all perished, or just disappeared!

This news sounded alarm bells ringing in her mind, and heralded a little guilt, as well.

She walked to a little chapel, off Montpellier, and prayed for them – lighting a few white tapering candles, for those she had known particularly well. She also lit a candle for Jacqui – which at last, brought forth her tears. Grateful that the chapel was empty, she wept uncontrollably. Then, suddenly she remembered the strange Deaconess in Brussels, and prayed for her too.

She thought of Robin and how the situation had sucked the romance out of their relationship, and left it in a vacuum.

Shivering slightly, she recalled Marcus Payne, and wondered where he was now, and what role he had played in the recent terrible events. She asked herself if she would ever hear from him again, and what her reaction might, or should, be if she did.

But now, she had to rebuild her life, after Jacqui, after Marcus, and yes... perhaps, after Robin too!

Above all, her task now was to re-establish her career, and her independence, on a very different basis from previously. Who knows, she thought, here there might be an opportunity to influence events at a critical time, and maybe to make amends for the past! For she had learned from her meeting with Ambassador Taylour, that there was to be a new government – a new Order, and that one of its (and principally her) foremost tasks, was to re-establish, international communications with the rest of the world. But what a pity they would almost certainly be covert, as before.

Drying her eyes, she walked out of the little Regency chapel and across the road into Montpellier Gardens. Above the falling leaves, the sun glinted in the trees, and a bird or two sang brightly. It gave her new hope, and she felt much better.

*   *   *

*"Bullies exist because
there are cowards."*

(Mahatma Ghandi)

Singapore

Before the Event

Having become increasingly suspicious since Payne's

disappearance, Hope–Watson was convinced that he was still alive.

More seriously, he began to suspect that Li Chan might know something about the tiresome South African's resurrection, or worse that she had assisted him – and, even now, may be harbouring him somewhere on the island. Initially he had dismissed this as stress-induced paranoia. But he had been watching his dutiful wife and noted her unexplained absences. On these occasions he had the lower terrace gardens searched, but without result. He in turn did not wish to arouse her suspicions or to alarm her unnecessarily, so he exercised some forbearance when he questioned her on her return. Indeed, he did not always do so.

Her answers were mostly convincing: shopping with Mi Ling; hairdressing and other personal care appointments; meetings with the Embassy Social Secretary. However, on the last point he knew *that* damn woman would lie to protect "the mistress" as she would insist on calling her – most unsuitably!

Yet, something was amiss... He would ask Mi Ling, his trusted assistant...

Then it hit him. What if "his girl" were involved? He paused to absorb this inward revelation. To sacrifice Li Chan would be terrible enough, but Mi Ling...? His Eastern Flower, his Fragrant Rose, his indomitable intellectual foil... and yes, his dearest, closest *friend...*, he hoped! For searching his mind, he had precious few friends. Acquaintances...? Yes. Associates...? A-plenty. Friends? No.

The terrible dilemma presented itself. If Li Chan and Mi Ling were allied with Payne, then they were a palpable threat to his momentous plans. If the FFEC should find out, they would demand their immediate liquidation – as a security threat.

He must think and then, sadly, set a trap for them. He experienced a fleeting loneliness until ire took over. How dare they betray him after all he had done for them? And for whom? A chancer, a vagabond of no fixed belief or abode?

But he was wrong. It was not for Payne that they had deceived him. It was for what *he* had done to Payne.

And so, by this logic, Hope–Watson was convinced. If his wife and stepdaughter were unable to stomach the attempted culling of a rascal such as Payne – himself a killer, what chance was there of their acceptance of a whole host of necessary deaths, in the much wider and lasting cause embodied in *Counter Strike!* ?

He briefly likened himself to John The Baptist, standing firm against a hail of decadence and mass abuse of everything he had held dear since childhood, and in the place that was still in his heart of hearts, "forever Eden."

In earlier justification, he had related his struggle to that other great, patriotic and eponymous Englishman, Cecil Rhodes! But if he was Rhodes, Payne was no longer his Dr Jameson.

But he had seldom been alone in his struggle! There were still stalwarts in the FFEC, as well as the waverers, and many supporters worldwide, as yet unidentified or counted – he was sure of that. When the deed was done, they would applaud. But they must never guess that he was even partly responsible, for that way lay perdition and disgrace. More importantly, the great act of faith that was *Counter Strike!* would be interpreted as just another act of wanton destruction – instead of making way for the New Jerusalem, or, as others would have it, the *Paradise* so persistently postponed!

Early the next day, before he could devise a trap for his wife and her daughter, he received a coded fax from the FFEC.

Apparently, through its devious links with the intelligence world, the communications cell had intercepted a long range high frequency, coded broadcast, on a secret diplomatic frequency, warning of an unsolicited and selective attack on Britain! But as far as could be determined, it had not been taken seriously, or acted upon. However, the fax made plain the FFEC's displeasure and stated that here indeed was evidence of a breach of security which certainly did not originate from them! Accordingly *Counter Strike!* should be cancelled, or at least postponed.

Hope–Watson decided the opposite. He began to draft the necessary message to all his field operatives to bring *Counter Strike!* forward – before it was too late! He decided to act first and inform the FFEC later. After all, what might they do without incriminating themselves? A dangerous supposition.

And so the deed was done.

Then he waited in Singapore, anticipating the summons to serve in any way he could, for he had been careful to lay the ground over preceding months ensuring that *he* would be the one selected. His remaining powerful friends in FFEC had seen to that. And yes, even those in official diplomatic circles, were not without his influence. In times of pressing emergency a man's "past" politics may be forgotten, while his abilities are remembered.

For Hope–Watson, Taylour's call could not come soon enough!

However, Payne, Li Chan and Mi Ling remained a threat, and he reluctantly decided that they would have to be dealt with. He had already shown that he had little compunction when it came to dealing with Payne. But dismissing his family? That was quite another matter. After all, he may need them!

34

*"Springtime is the land awakening.
The March winds are
the morning yawn."*

(Lewis Grizzard)

Hampshire, England
March 30th 1999

After the Event

On a crisp sunny morning, dressed in knitted silk tie and elegantly cut hounds–tooth jacket, stiff corduroy trousers and gleaming shoes, Hope-Watson was ensconced, relatively comfortably – considering the previous year's events – in his former country seat in the Test Valley, Hampshire. It was a Grade II listed house, brick built and timbered, low lying with lawns sloping down to a footbridge over a bright clear tributary of the River Test, which still yielded trout in the appropriate season.

Seated on one of several terraces, under one of the balconies, with views over the river and extensive gardens, the sun setting off his white hair and fresh complexion, he frowned momentarily at the parts of his domain still in need of some attention. However, there were new flowerbeds and bridges over the river, and clogging reeds had been cleared from the shallow water, sparkling brightly in the spring sunshine.

But it was strangely quiet..

In this soporific atmosphere, it was perhaps not surprising that he dozed off and as sleep came after a period of frenetic effort, it was also little wonder that he began to dream...

He was first of all, at Henley, as a young man, experiencing the balmy breezes rippling the surface of the river, and men in white boaters and gaudy striped blazers, supporting on their arms, expensively dressed women. They seemed to laugh incessantly, but in a manner that blended with the

245

gaiety of the surroundings, appearing in unison with nature and the environment – instead of offending against it, unlike the theme of nineteen nineties public gatherings.

This dream was obviously associated with the July Festival of Music and the Arts – a one time experience.

Then, he found himself at the Benson and Hedges Cricket Cup Final, at the hallowed green and white Lords ground, walking confidently and improbably into bat, pulling on his gloves with that wondrous willow instrument tucked firmly under his arm, when unaccountably, the scene and season changed to...

The Cenotaph
Whitehall, London, England

11am, Sunday November the 15th 1998

After the Event

Here was the actual event in which he had recently – in the international media's words – "bravely taken part!" The period between the Event and this milestone ceremony had been brief – the gathering barely safe. For among autumn leaves and blood red poppy wreaths of national mourning, were the detritus and paraphernalia of attack and subsequent rescue; plus the occasional whiff of gas and the background click of the Geiger counter.

He had flown in from New York, on an American transport plane with Taylour, for this much curtailed, though still impressive ceremony, held at the Whitehall Cenotaph – the white portland stone memorial to Britain's dead in two world wars.

A Remembrance Day, perhaps to end all Remembrance days...!

Attended by rescue teams, active servicemen of many nations, (few in the usual ceremonial regalia), and by one of the arch perpetrators!

Among the proud, and sadly borne red poppies, in the internationally attended service, some also wore the

246

English Tudor Rose – as a symbol of national loss. Others, poignantly, wore photographs of loved ones or comrades. Individual counties, cities and towns, sent representative groups of all ages, races and religious persuasion, – who marched past, solemnly, to familiar regional tunes.

Hope-Watson, a dignified figure, gave a moving speech, which history would judge, took hypocrisy to new depths! But, nevertheless, it provided a timely rallying call – after which, Taylour had congratulated him!

*   *   *

*"It is in his soul
that the swallow knows when to leave –
and in his heart that he chooses
a fitting time to return."*

(E.Cantona)

He awoke suddenly, and thought, involuntarily, of Mi Ling.

A darkish cloud scudded across the brightness of the springtime sun, and he shivered in spite of his heavy tweed jacket. He recalled a conversation with his erstwhile stepdaughter. They were on the terrace of the Residence, in far-off Singapore, under a very different, tropical, sun...

Its imagined warmth caused him to drift off once more...

She had looked, as always, quite stunningly beautiful and this had not made things easier for him.

'I had hoped you might see sense,' he said to her, sternly.

'A platitude, uncle,' she had replied, dangling her slender hand over the balustrade, and gazing down though the humid mists and trees, toward the sea.

'There's little time for the finer points of speech, my dear, we are at the turning point of our lives, you, me and...'

'And mother?' she said abruptly, turning to him, her dark eyes cold.

'Yes, of course, your mother, too...'

'And what would you have us do?' she countered.'Ignore what happened under this very roof? Attempted murder of

247

a guest in our own home?' Her shoulder quivered with the intensity of her delivery, and the dark eyes flashed, questioning..

'I think you may be getting matters a little out of proportion. After all, Payne himself is a killer.'

'At your behest,' shrilled Mi Ling, a trace of tears lingering between eye and cheek.

'That is not strictly true. I have had reports of his killing both in England and on his way out here.'

'But he was fleeing for his life.' Mi Ling sobbed defensively.

'Oh, so you know all about it then. What else did he tell you?' Hope-Watson tried to suppress his growing anger as he sensed signs of an affinity between her and Payne.

He reminded Mi Ling that, so far, he had killed no one, and that when he did, it would be indirectly – and in an essential cause, like any senior commander, or historic figure, who changes the course of history.

'Is that how you see yourself? Another Hannibal, or Napoleon? Or is it another Stalin... or Hitler!'

That had awoken him.

Getting his old house back had not been a random bonus – but more of a condition. Taylour, a traditionalist, had relented when told the house was originally the official home of a former Cabinet Minister. Hope-Watson had pointed out that his renewed occupancy was fitting on two counts: firstly because it was his natural home, and secondly, because he was now a Cabinet Minister – of sorts.

At first, the question of his title, or position, exercised him and confused others. He actually held several titles and many posts and delegation was vital – but only to those he could trust.

Chairman of the Political Council for Reconstruction (or PCR).

The truth was that he had not really made up his mind which best suited him. In this initial dynamic phase in the new nation's development, he told himself, it would be better to decide later – when the dust had literally settled!

For now, he resolved to put behind him his domestic problems and maintain clarity of political purpose, otherwise all would have been for nothing. Nor was it sufficient for his day to day actions alone to achieve that purpose. No! He knew he would need to embroil and persuade others to set up institutions which would last, and continue to deliver the policies and administration, he and his backers were convinced were needed. Meanwhile, countering external forces which might impose a path leading to the past. That, he determined, must never occur – in his life time, or beyond.

The ploy was to appease Taylour, Praed, Lammas and the EEC, by agreeing with them. Then, simply fail to implement their wishes – until such time that he, and the new nation, had sufficient strength (mainly financial) to ignore them. Then, to proceed with the real job in hand. By the time they had all realised they had given him virtual *carte blanche*, it would be too difficult to reverse matters.

Hope-Watson had set himself an even greater task than changing the nation's political economic and social structure. He also needed to reverse its culture.

Americanism and over-population had been but two deadly conditions, breeding not only political and economic expediency – at the expense of proletarian misery – but an unwillingness to take a chance on people, ideas, or unestablished products. Every bet had to be a certainty, or near certainty. Industry had been run by accountants – defeating creativity, and politics had been dominated by lawyers – at the expense of integrity!

At all events, Hope-Watson had quickly succeeded in one of his primary aims: namely, the elimination of the three traditional British political parties – who had collectively held sway for nearly ninety years! This was achieved in an indecently short time, through the relatively simple ploys of delegation and reverse psychology.

The new organ of government, was a hastily conceived provisional parliamentary legislature. This replaced the old Parliament, but used part of the Palace of Westminster buildings

– portions of which were still undergoing necessary repairs. This assembly retained delegates who were overtly independent (as in the Isle of Man Parliament), but were mainly nominated by the FFEC, the most vociferous of whom, were virtually under Hope-Watson's control, a control exercised through like-mindedness, financial support – and, if all else failed, by threats to their personal and economic future. This was nothing new!

A number of delegates put forward the radical changes which Hope-Watson required. Then, he publicly opposed them, to divert ownership of them. He was then overruled by a simple majority, and so his intended programme came about.

Hope-Watson could not quite believe such a subterfuge was historically unique – neither could he accept how easy it had been to achieve! But then his knowledge of political history was not particularly robust.

That well-tried excuse, the State of Emergency, soon carried the quest (temporary of course!) for a one-party state.

Quite rapidly, the Royal family (or what remained of it) had been constitutionally disenfranchised. On announcing the necessary decree, Hope-Watson had expressed public misgivings – while in reality he was its chief architect. A written constitution amended every five years, coinciding with the renewal of the Presidency, was introduced – with Sir Iain Taylour the first incumbent, due to Sir Percival Praed's recent failing health. This appointment pleased the Americans and the UN. While Hope-Watson remained tolerant of it, regarding it as temporary. For he was almost sure Taylour might be persuaded to step down, before his first term was complete. Indeed, it was just possible he too, might suffer ill health! Meanwhile, Taylour's internationally popular appointment, ensured at least the prospect of a much needed inflow of funds.

As Chairman of the Political Council for Reconstruction (or PCR), Hope-Watson's first task was to tone down its initial report to the new legislature. Some of its tenets even shocked him! And mindful of the fact that it would have to be released to the press – and thence the world – it was necessary to moderate it, otherwise overseas funding would be in jeopardy.

The starting point for the report was a view of the nation state, before the Event.

In a dusty room off Whitehall, Hope-Watson chaired an awkward and tiresome meeting called to ratify the report. The presence of remnants of the "old Civil Service" did not serve progress, except that they were necessary to verify the facts from remaining records..., and failing that, memory.

But, as is well known, memory is shot through with opinion...!

Hope-Watson gazed bleakly at the paper before him, and while agreeing with much of it, he could not be seen entirely to do so. He also judged its presentation as "over forthright".

Political Council for Reconstruction
Report on the
Political, economic & Social status of Great Britain,
prior to the Event of October 26, 1998.

Political scene

Concern is justified regarding the previous state of affairs, and steps to prevent its re-emergence would be desirable.

The former three political parties were merely a front, and only roughly coincided with the true political scene, which was disguised from the public's view.

Ostensibly a capitalist society, Britain had a strong, social liberal power camp that counterbalanced this, separate from the voter,and quite undemocratic. It exerted daily power through the educational establishment – quite simply by influencing the next generation! It had two public voices:-

(1) The former BBC, which exercised an unsubtle censorship of BBC radio and television news output –

mainly by a questionable and repetitive choice of subject. Apart from education, excessive time and emphasis were given to such subjects (to the exclusion of more relevant topics) which reflected the organization's internal politics and culture, rather than the public interest.

For example, there appeared to be a morbid interestinprisons,homosexuality, In vitro–fertilisation and child abuse, while geopolitical coverage dwelt disproportionately on Northern Island, Israel and Africa.

(2) The Guardian newspaper, part of a private company, legitimately championed social interest views. However, it was the exclusive and quite blatant use of this paper, by both the state educationalestablishment, and the BBC, for recruiting staff, that was unhealthy because this ensured that only a certain flavour of candidate was ever considered – let alone, recruited. A very efficient, self perpetuating process!

The above was the work of a young protege of the FFEC, named Carver, apparently a double first at Oxford..., or Cambridge, Hope-Watson could never remember which. What he was aware of, however, was that the man had little in the way of tact or circumspection, which during the present sensitive times, was a double first deficiency! The remaining Whitehall "old guard" present regarded him with a not unnatural, collective and healthy, disrespect.

Carver was presently on his feet, defending his piece...!

'Even before the Event, there was a body of academic opinion which believed the increasing failure of state education to properly educate British children – even in the fundamentals of literacy and numeracy – was a socialist plot thereby creating and maintaining a dependency culture, which would harry the Capitalists, and the decreasing few they chose to employ – with crime, and increasing taxation, to pay for their social benefits.'

'This theory was summarized crudely as – 'If you won't

let us play – we'll take it, anyway!'

Hope-Watson winced. He did not altogether subscribe to this theory, having met several members of the state teaching profession. Granted, he found some lacking in ability and general attitude, but he was aware that in many areas they were fighting a grim battle, which was not of their making – often with inadequate resources.

Later, he must have drifted off, because Carver had now changed the subject to the EEC... which he was attacking with some vigour!

'...On a more immediate, and serious note, the European Community, was (is!) beginning to suck the political power out of Britain. Like the life-blood of... well..., one may employ any analogy that comes to mind...'

But he did not do so.

'My first question is, *who*, or what, is *actually* the power and *motive* behind the European Economic Community? And can it *ever* be in the long term interests of our country?'

The civil servants blinked and Hope-Watson was mesmerised. He hovered between being impressed and appalled!

Carver was in full spate, 'Many may already *know* the answers to these questions...' He looked round the table but received only blank stares in return and continued, unabashed.

'It is that collective knowledge..., that will stiffen our resolve.'

Pausing for a sip of dusty water, he looked up at the flaking ceiling with distaste, then referred to his notes for a final flourish.

'I believe we can either embrace Europe and destroy it, Let Europe embrace Britain and destroy us! Or..., do the decent thing and withdraw!'

While the meeting attempted to digest this vaguely sexual metaphor, Carver concluded.

'We leave this topic temporarily, with an EEC Conference anecdote, where it was announced... that 95% of women in Europe, brought more money into the household than men did.' He paused for effect, looking up at his captive audience.

'Does that mean…, asked a Finnish lady delegate, that the men spend the money *before* they get home?'

He paused for applause, but there was none, apart from a rather slow hand clapping, predominantly from Hope-Watson, who decided it was high time to take charge.

Reviewing the immediate past, seemed a sterile exercise, yet Hope-Watson and his lieutenants gave it prominence – not merely to justify future measures, but also to put a stake in the ground, to which, he determined, New Britain must *never* return.

The civil servants brightened when Hope-Watson stood up.

'Gentlemen! Oh… I beg your pardon… and lady!' He peered over his glasses at a prim young woman, seated behind an overweight delegate. 'We now consider a summary of the British economy…. before the Event…' He adjusted his glasses and referred to the Paper before him. 'We note that up to 1997, Britain fell from 13th to 18th in the World economic League…, and that the UK net contribution to the EEC, including the Common Agricultural Policy, *may* have been a factor in this… unsatisfactory performance. Now…' He looked pointedly at Carver, who had written the text, and received a weak smile in return.

Hope-Watson then continued.

'It appears that a large part of the huge burden of government borrowing was spent on keeping a significant percentage of the community out of gainful employment…'

This brought forth various mutterings from the meeting, particularly the civil servants.

'… This had numerous negative effects. Unemployment led to crime and drugs – which begot more crime. The tax burden to finance borrowing, caused employers (particularly large companies) to cut costs to the bone and to transfer their business, or to import from cheaper countries, such as China.'

'Labour, being the most significant cost, forced

companies to "down size", the effect being that a large proportion of the over-forties were thrown out of work, taking with them a generation of experience and expertise...'

Hope-Watson put down the paper, an action which brought forth a look of concern from Carver, but he needn't have worried.

'Well, I think Mr Carver is to be congratulated, for thinking of us... the *older* generation...'

This warmed the temperature of the meeting a little, and Hope-Watson continued with mild gusto.

'....Consequently, many had to be supported by the tax payer – thereby creating a vicious circle.'

'If this were not serious enough, many employers replaced experienced staff with untrained and 90's educated young people.'

He put down the paper again and addressed Carve.

'Mr Carver, are we to take it that you discount all pre-Event, 90's education...?'

All eyes turned to Carver for his reply. But he was up to it.

'I was referring to state-educated young people, sir...'

'Oh, I see,' replied Hope-Watson, without qualification. But then, just as Carver thought he was safe, Hope-Watson said, 'It's just that you didn't actually say so.'

'I do cover it, quite comprehensively, a bit later on, sir,' Carver responded, smugly.

Had it been possible for a meeting to have emitted a collective groan, it would have done so at that point!

'Very well,' acknowledged Hope-Watson, 'I'm sure we shall all look forward to that! Now...'

'...bringing the level of service in many companies... to an all time low. Many have experienced being held on a telephone line... at the customer's expense..., obliged to listen to tasteless music, while awaiting service...'

'This is all very well sir,' interrupted a fierce looking civil servant, who displayed the demeanour of the senior man,

'But what are the foundations on which we are to rebuild the economy?'

'A pertinent question,' said Hope-Watson,' and at the risk

of pre-empting Mr Carver's later revelations, I shall attempt to answer that very briefly. I understand that London subsidised the rest of the economy in terms of many billions – and on its own would have been...' He turned to Carver, 'What was it Carver?'

'The sixth biggest economic unit in the European Union... That's more wealth produced than Sweden, Turkey and South Africa.' Carver answered, with unerring confidence.

This brought forth one or two gasps of surprise.

'So you see,' continued Hope-Watson, 'that will be our starting point...' and promptly sat down.

At the close of a long day, the report covering Exports, Export performance, the Environment, Population, Housing, Imports and Agriculture..., was amended and approved and went on to be presented to the New Parliament, a tedious but necessary process which laid the first cornerstone of the new State.

*   *   *

> *"Leave us to run our own ship,*
> *no matter how badly we do so!"*
>
> (Mahatma Ghandi)

Hampshire, England
April 30th 1999

After the Event

In international circles, the enquiry into of the causes of the Event was dragging on, known, of course, only to Hope-Watson and the FFEC – and a limited number of others. Even they were mystified by the extent of the disaster. There were mutterings in strictly closed circles about "overkill" and "miscalculation" and even "wanton slaughter". In fact, Hope-Watson had remarked that the matter had the political buck passing attributes of the allied bombing of Dresden in

World War 2, all over again.

Yet even he was not quite sure what had taken place, as he had not received all the reports which had been planned when he had conceived the outrage. He had been let down, and not only by Payne.

Also, there was something else...

And so, ironically, like the rest of the world, he had to rely increasingly on the press, for a post mortem picture of *Counter Strike!* until such time that a central intelligence gathering and communications centre could be re-established, a task, apparently, in the hands of someone to be appointed by Taylour, through his tiresome, British Overseas Services Contingent, or BOSC.

The re-constitution of the media had been a sensitive problem. Hope-Watson did not seek control, but influence, by releasing true, and occasionally exaggerated, leaks.

Taylour had also set up a new national broadcasting service. It provided both TV and Radio, with his own appointees in key posts. Hope-Watson thought it not quite as bad as the old BBC – which, he had once confided to Mi Ling, 'Needed a damn good clear out of all the politically correct harpies!' But when it was suggested that a new multi-channel cable TV system might be installed, Hope-Watson had retorted, 'We don't need 500 TV channels, just two good ones would suffice – minus police and hospital dramas!'

The press had quickly taken off – mainly owned and manned by expatriate Australians (which was not too much of a change!). However, control of the government-backed broadsheet, *New Britain Forward,* was retained. This featured a column, tucked way inside, entitled *Friend to Friend,* which purported to exchange international expatriate messages, but which in reality, was mainly used to transmit coded ciphers to FFEC members, who could not otherwise be contacted. At least a weekly perusal of this daily publication had become a condition of membership of the Funchal based cabal – and resignations were not allowed!

The press temporarily excepted, there were clauses Hope-Watson had insisted on, in the new written constitution, restricting foreign ownership of key industries. For example, he was determined that what remained of the motor industry would no longer be in foreign hands, as before, so putting into effect an opinion he had once expressed to Mi Ling, 'What other major country would sell its entire motor industry to foreigners? Could you imagine Germany giving away Mercedes, or BMW? Or the French selling us Renault, or the Italians, Fiat?'

'Well, they've sold most of Olivetti to the Americans and British,' retorted Mi Ling, countering while she thought of a more substantial *riposte.*

'Typewriters don't have quite the same cachet as motor cars, my dear.' Hope-Watson, had responded in a dangerously patronising tone.

He recalled sadly, the unabashed reply and the musical tone of her voice. He missed her. 'You're behind the times, Uncle Lloyd. They don't make typewriters any more! It's computers now – and many other products, besides.'

She had typically reinforced her argument by reminding him that actual ownership was of limited importance, provided the companies employed local people, paid taxes to the host nation and augmented national exports – thereby boosting the host nation's balance of payments. But Hope-Watson cited an earlier conversation of theirs, in which he had told her that multi-national companies had no national allegiances (even to their native countries) and that as soon as production costs rose beyond a certain point, they would close down the offending operation, take their subsidies and run.

Mi Ling had replied that was the nature of international business and that the Ford Motor Company had been in Britain for over fifty years. To which Hope-Watson had answered, turning to humour when defeated in argument, 'Oh they were founded by an Irishman, we'll never get rid of the Irish!' At this point, Mi Ling had thrown up her hands in mock horror and giggled.

He sighed, and with her memory, experienced one of his rare pangs of guilt, tinged with sadness.

*"Considering the number of Irish people
there are in England, compared with the number of
English in Ireland,
the question arises as to quite
who is occupying whom."*

(R.J.Williamson)

Belfast

At this point, Hope-Watson made a mental note that he would soon have to do something about the Northern Ireland problem, and in a far more forthright manner than had been employed in the previous decade. The key, he decided, were the Americans. They must think they are helping, when in reality they must be used – then excluded from the debate, and finally the Province, for good.

In considering the Northern Irish problem, Hope-Watson was of the simple opinion that people who killed were gangsters. (Of course he did not include himself in this category!) It was, he decided, nothing to do with political or religious problems; democratic society should have civilised ways of resolving those! But there is always the criminal element, which uses "political" disputes simply to make money. (He excused his own past actions by deciding that he had not made any money – in fact up to now, he was actually out of pocket!) Indeed, it was not in criminals' interests to see such problems resolved. If their so-called causes were settled, they simply moved on to others. They certainly would not go back to jobs as builders, shop keepers, accountants, or whatever their former professions had been – if they happened to have any. No, their life and living, was, is and will be terrorism, until somebody stops them. And that somebody was going to be Lloyd Hope-Watson - with a little help from the Americans!

*"The European Union,
from the economic standpoint,
is a giant.
Yet from the political point of view,
continues to be a dwarf."*

(La Vanguardia)

Barcelona

A guarded withdrawal from the EEC was among Hope-Watson's political aims, while at the same time, taking back as much from it as was possible – under the guises of reconstruction and inability to pay contributions. Then there was the simple impossibility of implementing the backlog of EEC directives – widely thought inappropriate at the best of times!

New British constitutional rules were supposed to be discussed (if not actually agreed) with the EEC Council of Ministers. Surviving members of the former British Government or Parliament were found, interviewed and the promptly isolated! Some were persuaded, and bought off with sinecures. Inevitably, a few were difficult and disappeared. Officially, they were consulted and their views recorded. Consultation with members of the British Commonwealth and various expatriate committees, took place but became mere talking shops.

The excuse given for the "temporary" elimination of the three main political parties (now replaced by a temporary, "citizens" party) was that it was necessary until such time as full and free elections could be properly held, the classic dictator's charter! But elections could hardly begin while the population and administration were being re-constituted.Meanwhile, the country had to be governed!

The "officially agreed" written constitution, to be amended every five years, coinciding with the renewal of the Presidency, was drafted, approved, and integrated with due ceremony at the Royal Albert Hall (The Palace of Westminster and Westminster Abbey, were both still under repair). All those attending, who were remotely entitled, wore full dress uniform. A military band was found, judiciously balanced by a childrens' choir, who sang – as might be expected – Parry's Jerusalem!

Hope-Watson resisted the rather obvious temptation to feature Land of Hope and Glory!

Immigration policy was an immediate priority. The first arrivals were mainly British expatriates. Perhaps surprisingly, colour was not an issue. However, policy dictated that they must be able to make an early economic contribution, through skills and/or their own capital; be fluent in English; physically healthy and fit; and not be the carriers of any known disease such as tuberculosis or AIDS.

Because they put practical matters before prejudice, neither Hope-Watson nor the FFEC could be accused of "conventional" racism; they paid little heed to colour as such. However, "an acceptable culture," consistent with British traditions, was expected! Otherwise, the new immigration criteria cloned the "points and sponsor system" currently operated by the USA, Australia, New Zealand and Canada.

The "Clean Slate Policy" – the central plank of the new administration – simply stated, was:

'The country will be refurbished using UN, US & EEC aid, and during this period will accede to any appropriate, and necessary constitutional changes, under the terms of the latest UN Resolution.'

However...,

Hope-Watson had negotiated a Charter, something akin to a Bill of Rights, with the FFEC (which still maintained potent world-wide influence) but Taylour, the UN and the EEC were barely consulted.

This Charter first appeared in *New Britain Forward*, and was debated in the launch week of the first restored television channel, NBBC One!

In written form, its primary phrases were to be found affixed to roadside telephone poles – those that were still standing.

"The New Parliament "– is a quintessential amalgam of the old and new!

New Britain will be,

An efficient state; a fair state with a strong sense of justice. People will have rights, but they will also have *responsibilities...*

Capital will not totally dominate, and labour will have fair reward...

Individual freedom is encouraged as long as it does not inconvenience others, or jeopardise the community (local and national) in any discernible way.

There will continue to be a Parliament with elected members.

New Britain will *not* be:

 A dictatorship!

 A regime where the innocent are punished, prosecuted or killed.

The New Citizens Party,

Will have a legal majority for the first five years only – the period of reconstruction.

Separation of power between the Executive, the Legislature (other parties together with us in Parliament) and the Judiciary, will continue.

The Judiciary,

However, fundamental reforms in the legal profession and the manner of the election of judges will be enacted immediately.

The Armed Forces

Will continue to reinforce the Civil Power – that is the police. All overseas deployed forces will return to home bases and remain there for the foreseeable future, with the exception of Northern Ireland.

The Police.

There will be a new *National* Police force.

The European Economic Community

Membership has not proved to be in Britain's long term interests. During the period of economic reconstruction we can no longer afford contributions, and we will be asking for the return of our foreign reserves, totalling some £30 billion (lodged at the Central European Bank before Monetary Union). A Bill will be placed before Parliament, for the withdrawal of New Britain from the EEC.

The Economy

Export markets to the English speaking nations will be vigorously promoted. The initial diminution of exports to the EEC will be counteracted by a price and quality campaign, and by releasing the full potential of *New British* companies set up in the EEC, before withdrawal. Any retaliatory action by the EEC, or member states, will be counteracted by the immediate nationalisation of EEC concerns in New Britain.

The Monarchy

His Royal Highness has graciously agreed to step down as head of state in favour of an elected President, whose term will run for 5 years. Any person who has held high office and has manifestly served the state or community may stand. However, an inaugural candidate has been chosen with the agreement of the supporting agencies of the international community.

35

Washington

After the Event

Having been temporarily suspended from his main duties by Scottdale, shortly after President Thomas's death, McIver made up his mind there and then to run for President. The primaries were the ideal platform, backed up by his hastily published memoirs, to crucify Scottdale with what he had learned about *Counter Strike!* during his long investigations with Hartog. All he had to worry about was the CIA, but if he was coerced, he might just reveal enough about their involvement to sink any attack before it got under-way. However, he was wise enough not to provoke them unecessarily.

He decided to bide his time and await developments.

He did not have long to wait. A few weeks after the President's death, McIver was sitting in the West Wing of the White House, next to the office of the new national security adviser to the Vice-President – his new boss.

While waiting, McIver opened his briefcase and glanced through the minutes of the first meeting on the now defunct operation, *Broken Arrow*.

SECRET

Chiefs' of Staff assessment of

Operation Broken Arrow

Things had changed. Since *Counter Strike!* no aspect of the Western alliance would remain as before. Many careers would also be affected – not least of all, his own. But as he read the report again, mentally correcting its assumptions, he reflected that in spite of recent events and revelations, perhaps not all of its insights were untrue after all...

(1) The possibility that Britain has been destroyed by a known or unknown enemy or by some accidental chain of events, needs to be determined.

(2) Some analysts say that expansionist China may be involved, following its shelling of Taiwan, the Hong Kong Accession, and news of the hand over of Macau.

The Chinese news agency is fighting a bitter rearguard action against world opinion, blaming them for the Event. This blame is exacerbated by Sino statements, films etc, openly declaring the West, but especially the USA, to be their enemy. This may have been started by the US Navy's past defensive action off Taiwan, and the 1996 Olympic Games which were staged in the USA rather than Bejing.

New Chinese long range missiles have been announced, and aircraft carriers planned, paid for by China's increasing economic strength.

(3) A possibility remains that the destruction was perpetrated by other than a covert force.

POST MORTEM QUESTIONS

How was it <u>allowed </u>to happen?

What were the warnings, (if any) oblique and direct? How were they received and acted upon?

McIver sighed deeply and looked up at the ornate white ceiling, then down at the deep red carpet under his highly polished shoes. He caught sight of himself in one of the long wall mirrors opposite. He looked very slightly haggard. The last five months had aged him – but he was still an impressive figure who could dominate any gathering. He was about to call on that attribute, and as many others as he could muster.

He was in the White House that Spring morning to brief the Vice-President on the lessons to be learned from *Counter Strike!*

While he waited, he took out his written summons to attend. It was printed on White House headed paper, a formal departure from the recent days of the late President Thomas. Then, a phone call would have sufficed.

The letter was addressed to:

General George Lee–McIver
Chairman of the National Defense Committee,
and the Joint Chiefs of the Defense Staff.

The first of these titles was already redundant, and he wondered how long it would be before the second would be also! Perhaps he was about to be told. Meanwhile, as he waited, he rehearsed what he hoped were some substantive answers to likely questions.

When he was eventually ushered in to the meeting room, the Vice–President stood up to greet him. He even shook his hand, appearing friendly enough, and neutral, but then McIver had no former relationship with him.

This was the first time since President Thomas's death that the new national security team had gathered. Chaired by the Vice-President, McIver thought it had a somewhat surprising membership.

There was Deputy Defense Secretary David Douglas, White House Chief of Staff Michael Denver, Deputy White House Chief of Staff Edwin Franks and President's Counsel James Stockman.

McIver was aware that there was a complete change of mood on security matters. In fact, he felt distinctly uncomfortable and sensed that former security policies were discredited. Worse, he felt he was somehow inextricably linked with them.

Nevertheless, he had been superficially welcomed, no doubt for his detailed memory of the recent past – particularly those details that might not have been officially recorded!

As a former National Security adviser, McIver had always run highly structured meetings, but this inaugural meeting was, at first, characterized by a measure of time-wasting banter, which led nowhere. However, one positive development arose; a new ambassador to the United Nations was appointed. This spared him the tricky task of back door meetings with Secretary General, Lammas.

McIver had started to deliver his carefully rehearsed homily on the lessons to be learned from *Counter Strike!*

'Historical examples of surprise attacks tell us that intelligence is acquired, but only rarely evaluated properly...'

As several pairs of not wholly friendly eyes contemplated him, it occurred to him that this might be seen as a past failing on his part, so he hastily reinforced his argument with some sound military advice.

'The capabilities of a likely, or known enemy can be measured – but *not* his *intentions!* The danger of making assumptions cannot be overemphasized. There is a natural tendency to project one's own sets of values upon others.'

'Despite an awareness that the enemy is different, it is hard to stop expecting him to act in the same way as oneself.'

Detecting signs of growing impatience, he concluded with a ringing finale.

'History gives many examples of this all too human failing'

The Vice-President thanked him, then, in a complete change of mood, dismissed several of the former banterers from the room, had a Marine guard put on the door, and got straight down to more serious business.

His first question was unexpected, and a considerable

shock. But it immediately made clear the real purpose of the meeting.

'What do we know about British Royal Navy Trident or Polaris submarine involvement in *Counter Strike!?*'

Although delivered to the meeting as a whole, this question was clearly directed at McIver, who had the distinct impression that his Chief already knew the answer. Whereas McIver had only unsubstantiated knowledge – for regardless of his lengthy conversations with Hartog, during which they had solved the puzzle, they had little or no evidence.

And before he could respond, the Vice-President followed up with an even more damning supplementary question, 'Was there an attempt to reprogramme, or retarget the onboard computers, to effect a Trident missile launch?'

McIver hastily countered, 'Mr Vice-President, I think that question would be better addressed to the Deputy Director of the CIA'

'Oh, why do you say that, General?'

'Because sir, he hinted at it during the President's meeting in California.'

'Which you attended?'

'Why yes, sir...But...'

'But you were not always admitted to the sub-committee discussions on various, er... top secret items on the agenda?'

'That's right, sir, I...'

'Didn't you think that strange... General?' The Vice-President added his rank, almost as an afterthought, staring at McIver inquisitorially, his head very slightly inclined to one side.

'Why yes, as a matter of fact, I did, and I protested at the time...'

'Who was it that *always* attended those sub-committees?'

'Well, the President... and the Agency Deputy Director...'

'Anybody else..., I mean, consistently...?'

'Secretary Scottdale, sir.'

'Thank you, General.'

It was at this point that McIver realised that Scottdale

was probably not going to attend the meeting. Up to that point he assumed he would be joining later. This knowledge caused him both puzzlement and some relief.

The Vice–President did not beat about the bush, and his following words were shocking for all present, including McIver. 'I can tell you that one Royal Navy vessel was taken out of line for test target marking. Also, that there was a clandestine computer replacement... And that this machine may have been reprogrammed, effecting a retargeting situation, culminating in a later firing... on a **drill only** launch command!'

'My God!' exclaimed the White House Chief of Staff.

The Vice-President continued, 'As a consequence, we believe that Admiral Kearns was going to Faslane to remove the "electronic key" which retargeted the Trident missiles.'

More gasps, during which McIver said nothing.

'He was a little late, wasn't he?' muttered President's Counsel James Stockman.

'Late, no, unsuccessful, yes...' replied the Vice-President. Then turning to McIver, 'Would you like to expand on this, General?'

As McIver cleared his throat to speak, it occurred to him that the Vice-President might be using this meeting to find out what he knew, and after all, knowledge was power!

'Sir, as I see it, Ted Kearns had two problems; number one, access to the base. He needed to remove the evidence which might incriminate him, but he was not sure how much damage *Counter Strike!* had done to the Faslane base. Whereas...,'

'Please go on, General,' prompted the Vice President with an oily smile.

'Well sir, as far as I know, what I'm about to say is uncorroborated...' McIver hesitated, he was not comfortable with the position in which he now found himself. He was about to divulge information which was the result of his unofficial research with Hartog.

'Well General? We're waiting...' The oily smile had gone.

'Sir, I have reason to believe that in Holy Loch, the old US nuclear submarine base, there was an old deserted and submerged Polaris submarine, and it was from that ship that specially adapted Polaris missiles were fired...'

'Yes, that fits...' interrupted Deputy Defence Secretary, David Douglas, 'we think missiles targeted on England, may have been fired automatically, by remote control, from such an area, and that demolition charges destroyed the launching site or vessel, immediately afterwards...'

'I'm obliged to the Deputy Secretary...' muttered McIver, simultaneously wondering where Douglas had obtained such information, why it had not been shared with him, and trying to absorb its implications.

'So what was his other problem?' enquired Stockman.

McIver replied with increasing caution, 'Although Kearns had used what influence he had to ensure otherwise, he could not be certain that the rigged Trident boat had not been sent to sea. The consequences of which would have been far worse perhaps than what already occurred...'

'What I can't understand are two things...,' enquired Deputy White House Chief of Staff, Edwin Franks, 'Why did he do all this, and two, why mess with all the difficulty of Trident when he had the old Polaris boat you mentioned, available...?'

The Vice–President supplied the answer, to McIver's considerable interest.

'The shortest possible answer is money and power. It was no secret he wanted General McIver's job. It is also thought that he was to be paid a fortune on results, by an as yet unidentified source.

Two, he was in a position, together with Captain Brannigan, over whom he had an unnatural hold, to access Trident secrets. It was only when he found the Trident route too difficult that he fell back on an original plan to use a modified Polaris solution.'

'Also, there remains a strong possibility that he had high official backing...'

Then, the Vice-President turned to a black leather folder before him and in a crisp, but slightly dramatic wrist movement, removed an official looking document from it and began to read, in soft measured tones....

McIver noticed that the document was stamped *Top Secret*, and bore the crest of the Central Intelligence Agency.

> *'The following is what is now believed to be the sequence of events that led up to the Event, Counter Strike! which was the code name used by one, if not all, of the perpetrators.*
>
> *This catastrophic attack culminated in the selective, but substantive, destruction of England as an industrial, commercial and political power.'*

He put down the document briefly and peered at his audience over rimless spectacles.

'As I think you already know, gentlemen, most of Scotland, Wales, Northern Ireland, Eire and the Channel Islands were not greatly affected, except for various military installations and communications centres, a repeated pattern of the attack.'

After looking hard at each man present, in turn, he continued...

> *'It is now believed that the order Counter Strike! was transmitted through the Internet. This initiated the fuses in many thousands of personal computers widely distributed throughout the country over the previous nine to twelve months, probably organized by a South African, named Payne. Many of these machines were in key government offices, including the military, the police and other security and emergency forces. Communications hubs were also hit by this method, but these were also the subject of "supplementary" targeting.*
>
> *There was an unknown number of ground agents recruited who had placed supplementary explosives in all main communications centres and sites, however remote.'*

The Vice–President's small select audience was transfixed by these revelations. Even McIver, who had pieced together much of what was revealed, was intrigued.

'Toxic diesel oil supplies, once again previously distributed to most rural areas, were activated by ground agentsinrespirators, twenty four hours before the main Event.'

'Given the twenty four to thirty six hour warning that Counter Strike! was imminent, it is possible (but not proven) that the late Admiral Kearns was alerted by the Internet broadcast. It is also suspected that he was in possession of a valid code capable of activating an old Star Wars defensive satellite. This device had been officially deleted from the Department of Defense inventory some time previously, and was thus listed as orbiting space debris!'

The Vice President raised his head, eyes cold and steady behind the rimless glasses, which glinted slightly as he delivered his next bombshell...

'The Agency has concluded that these actions might have been with the prior knowledge of these officers' superiors...'

At that point in the Vice–President's delivery, McIver experienced a nasty moment, when everyone present immediately looked at him!

'I should like to make it plain to this meeting,' announced the Vice–President with the merest trace of a wry smile, 'that General McIver is not under suspicion here, and that I *should* have said, *political* superiors.'

'I'm obliged to you, sir,' McIver acknowledged with some relief, leaning back in his chair and smiling.

'You mean, the late President knew about this?' gasped the White House Chief.

'I'm coming to that....,' the Vice–President continued.

'His superiors in this process were the late President, James D Thomas, and Defense Secretary, Richard Scottdale. The conclusion is that President Thomas may have known about this. However, evidence is still

being gathered. Meanwhile, Secretary Scottdale is being questioned, and has been taken to a place of safety.'

At this last revelation, McIver had to admit to mixed feelings: on the one hand, he had to suppress a rather childish feeling of being cheated. Following many weeks of work by himself and Hartog, he wanted to be the person to break the news! It was, in one way, a bitter pill to learn that the CIA had known all along... (or had they?). On the other hand, it was a great relief to have it out in the open, at long last.

But the Vice President had not yet finished...

'It is deduced that cover was needed for the activating of this device, and so a "hacker" was procured through third parties, in London, England, to access a Pentagon computer system. When a code is transmitted, this causes the 'Star Wars' device to descend from orbit and become dangerous. Previously, having had the twenty four to thirty six hour notice, the late Admiral Kearns then ordered Captain Brannigan, United States Navy, to bring forward Polaris missile firing from an off-line, Polaris submarine, officially scrapped and lying submerged, in the old US nuclear submarine base in Holy Loch, Scotland. The disposal records, for this ex-training vessel, are missing...'

'I'm still confused over this Polaris and Trident option.' stammered the White House Chief, Denver, temporarily over-come by the momentous revelations, which compromised his years of loyal service.

'With your permission, Mr Vice-President,' volunteered McIver, 'I'd like to answer that.'

The Vice-President seemed momentarily reluctant, but then nodded gravely, 'Very well, General..., please continue...'

'As has already been mentioned, we now believe that Trident was too difficult for them to procure and target, without arousing suspicion, and anyways, they did not have sufficient test firing data. Whereas, Polaris was obsolete, had many previous test firings, and Kearns was familiar with it... It was more his era.'

'But *why*, and for what purpose? Anyway, I thought the missile warheads were dummies?' queried Denver.

It passed through McIver's mind that the missiles were not the only dummies! But he answered evenly enough.

'The *Trident* warheads were dummies. That gave Kearns and Brannigan their first, and only test run, at the taxpayers' expense – just one month before the Event. But on the permanently submerged Polaris boat, in Holy Loch, no... the Polaris missiles *began* life as dummies, but Kearns authorised their relegation to scrap. Then through Brannigan, he had them removed from destruction, and fitted up with an array of fancy warhead fillings – including high explosives, sarin and phosgene gas. He recruited his own small special team, who were sworn to secrecy, for what he told them was a special contingency mission.

After Kearns' death, some of the procurement documents were traced by the CIA, and the leader of the special team interviewed. This provided the first main lead.'

'Have they been arrested?' Denver enquired, looking up, perplexed.

'No...!' said McIver, turning sharply, 'After all, they were acting under orders – from their Commander–in–Chief!' He realised he was beginning to sound indignant and moderated his tone, 'They thought they were fulfilling a special contingency mission...'

'We're obliged to you, General,' interrupted the Vice–President, wearily. He held up, what McIver hoped was the last page from the Top Secret document, and resumed reading it aloud...

'The reprogramming and retargeting of Trident Launch computers were probably based on a redundant cold war, joint US/British MI6 test scenario, covering a contingency, whereby if the United Kingdom was overrun...'

'Overrun. Who by, exactly?' enquired Deputy White House Chief of Staff, Edwin Franks, looking round the table, but avoiding the Vice–President's gaze.

'By an enemy, Ed! Who do you think?' Deputy Defense Secretary, David Douglas, replied sarcastically.

274

The Vice-President looked up and gave both men a withering glance, before resuming his address...

'They might be selectively launched to destroy strategic and tactical targets of use to, or occupied by, the enemy. However, incomplete evidence now suggests that Kearns and Brannigan brought that plan alive. Kearns probably did the detailed target planning and procured the highly specialised warhead fillings.'

'Excuse me, sir...,' said McIver.

'Yes, General?'

'Where is Brannigan, now?'

'You should know that, General. After all, you're still Chief of the Armed forces, are you not?'

The Vice-President's use of the word still, made McIver experience a shiver of insecurity, but he told himself he was getting paranoid.

'Sir, if he's not been detained, then he's still in command of the *Lexington!* I'll order his detention right away.' McIver began to get to his feet, but the Vice-President motioned him back to his seat, waving a deferential hand.

'It'll keep, General. It'll keep...'

'But, sir. He should be relieved of his command, and put under close arrest immediately...!'

But the Vice-President ignored him and continued reading.

McIver became very angry, and the others sensed it. There was a subdued and nervous coughing, to which the Vice-President appeared oblivious, his sonorous tones dominant, as he read on...

*   *   *

> *"A skilled politician does not
> always make a good leader."*

R.T.T.

McIver's attention began to falter in the warm room. Something the Vice-President had said, or read, reminded him of a late night conversation with Hartog.

'What actually happened?' McIver had asked. 'So far there were no less than three "aerial attacks," any one of which might have been responsible! The Russian Missiles; the Chinese satellite; the Polaris missiles...'

'Fylingdales' radar...!' Hartog answered excitedly 'Of course, their tape might answer that. The question is, who has that tape now?'

'Just a minute, are you telling me they could track missiles and satellites!' replied McIver.

'I believe they could,' said Hartog. 'It was a very special kind of radar – besides I think the Chinese satellite is a red herring.'

'Congratulations! You've just cracked a pun and mixed your metaphors at the same time!' McIver chuckled, grimly.

'Perhaps that's what they did.'

'Excuse me..?' replied McIver, puzzled by his companion's line of thought.

'Skip it,' said Hartog, sighing and getting up. He thrust his hands deep in his baggy trouser pockets, and thought deeply for a moment. 'I wonder where Captain Brannigan and this guy Payne are now, and what they're doing about Ambassador Hope–Watson?'

'Is that strictly relevant?' enquired McIver, 'Brannigan? Why, he's in still in command of the Lexington! Godammit! I'm going to have to do something about that!'

'Not until you can hang something on him, you can't,' Hartog reminded him. 'Where's your proof? It might be better to leave it to the CIA – at least for another day or two.'

'Oh fine. Meanwhile he's in command of a multi–million dollar killing machine! I should at least *suspend* him, immediately.'

'I don't think he's any *immediate* threat,' said Hartog, thoughtfully. 'He was acting completely under the influence of Kearns.'

There was a short silence while McIver fumed, paced the room and looked up at the ceiling. Meanwhile, Hartog appeared deep in thought. Eventually he spoke, changing the subject back to his original point.

'The old Ballistic Missile Early Warning Station at Fylingdales, Yorkshire, was ostensibly defunct. But did its radar monitor the Event? And if so, did the perpetrators know that? We still can't be sure whether they knew if it was operating at that time. Anyway..., my guess is that it's now p–r–o–b–a–b–l–y destroyed, but that *Counter Strike!* radar traffic *was* monitored from there...'

'Meaning?' enquired McIver impatiently, staring at him intently.

'That the main culprits did not know it was operating on that day!' enthused Hartog.

'You mean the Fylingdales' tape will provide the evidence as to what actually happened?' said McIver, turning round and regarding him steadily.

'Yes, and possibly more besides... *Counter Strike!* was heaven sent for the CIA, because it obscured the "Star Wars accident", triggered by hacking into the Pentagon computer, causing the trial to go live. Up till then they only had the "unauthorised" hacking as cover!'

'Trial? What trial ..?' enquired McIver, testily.

'I believe the reprogramming and retargeting of strategic weapons computers was based on a CIA/MI6 test scenario to destroy selected Socio/Political Targets, in the event of uncontrollable civil disobedience. The Star Wars satellite could have been a component which needed occasional testing. But up to the time of *Counter Strike!* any realistic test was out of the question! Scottdale and Kearns tried to use it for their own ends... and they needed good cover too. Well, they certainly got that!'

'Just a minute...,' stormed McIver, experiencing a whole mix of emotions he never knew he had. 'I can see that they got "cover" as you call it, from these... other things, the Russian Missiles, Chinese satellite and this madman Hope-Watson, but don't you think that Polaris missiles were something of an overkill?'

'No! They were the main destructive event. The satellites were likely to go off at half cock anyway,' said Hartog.

McIver took a deep breath, 'But I understood they just wanted to test the satellite, not blow up England!'

'You've got to realise there were two separate interests here, at least, let's assume they were separate for the moment!. One, was the CIA, representing what the political scientists might call "static America," that's the America that continues irrespective of which political party or President is in power...'

'Yes, I guess I know what it means!' replied McIver rather testily.

'Well...,' Hartog continued carefully, 'The second vested interest, was the renegade personal wealth and power of Scottdale and Kearns. Brannigan was just a pawn.'

'And the Russian missiles...?' McIver asked wearily, his brain in turmoil.

'I'll come to them in a minute', said Hartog. 'Perhaps the CIA knew about Hope-Watson in addition to Scottdale and Kearns. Maybe his methods were of interest to them.'

'Why, that's fantastic!' protested McIver. 'Anyway, hang his methods – exploding computers, nerve gas and laced diesel fuel – do you think the Agency would stand by and let him do what he did to England?'

'And what about President Thomas? If he knew, what was his motive?'

But Hartog was in full flow now.

'Scottdale and Kearns may have begun this... this... er... adventure, with the covert sanction of the state – after all they needed all the resources and influence that would bring. However, they were corrupted – perhaps from the beginning, perhaps later, with promises of wealth, power and office. Perhaps the ultimate power. Who knows?' Hartog paused to think and then resumed slowly.

'Now, assuming Scottdale chose Kearns – because he didn't like you, and knew that Kearns didn't either!'

'Thanks!' said McIver stoically, but flushing slightly.

Hartog continued, clasping his hands and hunched in concentration, 'Scottdale knew Kearns wanted your job and Scottdale wanted to be President...'

'I can't believe, that they would all have so little regard for the consequences for England,' interrupted McIver.

'Well, perhaps they didn't think things would get as far as they did. Now, the CIA? Well..., maybe... when they realised it was too late to stop the Hope–Watson scheme, it was allowed to continue, to cover their Star Wars satellite test.'

'Star Wars is history!' scoffed McIver.

'Maybe, maybe not. But they did spend 6.5 billion dollars on it!' replied Hartog pointedly.

'That much, huh? Tell me, is there *anything* you don't know?' McIver remarked grudgingly with a faint smile. 'Anyway, what about the Russians?'

'The Russians were an additional scapegoat – taking the blame with their supposedly misguided missiles, with the *quid pro quo* of a massive trade and aid deal, to help pay their armed forces. After all, it was very dangerous for them to have unpaid military manning their nuclear trigger...'

'And the small neutron weapons? Russia doesn't have any!'

'Who knows? Kearns may have gotten them from US Navy, or even British stocks.'

'That would be quite impossible!' exclaimed McIver, 'There's a strict inventory control on those things.'

'I'm relieved to hear it!' said Hartog. 'However, the short answer is, the neutron detonations are still being officially blamed on the alleged, orbiting Chinese satellite.'

'I'll say one thing for you Hog, you've sure got a vivid imagination!'

'Don't blame me, blame the State Department! I've done my homework,' replied Hartog defensively. 'Anyway, it's up to you now...'

'Yeah, how about that?' said McIver ruefully rubbing his chin.

*   *   *

The Vice–President was still droning on, when McIver mentally rejoined the meeting.

'... The Chinese authorities have not yet admitted to this accident... '

'And nor are they likely to!' the Vice-President commented, taking off his spectacles and rubbing his eyes. He replaced them carefully, then announced, 'I believe you were a signatory to that press release, General?'

McIver, taken unawares, hastily enquired, 'Er – which press release was that, Sir?'

'Come, come, General. The Pentagon press release of the 30th November 1998, subject, *Broken Arrow....!*'

'Why yes, sir, but I signed it under protest...' (He hoped he had not missed too much of what the Vice–President had been saying). At all events, he did not much care for the direction events were taking!

'Really?' replied the Vice–President, eyeing him coldly, 'And why was that?'

'Because I felt that it made too many assumptions,' McIver replied honestly.

'I see, and can you be more specific?'

'As I recall...' said McIver, clearing his throat.'

'I'll save you the trouble,' the Vice-President interrupted him abruptly, and fished back into the black document folder and took out the single sheet. 'I'll read it one more time, since you were obviously pre-occupied the first time round...'

He held the paper and shook it, as if it was somehow unclean, which in a sense, perhaps it was!

Then he re–read the press release.

'Secretary Scottdale, in consultation with the Chiefs of Staff, can now associate himself with an, as yet unconfirmed report–'

(McIver's recalled this as the one concession to his protests at the time!)

'that the destruction of the infrastructure of England, part of Great Britain, many of its citizens and government,was probably accidental, and caused by a Russian experimental intercontinental missile which exceeded its orbit, due to a malfunctioning propellent. Consequently the

missile took up a more northerly orbit that passed over the United Kingdom. An attempt to destroy the missile remotely, unfortunately caused an explosion, which in turn, damaged a Chinese satellite, in a higher orbit. This satellite, which was carrying an experimental kind of neutron power source and other chemical agents, plunged from its orbit and on contact with the atmosphere, caused the widespread damage and extensive loss of life, of which we are all painfully aware. For reasons yet to be explained, the Chinese authorities have not yet admitted to this accident.'

'That is all.'

The Vice-President carefully put away the document in the black leather folder, looked up, and clasping his long bony fingers before him on the polished table, remarked with a somewhat ominous smile, 'Well now, General, I hope you might be able to help us further, here...?'

A cold shiver ran down McIver's spine, a coldness which was reflected in the Vice-President's clear blue eyes.

Some gruelling hours later, as he left the White House and took the salute from the Marine guard in the entrance lobby, McIver happened to glance up at the motto, under the Presidential crest, which read, *'In God We Trust.'*

'Well...,' he muttered to himself, as he walked slowly out from the white colonnaded portico, and down the steps to one side, 'He's about the only one you *can* trust around here! And hey..., I'm not even sure about *that!'*

36

"There's a divinity that shapes our ends,
rough hew them how we will..."

(William Shakespeare)

Singapore

After the Event

An emptiness, so vast and forbidding, it was almost un-
bearable. Deprived of home (if not its fabric, then its
meaning), her studies complete, together with her work...
these were the thoughts of Mi Ling as she stared across the
grey blue waters of the Straits.

He was not there at her graduation, which he had
promised for so long. Therefore, receiving her degree was
an empty moment rather than a happy and triumphal one.

Such is life.

'Come, have some tea...' her mother called from the
terrace. 'You must not be sad,' Li Chan chided gently, taking her daughter's hand as she sat and joined her, head
bowed. 'A new way is before us. But meanwhile, we have a
position to maintain!' said her mother proudly.

'What position is that?' Mi Ling enquired mournfully.

'Why child, you are the Ambassador's daughter, and I am
still his wife. In his absence we must....'

'Must, must!' shrieked Mi Ling getting up, causing the
fine china to chink musically on the white tablecloth, 'Why?
We are betrayed! We must think of ourselves now, and get
away from here!'

'But daughter,' cooed Li Chan, stretching out her hand.
Her long upbringing meant duty came first. 'It is our duty...'

'Mother,' announced Mi Ling firmly, sitting once more and
smoothing her skirt, *'Our* duty is *over!* Why can't you see
this? It ended when we found Marcus...'

'I think perhaps, Marcus found you!' chided her mother, not unkindly.

'Nonsense!' stormed her daughter, looking up fiercely, 'But he is right about one thing...'

'Oh, and what is that?' enquired Li Chan, calmly pouring the tea.

'He says we must go away from here.'

'Go away with him, perhaps. Is that what he means?' Li Chan's voice was suddenly cold.

Mi Ling flushed and bowed her head. Li Chan reached for her once more, 'Child, we...'

'Do not call me that! My childhood is well and truly past!'

'Well..., yes...,' admitted her mother, withdrawing her hand.

'He has asked me to go with him to Hong Kong,' declared Mi Ling, defiantly.

'Indeed! And why should he ask you this?' demanded Li Chan, setting down the teapot with a clatter.

'Because he is concerned for my safety.'

'Is he now...?' replied her mother, impassively, 'and does he say precisely why he is so concerned?'

'Why? Because *your husband,* Her Majesty's Ambassador to Singapore State, is a murderer!' raged Mi Ling.

Her mother rose and taking the short step to the balcony, turned and spoke, clearly trembling with controlled wrath, 'And you think he is *not?*' Then, before Mi Ling could answer, 'Go to him, then..., but do not return here, ever again, *takut kalau!'*

Li Chan did not complete her uttered threat, but left the terrace in floods of embittered tears. Mi Ling's first instinct was to run after her mother and embrace her.

But she did not.

*   *   *

Marcus Payne had now smoked two cigarettes consecutively, a rare and mildly disturbing event for him! Something was wrong. She had not rung. Her image had replaced that of Julia in his thoughts. A man without a home, family – or country, needs something or somebody, to hold on to, even if it is only in his memory. For without memories, we don't know who we are, and nothing makes sense any more.

Presently, for Marcus Payne, in an impersonal hotel room in a foreign country, sweating slightly and trembling..., that somebody was Mi Ling.

He looked at the phone, which remained stubbornly silent.

He must take a grip of himself. A drink! That was it. He advanced to the bottle. He felt its coolness, he unscrewed the cap... held the glass...

Then..., the phone rang, at last!

*　　*　　*

On the way to the airport, Payne had the distinct impression they were being followed, but Mi Ling told him he was being fanciful.

'What about your mother?' he asked tactfully.

'She would not come.'

'But I thought she came from Hong Kong.'

'She does...'

'Well?'

'She is suffering from a sense of duty.'

'Really?'

'Well, she is still the Ambassador's wife,' proclaimed Mi Ling defensively,' She cannot desert her position at a moment's notice.'

'I suppose not... But...'

'Yes?'

'You're worried about her?'

'Of course....,' Mi Ling sniffed, and clasping her delicate hands together, looked down demurely, in the manner some Eastern women have.

'Here,' said Payne softly, passing her a freshly laundered

white handkerchief. The 'MP' in the corner, embroidered in blue silk, reminded him of better days.

Without warning, a blue and white police car joined the road behind them, flashed its lights and gave several blasts on its siren.

'You must stop, I think,' said Mi Ling.

Payne cursed and brought the hire car to a halt under a palm tree.

The two officers approached them in the manner of police patrol men worldwide, slowly, deliberately and with menace.

'Great!' exclaimed Payne, and hit the steering wheel hard with the heel of his hand.

'May I see your passport please?' said the first officer, holding out his hand.

'Is this necessary?' replied Payne, 'We are in a hurry to catch a plane.'

'Is that why you exceed the speed limit?' remarked the officer coldly.

'Your passport please?' he repeated.

The policeman seemed to take an inordinately long time to examine the document, while his companion stood one pace behind him and stared fixedly at Mi Ling.

*   *   *

Comfortably seated in the Singapore Airways Boeing, climbing steeply *en route* to Hong Kong, Payne was still livid. 'Well..., now we *know* that he's out to get us' he fumed.

'Well, we are free now anyway,' replied Mi Ling, without conviction, staring out of the window at her receding home.

They were both thinking the same thing. Hong Kong was now in Chinese hands. Things would be different there now. Different from Mi Ling's upbringing in Kowloon. Different from Payne's last visit, many years past.

'You were great.,' he said gently turning to her, clasping her hand.

'It was lucky... I... we... know the Chief of Police. He has a son... we used to...'

'Spare me the details,' said Payne stiffly, withdrawing his hand.

'You... you are like the little boy!' she hissed, chiding him.

'You mean, I'm jealous?' he said, simply, his face suddenly pale – the jawline tense.

'Yes, jealous!'

'OK, I admit it.'

'You must be...'

'Yes?'

'More... dignified,' she whispered primly, crossing her legs with difficulty in the restricted space.

'Oh,' said Payne, 'is that all?' Then feeling warm and mildly reassured, his many tensions momentarily released, he promptly fell asleep.

When they arrived at Kai Tak airport, with its dramatic approach over North Bay, its runway jutting out into the sea, they held hands tightly. She, because she was tense, and he, because he loved her.

* * *

"Better to live in the certainty of misery than the misery of uncertainty!"

Anon

———

Hong Kong

After the Event

With the arrival formalities and frustrations behind them, they finally reached their hotel. Mi Ling had insisted on separate rooms, but the hotel was full. Anyway, she decided that was her mother talking!

After they had unpacked, they allowed themselves a few hours' relaxation before considering their immediate and uncertain future. This release of tension, which had built up in both of them over the preceding weeks, was expressed in the act of love.

It happened quickly...

She emerged from the bath, newly scented and wrapped in a thick white towel, so large that it trailed behind her. Payne had simply, and unwittingly, stepped on the trailing towel. In the next instant she fell naked into his aching arms. They were both overtaken by the unexpectness and beauty of the moment. For when life offers its rarer gifts, it is often at a moment's notice...

As Payne took her, Mi Ling gave herself willingly – or rather her body did! While she, the strictly brought up Eastern girl, was shocked. Yet even that persona was furnished with an excuse, the suddenness of a circumstantial accident, the relief of mutual stress and tension?

Perhaps, perhaps not...! But it sufficed, for the moment. to salve her prudish conscience.

It was good.

Her body screamed its approval, using her full lips as its agent..., her long fingernails raked his back through the thin shirt..., unmercifully, until he too cried out in unison with her, as he filled and fulfilled her in *all* senses..., and in all *her* senses – at least for that instant.

But the ecstatic moment died quickly, and the next assailed her with a message, sharp, like a dash of iced water.

For she knew then she must leave him. It was only her body that returned his love.

*   *   *

In the thirty years before 1997 no one was executed in Hong Kong, but already the show trials, ritual humiliations, bullets in the head and wasteland killings had begun. But the dismayed, hand-wringing West did absolutely nothing about it.

In some parts of the ex-colony the right connections were needed to survive! This applied to many who were fearful, without proper papers, fugitives or merely *persona non grata*.

Meanwhile, in the Hutongs, or alleyways of Shenzhem, a Hong Kong Chinese border city, the rape and murder capital of China, with its hideous concrete sky scrapers, spivs, drug dealers, and Armani clad prostitutes, toting "big-sister-bigs," pigeon English for mobile cell phones, nearly a thousand murders were committed each year, increasing nearly 40 per cent, year on year.

A South African business man, found dead in the five star Shangri La Hotel, was an uncommon, but not unknown event, to the indifferent authorities. Another foreigner who had ventured too far? Taken too much and given too little...? Who knows? Investigations cost money. At all events, it was too late for him!

It appeared he was alone and the hotel bill unpaid. The Chinese girl who had checked in with him had left some time before his death – that much at least was forensically proven. His body was eventually handed over to the South African Embassy, but in spite of their exhaustive enquiries and numerous advertisements in various international journals, his body and few personal possessions remained unclaimed.

However, many weeks later at his eventual burial in Pretoria, an anonymous single wreath of white Chincherinchees appeared on his grave.

*   *   *

Great Britain

After the Event

New Britain was indeed beginning to emerge.

The roads carried half the traffic of hitherto. Gone were the grinding, frustrating and polluting traffic jams. Diesel lorries were being replaced by an ingenious new form of transportation – the Side Track system, comprising a light railway with two lower conventional tracks and two upper, erected at the side of thoroughfares carrying standard freight containers in almost continous trains – computer-controlled from intermediate depots and terminals where the containers were loaded and unloaded, similar to alpine ski gondolas. These "trains" never stopped, apart from maintenance and break-down, rather like vehicle production lines. However, their speed, loading and unloading were governed by clutches and special cranes. The system also carried occasional passenger cars of identical dimension to the international standard freight container, which were patronised by those who required ultra cheap, but not particularly rapid transportation.

On the motorways, automobiles and trucks were entirely separated by the simple allocation of separate carriageways and lanes, obviating one of the former causes of fatal accident – cars crushed by heavy lorries – particularly in fog.

Town and city parking problems were all but eliminated by greater restriction on vehicle ownership – licences being granted on a points system according to need – and the banning of all on-street parking in central areas, and where road width was below a minimum. Thus at a stroke, the former problem of car clogged streets, where vehicles were often parked on both sides of narrow city streets, and on

289

pavements, was eliminated.

New laws included the confiscation of vehicles from persistent offenders.

New Britain was also a much quieter place. High decibel "ghetto blasters" were banned, together with multi-watt in-car sound systems, where audible thumping could be heard outside the vehicle.

Hope-Watson's radical remedy for the inner city problems – those that remained after *Counter Strike!* – consisted simply of bulldozing derelict, run down, or crime-infested areas, and landscaping them with trees and flowers, together with the later introduction of natural wildlife. Ugly sixties style architecture began to be replaced by more visually sympathetic, and homely structures.

Wild bird and mammal breeding centres had been set up to replenish the dramatic, and sad declines, in these native creatures recorded before the Event.

Already a few larks began to sing again, high above the formerly over-populated and commercialised, Home Counties.

In London itself, the best architectural features were passionately preserved and repaired, while many of the aggressively abhorrent towers, were systematically blown up.

The new regime soon became aware, after the reconstruction and rehabilitation phase, (a matter of weeks after the UN had left), that a great many "undesirable" criminal and non - conformist elements had survived.

Swift and decisive action was soon taken to remedy the situation.

> 'All the festering sores of drug distribution, violent crime, especially street and inner city crime, will be ruthlessly dealt with. Liberalistic shilly-shallying and persecution of the weak and defenceless by hard, commercially-driven criminals, is at an end..'

Hope-Watson was as good as his word. Armed police

entered the most notorious parts of South East London, Manchester and Liverpool (those still intact), where hitherto the Triad and other factional youth gangs had held sway...

At first the police were harried, occasionally isolated, cornered and victims of the knife, sword and even automatic weapons, but they soon became acclimatised to their task, and to the previously damaged and unfamiliar streets.

Within an unanticipated short time, it became a "Turkey shoot..."

House to house clearance began, day and night, with ever more reinforcements. Helicopters with powerful spotlights and heat-seeking equipment ranged noisily above.

Gradually truck after truck brought out dead and dying baggy trousered bodies. Gang and drug barons, were rounded up at railway and underground stations, ports and airports. The most powerful and affluent took flight in private planes, only to be shot down by two special squadrons of the BAF (British Air Force), with night flying helicopter gunships.

Darkened nocturnal yachts and luxury cruisers sailing secretly across the English and Irish Channels, and the North Sea, were challenged and boarded. Those that resisted or tried to flee, were blown out of the water, by naval patrol vessels. The white gloves were off!

In spite of a media embargo, news of these actions eventually reached the World's press. The UN and EEC, as can be imagined, were appalled.

'New Britain steps out of line!' screamed the banner headline of the *Washington Post.*

> 'The New British government under strong man Hope-Watson kicks sand in the face of 50 years of liberal democracy...'

However, some elements considered it a triumph. The white-controlled, *Johannesburg Times* railed...

'At last, the rotten stinking heart of Britain, has been cut out! Who knows, perhaps one day, women and children may safely walk British streets once more....!'

'The end of decades of dithering....!' said another.

However, this was only the beginning. The very next day after the country's Foreign Currency Reserves had reached pre-1998 levels, commercial war was declared on the EEC.

The first action was that all contributions ceased.

A Bill was introduced in the new legislature to this effect, and Value Added Tax, the previously prime source of Britain's contributions, reduced to 10%. A few days later, two Spanish trawlers fishing in British waters, were boarded and their catches confiscated, while an absconding third, was summarily sunk off the Scilly Isles.

When the Spanish fishermen were rescued, the New British Foreign Office sent a facsimile message to Senõr Vargas, the Spanish fisheries minister, saying that they would be returned on payment of a substantial fine (a 'ransom', Vargas had called it) of £250,000. The next day it was announced that the Euro had ceased to be legal tender in New Britain.

More was to come..., a significant example of which was as follows:

Orders in Council

Emergency Directive 99/10

.Jurisdiction. England, Wales and Northern Ireland,Only.

The Liberalistic Judiciary is to be replaced with local Tribunals whose strength and power will be augmented to fit the seriousness of any particular offence brought before them.

Emergency Directive 99/11. Jurisdiction. England, Scotland, Wales and Northern Ireland

The following activities are hereby proscribed and will be unlawful as from midnight on June 30th 1999.

Drug addiction.

All affected persons must register for rehabilitation.

Juvenile Delinquency.

All children of school age, in term time, will be stopped and questioned and if in default of attendance will be taken to a local care centre. Their parents will be informed. Parents, on collection of the defaulting child, will be fined. Fines will increase for every incidence of the same offence.

Vehicle Ownership

All vehicle ownership and operation by any person under twenty five years of age is prohibited on the grounds that this age group, although representing only 20 per cent of the driving community, cause over 50 per cent of motoring offences and accidents. Any person found operating or owning a vehicle under the age of twenty five years, even under a previously issued licence, will have such vehicle confiscated. Motor cycles under 250 cc's are not included in this Directive. However, all motor cycles over 250 cc's count as motor vehicles.

Diesel Vehicles

On the basis of scientific evidence and research, the government is determined to progressively reduce the number of vehicles in use powered by diesel engines, which have been shown to emit dangerous microscopic particles, which are ingested into the lungs and cause cancer and other diseases, notably asthma in children.

Accordingly, the installation and operation of diesel engines in motor cars is prohibited and will be unlawful as from midnight on September 30th 1999. All those who own such a vehicle may apply for a grant of up to 30% of the cost of replacing diesel engines with catalytically controlled petrol or natural gas fuelled engines. Forms for obtaining this grant will be available in post offices from June 30th, 1999.

Other forms of transport did not escape the new regime's attention...On the Underground system, all graffiti was removed, often by former perpetrators – where they could be found. No passenger was allowed on the system who sported, what specially selected ticket barrier staff judged to be, an unacceptable standard of dress or demeanour. In the trains themselves, it was reported that some rush hour passengers (those who were admitted) including commuters, were actually seen to smile occasionally – a long forgotten phenomenon!

*   *   *

1900hrs May 30th 1999

After the Event

After a tiring day, a few days after his meeting with the Vice-President, McIver was trying to relax in his apartment in the Pentagon. But as he poured himself a Jack Daniels, he was distracted by the television news. He had switched the set on merely for company with the sound turned down. It was the evening news broadcast, and two names, though muted, caught his ear and set his pulse and mind, racing…

'…Secretary Scottdale and Captain Wade Brannigan, United States Navy…!'

He grabbed the remote control and increased the sound.
'…while travelling from the White House to the Pentagon, their car skidded on wet leaves, or oil…. left the carriageway opposite the Arlington Cemetery, demolished a barrier and plunged into the Potomac River… which unfortunately is in full spring, flood.

The car and its two occupants were recovered but they were found to be dead on arrival at the hospital…'

McIver, made a grab for the phone, knocking over his drink in the process.

*   *   *

Hampshire, England

Summer 1999

After the Event

Although Hope-Watson was still aware of the risk of exposure for his pivotal role in *Counter Strike!* from his wife, Payne and sadly, even Mi Ling, nevertheless one by one, he began to discount them and relax. After all, Payne was dead – at last! Li Chan was isolated, and congenitally loyal... while Mi Ling...?

Then he received a telephone call from immigration at London's Heathrow Airport.

*   *   *

She had some difficulty in finding his address, and her motive for seeking him out was unclear to her, more emotionally-based than rational or practical.

It was raining as she emerged from the terminal, with her minimal luggage and confidence. Then she noticed a man watching her. She tried to avoid his gaze but eventually he advanced toward her.

'Excuse me miss, would you be ...?' He fished a notebook from his raincoat pocket,'... Miss Mi Ling...er?'

'Why yes, but who...?'

'I've been sent to collect you by the Admiral. You're his stepdaughter, I believe?' The man was short, smartly dressed, clean shaven and smiled kindly.

'But how do I know who you are?' Mi Ling began uncertainly.

'Oh of course, you'll need some identification.' This time, he took a small black wallet from his inside jacket pocket, opened it and presented it to her. The government pass bore his photograph and Hope-Watson's signature.

With Mi Ling reclining on its blue leather cushions, the Bentley Azure swished its way down the half empty M3 motorway, in a spring shower, the clouds black on the horizon against a brilliant sky, the bright sun hiding mockingly, before illuminating a vivid rainbow and the vernal green of the Southern English countryside.

She was unsure of what her stepfather's reaction would be towards her. Did he still consider her a threat? She knew he had not approved of her association with Payne – for obvious reasons! Now, to her great sorrow, Payne was dead. Where else was she to go? Back to her mother and Singapore – her old home? No, for although her mother's parting threat was probably empty, she felt stifled there. She needed to move on, to find new stimuli, and to use her brain and her education. In spite of herself, she was drawn to her stepfather – the figure of power and purpose.

In short, she knew no other course, but her mind and being were in conflict.

This conflict concerned responsibility for so many deaths – perhaps even Payne's. When she had read of his death in, of all things, a hotel chain magazine, she experienced a deep sadness and not a little guilt, although when she had left him, he seemed to understand. Of course, she did not reveal her final destination. Indeed, at the time, she barely knew it herself.

She must find the answer to this and many other questions, but she needed to work, and she was sure that there would be work for her here – perhaps with her stepfather, perhaps not. But again a conflict arose between her needs and the betrayal of her mother; her memory of Marcus Payne, and of her finer instincts.

But worldly maturity was being forced upon her; Mi Ling was growing up. She had discovered, through unyielding experience, as well as academe, that the world was imperfect, and compromise was often the price of survival.

Thus was her conflict salved...

Her feelings sought succour in rationalization. What was done was done, and all that followed now, was to make the best of things.

Who would believe what she knew? Where was her evidence? She felt now, that her mother would never speak out against her husband and his position – which in many ways seemed more important to her. Li Chan would always be the Ambassador's wife. It was her life. She had grown used to it, and that was how she would die.

She emerged from the Bentley before the grandeur of Testcombe House. The air had that soft balminess of an early English May evening. A blackbird and a chaffinch sang and she marvelled at the spacious glory of a great English country house.

She gazed about her, temporarily enchanted, then shivered slightly as she focused on the figure emerging to greet her, from the ornate wooden porch.

Her relationship with her stepfather, her "uncle" Lloyd had recommenced...

* * *

Washington

1900hrs, May 1st, 1999

After the Event

Later, at the Pentagon police post, Agent Clarke presented his identification to the guard. Ushered into the dismal office, he stated his business.

In the background, a radio played softly. It was Elton John's, *No Sacrifice*

> *'...just passing through*
> *and it's no s-a-c-r-i -f-i-c-e*
> *Just a simple word...'*

'Is that all?' enquired Clarke, dispassionately.

'I reckon,' said the policeman.

Clarke scooped up the cardboard box containing the men's personal possessions, and tucked it under his arm.

'No – hold on there...!' The policeman turned and scurried into the back office.

He returned with a small brown sealed envelope...

'This fell out of the tall feller's top pocket...'

'Next to his heart, eh?' cracked Clarke with a limpid smile.

> *'It's two hearts living ....*
> *In two separate worlds...*
> *But – it's no sacrifice...'*

'I guess so,' replied the policeman. Clarke was making him nervous.

Clarke opened the envelope and a photograph fell out and fluttered down to the dusty floor.

He stooped, uttering a mild groan from the effort, and swept it up. It was a photograph, a portrait photograph of a young woman.

'Good looker!' remarked the policeman, peering at it between the agent's fingers.

Clarke turned the photograph over disinterestedly. On the reverse side was a line of handwriting in smudged black ink. The envelope had protected the print from the water sufficiently to render it just readable. It said... *'To Richard, with love from Julia & Uncle Lloyd.'*

> *'...No sacrifice*
> *It's no s-a-c-r-i-f-i-c-e*
> *a-at all!'*

'What about the car?'

'Which one is it?'

'It's in the yard... , a maroon Buick.'

'...in the final act
We loose di-rection
No stone unturned...
No teeth to damn you
when jealousy burns...
Cold, cold heart
Hard done by you...
some things look'in' better, baby
Just passing through...'

*　　*　　*

Meanwhile, somewhere in England, a lark soared high above a chemical-free, long-grassed meadow, abundant with wild flowers and began to sing once more. While below, over a poppy-strewn hill, the first grass appeared between the growing cracks of a deserted motorway.

A mile distant in a splendid gabled country house, an old fashioned black telephone rang repeatedly in the beeswaxed, oak-decorated hall. A village constable and a security man entered through the shafts of sunlight, paused, then made their way toward the open gunroom door.

A faint odour of smokeless shotgun powder, mingled incongruously with Chanel and Jasmine...

Three bodies there...

Lying on the dark, polished wooden floor, a beautiful young Chinese girl in a cream silk dress; the tweed-suited, recumbent figure of an English country gentleman – a look of startled surprise on his strong featured face; and in the corner – quite dead – an elegant, English woman in a brilliant red suit, embracing a very expensive shotgun!

Under her body a scrap of an official looking document, resembling a secret diplomatic report, was found...

It read:

'A letter was sent by the US Consul in Brussels to CIA Headquarters in Washington.

Some months later, the Agency began intercepting communications to and from Singapore—following information contained in that letter.

This later led them to Madeira, and later still to open a dossier on Her ex-Majesty's Ambassador to Singapore, Sir Lloyd Hope-Watson, a retired Royal Navy Admiral, who it is now thought, was the principal architect of the catastrophic event, Counter Strike!, which almost destroyed England, killing millions. The Agency then informed US Defense Secretary Scottdale, who apparently failed to act on the information.Secretary Scottdale was today placed under arrest…'

All Hedgehog Books are available at your local bookshop or newsagent, but check publication dates. They can also be ordered direct from the publisher. Please indicate the number of copies required and complete the simple form below.

Send to: Hedgehog Books
                         Stable Cottage
                         Maunditts Park Farm
                         Little Somerford
                         Chippenham
                         Wilts, SN15 5BH

or phone: 0800 545606 (Free 24 hrs 365 days)
Or fax: 01666 822192
Please give title, author & credit card number.

When ordering by post, enclose a remittance to the value of the cover price, plus £1.00 per book for post and packing. Overseas customers add £1.75 for post and packing.
    Payment may be made in sterling by UK personal cheque, Eurocheque, postal order, sterling draft, or international money order, made payable to Hedgehog Books. For payment by VISA or MasterCard, give Card No.,Name on Card and Expiry Date.

Card No ☐☐☐☐☐☐☐☐☐☐☐☐☐☐☐☐☐☐

Exp.Date ☐☐☐☐☐☐☐☐☐☐☐☐☐☐☐☐☐☐

Signature _____

Name & Address in BLOCK CAPITALS please. ....
Address...
....
....
Please allow 28 days for delivery. Please tick box for catalogue ☐ 2/98